"Knock off the act," Cutter said gruffly.

"Act? How do you know it's an act? After all, you really don't know me very well."

"Don't I? I think I do. I admit I had some preconceived opinions regarding you, but I realize that wasn't quite fair. I know you, Hollis, because I held you when you cried tears that were honest and real. I know you because you responded to my kisses, then were shocked and embarrassed that you had. Oh, yes, I know you. The more important question is . . . do *you*? Do you know who you are, what you really want?"

"That," she said tightly, "is none of your business. I *do* know that I'll be leaving for Mexico City. Bear in mind, Mr. McKenzie, that I *will* be coming back."

Cutter grinned. "I'm counting on it, darlin'. Oh, yes, I'm looking forward to it."

Dear Reader,

When two people fall in love, the world is suddenly new and exciting, and it's that same excitement we bring to you in Silhouette Intimate Moments. These are stories with scope, with grandeur. The characters lead the lives we all dream of, and everything they do reflects the wonder of being in love.

Longer and more sensuous than most romances, Silhouette Intimate Moments novels take you away from everyday life and let you share the magic of love. Adventure, glamour, drama, even suspense— these are the passwords that let you into a world where love has a power beyond the ordinary, where the best authors in the field today create stories of love and commitment that will stay with you always.

In coming months look for novels by your favorite authors: Maura Seger, Parris Afton Bonds, Linda Howard, and Nora Roberts, to name just a few. And whenever you buy books, look for all the Silhouette Intimate Moments, love stories *for* today's women *by* today's women.

Leslie J. Wainger
Senior Editor
Silhouette Books

Robin Elliott
Gauntlet Run

Silhouette Intimate Moments
Published by Silhouette Books New York
America's Publisher of Contemporary Romance

SILHOUETTE BOOKS
300 East 42nd St., New York, N.Y. 10017

ISBN: 0-373-07206-6

First Silhouette Books printing September 1987

America's Publisher of Contemporary Romance

Printed in the U.S.A.

ROBIN ELLIOTT

lives in Arizona with her husband and three daughters. Formerly employed in a high school library, she is now devoting her time to writing romance novels. She also writes under her own name, Joan Elliott Pickart.

For Tara Hughes,
who believed in this book
when it was still a dream.

And for Anne Leiner,
who helped the dream come true.

Chapter 1

It rained the day of the funeral.

A steady, quiet rain, it darkened the sky and matched the somber mood of those in the state of Texas and beyond. The rain fell like tears in a hushed flow as the people mourned. They, too, cried as they sat in schools, office buildings, bars; eyes riveted on the television and the somber scene before them. In mansions, tenements, and all in between, the tears fell. The people huddled together, seeking solace from those around them; the gnarled hands of the old clutched those of the young.

The procession of black limousines snaked slowly through the rain-slick streets, led by police officers on motorcycles with lights flashing. Onlookers lined the sidewalks, some holding umbrellas, others oblivious to the inclement weather.

And all were silent.

Men, women, children, of every race and creed were shoulder to shoulder, eyes misting, hearts aching. The television crews worked efficiently, but there was none of the usual banter among the cameramen, no joking or arrangements being made to meet for drinks at a favorite bar.

There was only silence.

The TV anchorman droned on, identifying some of the limousine occupants by the flags attached to the hoods: the governor, an ambassador, a senator, a congressman. And, with additional motorcycles flanking the large car, the vice president of the United States.

The rain continued to fall.

As the procession entered the cemetery, the cars stopped in the middle of the narrow road and the doors were opened. Dressed in black, the occupants emerged, umbrellas lifted to shield them from the cold drizzle. Black umbrellas. In all directions there was only black.

"The doors of the lead car are opening now," the anchorman said, "and Buck Champion's family is emerging. Floyd Barnett is assisting his wife, Kathleen Champion Barnett, Buck Champion's sister, from the vehicle. There's been much speculation here in Houston as to whether Buck Champion's daughter, Hollis Champion Ramirez, would return from Mexico to attend her father's funeral. We don't know as yet if she— Yes, I believe that is she now being assisted from the car by Mr. Barnett. If that is, indeed, Hollis Champion Ramirez, it has been seven years since she has stepped on Texas soil.

"Buck Champion," the anchorman continued, "made no attempt to hide his disapproval of his daughter's marriage to Raymond Ramirez seven years ago. It was assumed by many when Mr. Ramirez died, five years ago, that Hollis Champion Ramirez would return to Texas to mend the shattered relationship with her father. According to sources close to Buck Champion, a reconciliation did not take place. To the best of this reporter's knowledge, father and daughter have not spoken during the entire seven years.

"Everyone is gathered at the graveside now, and the minister is speaking, although we won't be able to hear what is being said. It is reported that the vice president will say a few words.

"Buck Champion is dead," the man said, then cleared his throat roughly. "One minute vibrantly alive; the next, struck down by a heart attack at the age of fifty. Buck Champion's millions touched many lives with his tireless campaigns for the underprivileged. None of us, I'm sure, will ever forget his impassioned speech many years ago declaring that no man, woman, or child would ever go hungry in the state of Texas. He loved this land and its people. He was a Texan. He was Texas. Buck Champion was all things to all people, almost larger than life, and now he's gone. He will be sorely missed."

The announcer stopped speaking, his voice choked with emotion. No one moved to take the microphone from his hand. Across the state, the people watched the scenario unfolding on their television screens with no commentary, no human voice to bring a sense of reality to what they were witnessing. Their hero, their hope, had been taken from them, and many wished to rage in anger to mask their fear. Buck Champion had belonged to the people, and they ached with the chill of their loss.

Thunder rumbled through the sky as though nature, too, did not accept what was taking place. The rain was swirled into biting whips, tearing at the clothes of the graveside mourners. The leaves on the trees rustled with an eerie sound that seemed to come from a distant place as though voicing the presence of ghosts. The minister's words were carried into oblivion, heard only by those closest to him.

Hollis Champion Ramirez lifted a slender hand to the crown of her large black hat to hold it firmly in place. In spite of the umbrella that Floyd Barnett held above her and

Kathleen, the rain pelted Hollis's long-sleeved black wool dress, soaking the rich material.

Hollis felt a chill course through her, partially from the cold and dampness and partially from the ominous aura in the cemetery, and she shivered. She swept her gaze over the flower-draped casket and waited; waited for an emotion, any emotion, to assault her. But deep within her was nothing; not sorrow, not hate, only a void, an empty darkness. Her father was dead. Buck Champion's reign was over. And she felt nothing.

He'd been human, after all, Hollis thought dryly. He'd died. His heart had stopped functioning like any mortal man's and he'd ceased to exist. Oh, how the people had worshiped this man, had been awed by his money and power, his ability to change the course of so many lives. *Time* magazine had put his picture on the cover with the caption, "Buck Champion...the People's Champion." Fools.

Hollis tore her gaze from the casket, her jaw clenched so tightly her teeth ached. The vice president began to speak, and Hollis closed her mind to the eloquent eulogy, which she knew would declare Buck to be the finest of men, a breed unto himself, one among the multitudes. Buck would be lauded for his quest to end the suffering of his fellow man, for...

Enough, Hollis thought fiercely. Anger was depleting, exhausting, and she had no intention of draining herself of energies. It was difficult as it was just being back in Texas, back...home? No, never that. Not any longer. Neither Texas nor Gauntlet Run was home.

The wind quieted, and the rain slackened to a chilly drizzle. Hollis dropped her hand back to her side and lifted her chin, her eyes scanning the faces of the somber people around the casket.

What were they all thinking? she wondered. Here they stood, cold and wet, men and women of power and money paying their last respects to a man who'd died in his prime of life. Had they loved or hated him, feared or revered him? Were they registering a sense of loss or relief that Buck Champion would never again walk among them?

Hollis's gaze swept quickly over the faces before her, then her eyes collided with blue ones that were staring directly at her. They were the coldest eyes she had ever seen. By sheer force of will she tore her gaze from the winter chill of the mesmerizing eyes and redirected her attention to the casket. In the next instant she realized that she had somehow etched into her mind every detail of his face.

His image danced in Hollis's mental vision: tall, tanned, with thick black hair tousled by the insistent wind. His features were rough-hewn, as though they'd been chiseled from stone before being bronzed by the sun. His black suit, western-cut and of obviously expensive material, stretched across his broad shoulders and encased his muscled legs. Tucked under his arm was a black Stetson. He appeared to be in his late thirties, and every rugged inch of him shouted Texas. Hollis had never seen him before, but as a shiver feathered along her spine, she knew he despised her. The message had been clear in his look, and waves of animosity seemed to emanate from him and touch her despite the distance between them.

Hollis snapped her head around to meet the man's stare once again, anger now flashing in her eyes. Who was this man? Why was a stranger holding her in such obvious contempt? Had her father wronged him in some way, and now she was to bear the brunt of this man's wrath, reap the sins of her father? No, that didn't make sense. Those standing at Buck Champion's graveside were there by invitation only, according to Buck's instructions executed by his attorney. The stranger was there by Buck's choosing, which indicated clearly that the tall man's disdain was directed at her.

"May he rest in peace," the minister said quietly.

Hollis's attention was riveted again on the casket, the hostile, unknown man across from her forgotten.

"God bless his soul," the minister intoned. "May Buck Champion be remembered always."

Unexpected and unwelcome tears sprung to Hollis's eyes, and she blinked them away angrily. Oh, please, Daddy, she thought frantically, don't leave me, not again, not forever this time. Dear heaven, she would never see him again. She was alone, so incredibly alone and . . . No! It didn't matter. It had been seven years since he'd forced her to choose between him and Raymond Ramirez. Seven years since he'd shut the door on Gauntlet Run and on his heart, on his love for his daughter, telling her never to return.

And so she'd gone, Hollis thought. And now she was back to witness Buck Champion's final moment, his grand exit from the world he had controlled down to the most minute detail. She was truly free now, out from under the dictatorial hand of this powerful man. There was nothing more he could do to her to cause her heartache and pain. She should be registering a rush of relief, but instead . . . Why? Why this sense of emptiness, of desolate loneliness?

No, she was only tired, Hollis rationalized. She'd arrived from Mexico City with only enough time to change clothes and join Kathleen and Floyd in the limousine. Hollis had entered Gauntlet Run, hurried to her old room, and showered and changed. There had been no time for memories to assault her, no time for emotions to confront her. She felt disoriented, off-kilter, and a steady pain was beginning to beat at her temples.

Hollis closed her eyes for a moment, gathering her strength, then opened them again, knowing she now had a cool, unreadable, aloof expression on her face. She was in control again. She was fine. Soon, very soon, this nightmare would be over and she could leave. Leave Texas,

Gauntlet Run, and the memories of Buck Champion far behind.

Cutter McKenzie stared at the woman across from him, a muscle jumping along his clenched jaw.

So this was Hollis, he thought. Hollis Champion Ramirez, Buck's daughter, the prodigal, returning home at age twenty-seven. He'd seen pictures of her, of course, but they hadn't done her justice. A camera couldn't capture her gracefulness, that intangible aura that said money, breeding, class. She was a Champion, all right. It showed.

And he'd like to wring her neck!

Cutter's gaze flickered over Hollis's figure, seeing her full breasts pushing against the soft fabric of her dress, the gentle slope of her hips, the shapely calves of her legs, which were obviously long and slender. She was tall, maybe five seven, and her skin was like ivory in contrast to her black hair, which she wore in a tight chignon.

Hollis had the Champion temper, Cutter mused. He'd noticed the ire flashing in her green eyes when their gaze had met. He'd done nothing to mask his distaste of her, and he knew she'd seen it on his face, in his eyes. She'd seemed to be challenging him, daring him to continue his angry look, waiting for him to back down, avert his eyes first. But she had been the one to turn back to the casket, and for a fleeting moment he thought he'd seen a flicker of sorrow, of vulnerability in her. But then she'd stiffened again and retreated behind an invisible wall.

Hollis was beautiful, Cutter admitted. One of the most beautiful women he'd ever seen. And he had a knot of cold fury in his gut at the mere sight of her. Damn her and her icy facade, her expression of near boredom as she looked at the box containing her father. Buck Champion was dead, and his almighty daughter obviously didn't give a damn.

Oh, yes, he would gladly wring her lovely neck.

" . . . Amen," the minister said.

Hollis jerked in surprise as Kathleen touched her arm. She looked at her aunt and saw the tears shimmering in her eyes.

"Everyone will speak to us here," Kathleen told her quietly. "Buck's instructions stated that no one was to come back to Gauntlet Run after the service. Dear God, Hollis, I can't believe he's really gone. I expect him to appear any minute and start barking orders. I'm so glad you're here."

Before Hollis could reply, they were approached by the vice president. Hollis smiled politely, murmured her thanks at the condolences expressed, then greeted the governor as he stepped forward. She tuned out their words and went through the motions of social protocol, feeling like a robot. She was damp, cold and tired and wanted nothing more than to escape from the dreary scene.

Hollis suddenly thought of the angry stranger, her eyes darting quickly over the throng of people. He wasn't there. Without having gone through the proper procedure of expressing his sympathies to Buck Champion's family, the man had simply disappeared. He was rude, Hollis fumed. Insolent and rude. How dare he stare at her with such obvious disapproval, then snub her, Kathleen and Floyd, as though he were too good, too far above them, to pay his respects. Forget it. Why she was wasting her mental energies on an arrogant stranger, she didn't know, and she refused to give him another moment of her time.

He *was* handsome, she had to admit. He'd exuded a raw virility, an aura of masculinity, that was nearly palpable—

Enough, she ordered herself. She would *not* think about him anymore.

"Thank you for coming." Hollis shook a woman's hand.

"He was a wonderful man." The woman dabbed at her eyes with a hankie. "We'll miss Buck Champion. All of Texas will miss him."

"Yes," Hollis said, gritting her teeth.

"It's so wonderful that you're home at last, dear," the woman said. "Buck would be so pleased. I only wish...well, at least you're back where you belong. Goodbye, dear."

Floyd Barnett cleared his throat. "Kathleen, Hollis, let's get to the limousine. It's going to start pouring again any second."

"Yes, I'm chilled to the bone," Kathleen agreed.

"I'll be there in a minute," Hollis said.

Kathleen looked concerned. "Hollis?"

"Let her have a moment alone, Kathleen," Floyd suggested, taking his wife's arm.

Hollis walked slowly to the casket and ran her fingertip over a velvety petal of one of the multitude of yellow roses. Her throat tightened, and she drew a steadying breath as she fought her tears. She had the urge to bury her face in the fragrant flowers and cry. Yet who would she be crying for? she wondered. For Buck, her father, so dynamically alive one minute and gone the next? Or would the tears be turned inward to herself, for all that wasn't and all that might have been?

No, Hollis thought, no tears. They would serve no purpose, only stir up old, painful memories that would rip at her soul.

"Goodbye, Buck Champion," she whispered. "Goodbye, Daddy."

As Hollis turned to leave, she looked at her hand in shock. Without realizing it, she had tightened her hold on the roses, crushing the soft petals. A breeze flicked the broken flowers from her palm and scattered them on the wet ground. Hollis stared at them for a long moment, then squared her shoulders, lifted her chin and walked to the waiting car.

"Amen," the television announcer said in a hushed voice, then said no more.

Inside the limousine, Hollis took her hat from her head and grasped her aunt's hand for a moment as the huge car started to move.

Kathleen Champion Barnett was forty-five years old, looked every bit of her age, and didn't care. She was fifteen pounds overweight, as was her husband, and she didn't care about that, either. Kathleen refused to patronize the "fat farms," as she called them, that were so popular with her friends. She was glad to know that Floyd thought her to be as sexy as when they'd been married twenty years before, so she figured the heck with starving to death on carrot sticks and lettuce.

Kathleen looked at her niece and frowned. "You're exhausted, Hollis. I'm sure Mattie will have some lunch prepared, then you can rest until the reading of Buck's will at four. Leave it to Buck to have this programmed down to the last detail. Can you imagine not inviting anyone back to the house after the funeral? Talk about insulting some big shots. Oh, well, what the heck. I'm going to miss that brother of mine."

"Bastard that he was." Floyd chuckled.

"Indeed he was," Kathleen said. "No one knows that better than Hollis. When I think of how Buck—"

"Kathleen, don't," Hollis murmured. "Don't rake it all up again. Think of the lovely times you and I had when you came to visit me in Mexico City." She laughed softly. "Even though you did nag me unmercifully to come back to Texas."

"And back to Gauntlet Run," Kathleen said decisively. "I still say you should've come home after Raymond was killed. You're as stubborn as Buck was."

"And you're not?" Floyd said, smiling.

"Don't be silly," Kathleen scoffed. "I'm the calm, even-tempered Champion."

"My dear wife." Floyd was hooting with laughter. "You're full of it."

"I'm ignoring you, Floyd." Kathleen rapped him playfully on the knee. "Hollis, I'm almost afraid to ask you this, for fear I won't like the answer, but how long are you planning on staying? Please, darling, tell me you're home for good."

Hollis shook her head. "You know better than that. I'll stay a few days to have a nice visit with you, but that's it."

"Oh, Hollis, why?" Kathleen wanted to know. "You can paint here, get involved in charities, just as you have in Mexico City. I doubt that you've made a dent in the trust fund your mother left you. You could pursue all your interests, yet be close to me and Floyd."

"My home is in Mexico City now."

"But what about Gauntlet Run?" Kathleen said.

"What makes you think my father left it to me?" Hollis asked. "He ordered me off of Gauntlet Run seven years ago, remember? I can't picture him handing it over to me now."

"Well, we'll know at four o'clock," Floyd said, "when the will is read. I suppose you'll inherit a bundle, Kathleen. Our poor accountant will go crazy trying to find more tax shelters for us."

"Buck had better have provided well for me in that will," Kathleen said. "I certainly earned it, being his sister. There were times when I despised him, probably even hated him. But I'm going to miss him. Oh, how I'm going to miss him."

Floyd nodded, then gently held Kathleen's hand as a silence fell over the car. Hollis turned to look out the side window as they left the city limits of Houston. The land stretched as far as the eye could see—Texas land.

Hollis sighed, a deep, weary-sounding sigh that seemed to come from the very depths of her soul. How she had loved all this as a young girl, she mused. She'd been Texas-born, a Champion. Gauntlet Run had been her home, her haven, and Buck Champion her knight in shining armor.

No, she admitted, he'd never had much time for her, but she'd cherished the stolen moments they'd had together. After Marilyn Champion had died of pneumonia, when Hollis was four, Mattie had raised her, and Hollis had been a happy little girl.

It hadn't been until her teenage years that she'd begun to feel the sting of Buck's neglect. It seemed as though he was never home to share, listen to her, just be there for her. There was always a plane to catch, a meeting to attend, people to see. Everyone wanted Buck Champion. Everyone had him except Hollis.

She'd done everything she could to gain Buck's attention, Hollis recalled dryly. She'd gotten in trouble at school, collected an exorbitant number of speeding tickets, dressed outrageously. But Buck's cold, silent fury at her actions had cut her to the quick, and she'd rapidly fallen back into her dutiful role, trying desperately to please him, to hear a word of praise, be rewarded with a smile or hug.

Then there was Raymond Ramirez, Hollis thought, watching the scenery as the car sped along. Raymond. He'd come into her life just before her twentieth birthday, and he'd loved her. Even more, he'd needed her. She had been the focal point of his existence, and she'd basked in his undivided attention. Raymond had . . .

Hollis's mind was pulled from the past as the first sight of the pristine white-planked fence came into view, marking the boundary of Champion land, of Gauntlet Run. Her mind had been a blur as she'd come to Gauntlet Run in the taxi from the airport, then entered the limousine shortly thereafter. But now she saw it clearly, sweeping before her in majestic beauty.

Cattle and horses grazed in the distance, and windmills dotted the expanse, churning up the precious commodity of water. Patches of blue sky peeked from between the gray clouds as though declaring that Champion land demanded sunshine even on a rainy day, land that stretched for miles and miles, making up one of the biggest, richest spreads in the state. Gauntlet Run.

In her dash to be ready for the funeral, there had been no time for Hollis to be affected by the view earlier. Hollis's heart quickened now as the sprawling, one-story ranch house came into view. It was enormous, built with numerous wings extending off from the main area. Hollis had seen it once from an airplane and decided it looked like a pinwheel at the center of which stood Buck Champion.

But no more, Hollis mused. Buck was gone. Gauntlet Run stood empty, except for Mattie. Oh, the parties Buck had given in that house, on that land, she remembered. Texas barbecues were his specialty, with people flying in from all over the state to attend. From the time she was a child, Hollis had moved among the rich and powerful, not realizing the importance of those who acted at her father's command. Thousands of dollars would be spent for a Sunday afternoon's festivities, where champagne flowed and food was in abundance. Hollis grew to love the parties, as Buck kept her close to his side for hours and she glowed with happiness. It wasn't until years later that Hollis realized he'd been showing her off as just another of his possessions, as a prize he held that no man was to take away from him.

"I want food," Kathleen said, bringing Hollis from her reverie, "and a hot shower. I'm glad I keep some clothes out here. This suit is soaked. How does Gauntlet Run look, Hollis? Seven years is a long time. Does the house seem smaller?''

"No, actually, it appears larger.''

The driver turned under a wrought-iron archway and drove toward the house, which was set far back from the road.

"Much larger,'' Hollis said as the limousine followed the curve of the circular drive.

"That's strange,'' Floyd said. "People usually remember houses as being bigger than they actually are.''

"My father had a way of filling it to overflowing,'' Hollis explained. "Does that make sense?''

"Oh, yes,'' Kathleen said.

The driver stopped in front of the sweeping front porch and bounded out of the car to open the car door for his passengers. Hollis stepped out and walked forward, aware once again of the throbbing pain in her temples. She ascended the three wide steps and crossed the porch. Mattie pulled open the double hand-carved wooden doors.

"Come in, come in,'' she said. "You're damp and cold, all of you. Change into dry things, then have a hot lunch. I watched the funeral on television. Mr. Champion would have liked it, with all those important people getting soaked to the skin because of him. Go, go!'' She flapped her hands at the trio.

Mattie spun around and scurried back in the direction of the kitchen. She was short and round, and her hair was a frizzy mass of gray curls on her head. She'd admit to having seen her sixtieth birthday but refused to divulge her age beyond that. Hollis loved Mattie and had literally flown into the housekeeper's arms earlier that morning.

"Thank God some things never change,'' Hollis said, turning to Kathleen and Floyd. "She's so wonderful.''

"And she'll whop your fanny if you don't get out of those wet clothes," Kathleen said. "And hurry. I'm starving. We'll meet you in the dining room."

Hollis smiled and left the foyer, which had Spanish tile on the floor and a chandelier overhead. Hollis went down a thickly carpeted hallway and entered the bedroom that had been hers since childhood. She saw that Mattie had unpacked the small suitcase Hollis had tossed on the bed. Everything would be in the dresser and closet, Hollis knew; it was Mattie's message that she wanted Hollis to stay on at Gauntlet Run.

"It's too late for that, my sweet Mattie," Hollis said as she tugged at the back zipper of her dress. "Much too late." Nothing had been changed in her room, she realized. It was still decorated in white eyelet, with accents of pale yellow and mint green. A glance into her closet revealed an extensive seven-year-old wardrobe encased in clear plastic bags. Knickknacks and expensive perfumes were on the white French provincial dressing table, along with a pearl-handled brush and comb set that had belonged to her mother.

A few minutes later, Hollis was standing under the warm spray of water in the shower, feeling the chill leave her body. When she was finished, she dried off with a large, fluffy yellow towel, then went back into the bedroom to gather the clothes she'd brought with her from Mexico City. As she pulled on pale pink bikini panties and a matching bra, her gaze took in the large, airy room.

Memories, memories, memories, she thought. Hollis the little girl had slept there, then Hollis the adolescent, then Hollis the woman. And it had been from this room that she had fled, had snuck away in the night through the French doors to meet Raymond and leave Gauntlet Run. How long ago it all was; how like only yesterday it suddenly seemed.

Dressed in doe-colored suede pants and blazer and a dark brown silk blouse, Hollis sat down at her dressing table to smooth her hair into place. Pulled tightly back from her forehead, it was twisted into a chignon at the nape of her neck, and her green eyes suddenly appeared to her to be too large for her face. The shadows under her eyes attested to her fatigue, and she got wearily to her feet. She was definitely going to take a nap, she decided, before enduring the ordeal of the reading of her father's will.

Hollis left the bedroom and went down the long hall, across the foyer, and down another hall to the dining room. The murmur of voices reached her, and she quickened her step as she realized that Kathleen and Floyd were waiting for her. At the doorway to the dining room she stopped abruptly, nearly stumbling as she saw who was talking to Kathleen and Floyd.

It was him...the man...the angry, rude, arrogant man from the cemetery, Hollis thought incredulously. What in heaven's name was he doing at Gauntlet Run? He'd changed his clothes, was wearing faded jeans, boots and a royal blue western shirt. He was handsome, rugged, with those clothes molded to his muscled body like a second skin, and... But who was he? And what was he doing there?

"Oh, Hollis," Kathleen said when she saw her in the doorway, "thank goodness. I'm about to die from hunger. Floyd, will you tell Mattie that we're ready to eat?"

Hollis moved slowly forward, her eyes riveted on the tall man, who was looking at her steadily, with no readable expression on his face.

"I believe introductions are needed, Kathleen," Hollis said coolly.

"Oh, of course," Kathleen said. "I'm sorry. Hollis Champion Ramirez, this is Cutter McKenzie. Hollis, Cutter is the foreman, manager—whatever you want to call it—of Gauntlet Run. Cutter, this is Buck's daughter, Hollis."

"Mrs. Ramirez." Cutter extended his large hand.

Hollis had placed her hand in his before she realized she'd done it. "You run the ranch?" she asked. "How long have you . . . My father was always in full control of Gauntlet Run, Mr. McKenzie."

"Goodness, how formal you two sound," Kathleen said. "Use first names, for heaven's sake. We're all family here."

"Family?" Hollis repeated.

"I've been here for six years," Cutter said, tightening his hold on Hollis's hand. "Apparently Kathleen didn't mention me to you during any of her visits."

"I thought I had," Kathleen said, shrugging. "Oh, good, here's lunch."

Hollis, acutely aware that Cutter McKenzie was still holding her hand, attempted to pull free, only to have his grip grow tighter yet. His callused fingers felt abrasive against her soft skin, and his entire hand was warm, very warm, and sent a tingling heat up her arm and across her breasts.

"My hand, please?" she said stiffly.

He nodded and smiled slightly as he slowly relinquished his hold. It was a smile, Hollis decided, that appeared smug, cocky. She couldn't believe this! Buck Champion had placed the running of Gauntlet Run in the hands of this muscle-bound cowboy? Cutter McKenzie had been in charge for six years? It didn't make sense. No matter how busy Buck was with outside activities, nothing had come before Gauntlet Run. *She* certainly had never come before the ranch.

"Hollis, sit," Mattie said sternly. "You were a million miles away."

"What? Oh, I'm sorry. You'll excuse us, Mr. McKenzie?"

"I'm only waiting for you to be seated, Mrs. Ramirez," he said, grinning at her, "so I might take my own chair."

"You're what?" Hollis sat down heavily next to Kathleen. Her eyes widened as Cutter walked around the table and sat opposite her.

"Eat up now," Mattie said. "Cutter, I've got your favorite peach cobbler for dessert."

"You're my best girlfriend, Mattie."

"I wouldn't be one of your women, Cutter McKenzie," Mattie said. "The line is too long."

Cutter chuckled, then looked over at Hollis, who was still staring at him. "Is something wrong, Mrs. Ramirez?" he asked pleasantly.

"Call each other Hollis and Cutter," Kathleen suggested.

"All right," Cutter said. "Hollis. Do I have a bug on my nose, Hollis? You seem to be staring at me."

"What? Oh, no, I'm sorry. This is a surprise to me, that's all. I'm having a difficult time believing that my father relinquished control of the management of Gauntlet Run. Men in charge of various duties on the ranch used to report in at dawn and dusk. Nothing happened here except under my father's direct orders. He even called when he was halfway around the world." He called them, she thought, but he would never just call to talk to me.

"As of six years ago, those orders have come from me," Cutter said, his jaw tightening slightly. "I was the only one reporting in to Buck, and not necessarily on a daily basis."

"I was sure I told you about Cutter," Kathleen said. "Well, it doesn't matter. You've met each other now, and that's what counts. Cutter has done marvelous things here at Gauntlet Run, Hollis. You must have him give you a tour. He's brought in some of the most incredible mares, and the babies are gorgeous. Gauntlet Run has its own stallions now, too, and Cutter gets calls from across the state wanting stud service from a Gauntlet Run stallion. It's all very exciting.''

"Yes, I'm sure it is." Hollis was frowning. "We were always known more for our beef than our horses, though."

"Things change," Cutter said.

Their eyes met, and Hollis's flashed with anger. "Yes, they certainly do," she said. "I can remember when the ranch hands ate in the bunkhouse." She didn't know why or how, but this man was a threat to her.

"Hollis," Kathleen gasped, "that was uncalled for. Maybe you don't understand, dear. Cutter runs this ranch and has for years. He eats at this table and sleeps under this roof."

"I beg your pardon?" Hollis wasn't sure she'd heard right.

"That's right," Cutter said. "Just like one of the family." And it was bugging the hell out of Miss High-and-Mighty, he thought. She hadn't stepped foot in that house in seven years, yet she resented the fact that someone other than a Champion had been made to feel welcome. She was a rich snob. He knew he was goading her, rubbing in his status, but it served her right. She needed to be taken down a peg or two. "How're things in the investment business, Floyd?"

Hollis fumed as Floyd launched into a dissertation on a new condominium project he was putting together. Who in the blazes did Cutter McKenzie think he was? He'd been running Gauntlet Run for six years! Why? Why had Buck done it? And Cutter slept in the house, had Mattie prepare his meals? None of it made sense. Buck Champion would never have... But he had. Cutter was proof of that. There he sat with his smug smile, letting her know just how all-fired important he was around there.

"It's a beauty of a deal," Floyd was saying.

"It sounds like it," Cutter said. "Hollis, aren't you hungry? You haven't touched a thing on your plate."

Hollis got to her feet and tossed her napkin onto the table. "No, Mr. McKenzie, I am *not* hungry. It seems that I've lost my appetite. If all of you will excuse me, I believe I'll go take a nap."

As Hollis marched from the room, her fury reached the boiling point as Cutter's throaty chuckle drifted after her, taunting her with its rich, masculine rumble.

Chapter 2

Hollis," Kathleen said, "wake up. Hollis?"

Hollis slowly lifted her lashes. "What? Oh, Kathleen. Goodness, I was so sound asleep I didn't remember where I was for a moment."

"It's after three. I thought I should wake you so you'll have time to come out of your fog before the reading of the will. I hate to take naps. I feel groggy for the rest of the day."

Hollis pushed herself up and leaned against the headboard, recalling when she'd come to take the nap. After leaving the dining room, she'd hurried to her bedroom, stripped off her clothes and donned a lavender satin nightgown. Despite her anger at Cutter McKenzie, she'd fallen asleep moments after crawling into bed.

"Feeling better?" Kathleen asked.

"Much. I was even more tired than I realized."

"This has been emotionally draining as well as physically." Kathleen sat on the edge of the bed.

"Ugh, my hair. I'll have to undo it and start over," Hollis said, fingering the loose chignon. "Kathleen, who is Cutter McKenzie?"

Kathleen sighed. "I was so sure I'd told you about him. I realize now that Buck hired him while Floyd and I were on our Caribbean cruise. By the time I visited you again the following year, Cutter was so much a part of this place it didn't occur to me to make a newsflash-type announcement to you about him. I'm sorry, Hollis. I realize that his being here has come as a shock to you."

"Weren't you surprised when Buck first hired him? Didn't you ask my father why he was relinquishing his authority of Gauntlet Run?"

Kathleen shrugged. "Yes, I was surprised, but I didn't push Buck about it. You know how he was. Once he made a decision, that was it. Cutter has done marvelous things here, Hollis."

"But why does he live in the house? He is, after all, the ranch foreman. He could stay in one of the cottages that the married hands use."

"I never questioned Buck about it, Hollis. I would guess, though, that this place seemed awfully big and empty after you left. Perhaps Buck liked the idea of having someone else under the roof besides him and Mattie."

"Oh, please, spare me," Hollis said, crossing her arms over her breasts. "Don't give me a hearts-and-flowers number about how much my father missed me. He didn't have time for me when I was here. What's next? Cutter is like the son Buck always wished he had? After my mother died, Buck could have married again and filled this place with children. He was just too selfish with his time to devote himself to a serious relationship."

"All right, Hollis," Kathleen said wearily, getting to her feet. "I don't want to get into an argument as to why Buck treated Cutter like family. Truth remains that he *is* like family, and we all admire him. Per Buck's instructions,

Cutter will be at the reading of the will, and I'll expect you to behave. You were very rude to him at lunch, but we've all dismissed it as your being tired. I'll see you in the living room.'' She turned and left the room, shutting the door behind her.

Hollis opened her mouth, then snapped it closed. She'd just been scolded, she realized. There she'd sat in her frilly, little-girl bed being told she was a naughty child for having been rude to the great Cutter McKenzie. He'd certainly charmed the socks off Kathleen and Floyd, and Mattie made his favorite dessert and ... What was wrong with these people? Couldn't they see Cutter's smug smiles? Surely they were aware of how cocky and arrogant he was. *He* had been rude to *her* at lunch with his condescending remarks.

''And you sound like a kid throwing a tantrum,'' Hollis muttered, flipping back the blankets on the bed.

As Hollis dressed in the suede suit, then sat at the dressing table to fix her hair, she concentrated on the subject of Cutter McKenzie. She still didn't understand her father's motivation behind hiring Cutter, but she apparently wasn't going to get any answers to that riddle. Since everyone seemed to adore Mr. McKenzie, she'd only come across as a spoiled brat if she were to continually voice her displeasure as to his status at Gauntlet Run. So, she'd pretend he was invisible during the next few days, then return to Mexico City.

Cutter invisible? Hollis repeated in her mind. He was hardly that. The man was so incredibly male, so...there, it was a bit disconcerting. Everything about him gave testimony to his masculinity. He exuded a raw, sensual virility that must have the women of Houston fighting to get near him. And those damnable blue eyes of his. She'd already seen that they could speak volumes: icy cold in anger, sky blue when dancing with amusement. What color were those eyes, she wondered, when they reflected Cutter's desire, his physical want and need of a woman? What would it be like to be made love to by him, by a man of such power and strength?

Hollis jumped to her feet as she felt a warm flush on her cheeks. "What an absurd thought!" And totally unlike her. She didn't go around fantasizing about making love with men she didn't know—or men she did know, for that matter. She hadn't been to bed with a man since Raymond's death. She kept her relationships light, friendly, and the men who pushed for more were sent on their way. Where the image in her mind of making love with Cutter had come from, she didn't know. But enough was enough. From that moment on, she would be only polite to the man.

"So there," Hollis said, going to the door. Super. She sounded like a little girl again. If she didn't get her act together, she'd end up sticking her tongue out at the gorgeous Mr. McKenzie. The way things were going, Kathleen would probably send her to bed without any dinner.

Hollis shook her head in disgust and left the bedroom. She found Kathleen and Floyd in the living room.

"Ah, Hollis," Floyd greeted her, "you look much better, very rested, very lovely. Would you like a drink? It's early in the day, but we felt the occasion called for it. Buck's attorney should be along soon."

"I'll have some sherry, please," Hollis said, sitting down in a soft velveteen-covered chair. "Kathleen tells me that Cutter is to be at the reading of the will."

"That's right," said a deep voice behind her. "I'll have Scotch if you're playing bartender, Floyd."

Hollis's gaze flickered over Cutter as he moved past her chair to the bar across the room. She caught the aroma of soap and a woodsy after-shave and saw that his hair was slightly damp. He'd changed into black western-cut slacks that molded to his narrow hips and muscled legs and wore a gray western shirt that strained across his shoulders and back. To Hollis's annoyance, she felt a shiver dance along her spine, and she averted her eyes from Cutter's magnificent body.

"Your sherry," Cutter said, interrupting her reverie.

Hollis looked up quickly to see him standing directly in front of her, holding a small crystal glass that seemed dwarfed in his large hand.

"Thank you," she said, directing her attention to the glass. As her fingers closed around it, Cutter didn't immediately relinquish his hold. When their fingers met, the heat shot up Hollis's arm and across her breasts.

"You do want it, don't you?" Cutter asked, his voice low.

As Hollis looked into his eyes and saw the amusement dancing in the blue pools, anger flashed in her emerald-green ones. Why did he insist on taunting her? She almost preferred the unexplained anger she'd seen on his face and in his eyes at the cemetery to this smirking smugness. Well, she had news for Mr. McKenzie. She couldn't care less what he did.

"My glass, please, Mr. McKenzie," she said, tilting her chin up.

"Of course, Hollis." He withdrew his hand. "I simply didn't wish to see you spill it on that lovely suit. That's genuine suede, isn't it?"

"It is. An original."

"Only the best for a Champion." He lifted his glass in a salute.

"And a Ramirez. Surely you haven't forgotten that my last name is Ramirez."

"Widow of Raymond," Cutter said, nodding. "The son of one of the wealthiest families in Mexico. I understand that you met Raymond Ramirez when he came to Gauntlet Run with his father to negotiate the buying of a valuable bull. You were home for the summer after your freshman year at college."

"That's correct," Hollis said, then stared into her glass. "Not that it's any of your business, Mr. McKenzie."

"Hollis," Kathleen interrupted her sharply, "Mac Winston just drove up. I'd appreciate it if you and Cutter declared a truce while he's here."

"I apologize, Kathleen," Cutter said. "This wasn't the time to bring up what happened seven years ago."

"There will never be a time," Hollis said. "I have no intention of discussing it with you. Ever."

Wrong, Cutter thought, then took a swallow of his drink. We *are* going to discuss it, Hollis. Every detail.

"Hollis." There was a warning tone in Kathleen's voice.

Floyd laughed. "Kathleen, quit acting like a mother hen."

"I would," she replied, "if these two would refrain from squabbling like children. This is ridiculous."

Cutter chuckled and crossed the room to place his glass on the bar, while Hollis frowned and got to her feet just as Buck's attorney was shown into the room by Mattie. Mac Winston was short and thin, had just celebrated his sixty-third birthday, and was one of the sharpest, highest-paid lawyers in Texas.

"Hollis," he said, smiling broadly, "what a delight to see you. You've gotten even more beautiful, my dear."

"Thank you, Mac." She kissed him on the cheek. "It's good to see you, too."

"I wish it hadn't taken Buck's death to bring you home," Mac said. "Well, what's done is done. Shall we go into Buck's office? I'll feel much more important if I sit behind that massive desk of his."

What Mac had referred to as Buck's office was actually a library with floor-to-ceiling shelves full of books. It had been decorated with a totally masculine flair, and Hollis could remember her father spending countless hours in the large room. As a child, she had not been allowed to enter this private domain without Buck's permission.

The group settled into large leather chairs as Mac took his place behind the desk. He opened his briefcase and withdrew a blue folder.

"It's hard to believe that Buck is gone," Mac said, opening the folder and taking out the papers, "but he is, and my instructions were to come to Gauntlet Run today and read his will to you. The first six pages contain donations to be made to Buck's favorite charities and the projects for the underprivileged that he was involved in. He said you'd be bored to tears if I read all that, and I was to skip over it. You will all be receiving copies of this document if you care to examine the bequeaths."

"That's fine," Kathleen said.

Mac put on wire-rimmed reading glasses. "All right, we'll proceed. Floyd, would you ask Mattie to join us, please?"

"Certainly."

A few minutes later a somewhat flustered Mattie came into the room, and Cutter rose, motioning for the housekeeper to sit in his chair. Cutter leaned against a bookshelf and crossed his arms loosely over his chest.

Mac cleared his throat and began to read from the papers. "To my housekeeper and friend Matilda—Mattie—Henderson, I leave the sum of one hundred thousand dollars."

"Dear heavenly angels!" Mattie gasped.

"I also guarantee her a home at Gauntlet Run for the remainder of her days or until such time as Gauntlet Run is no longer occupied. This is but a small token compared to the love and warmth Mattie has given to Gauntlet Run."

"Bless his heart," Mattie said, sniffling into her hankie.

"To my sister, Kathleen," Mac continued, "I leave the sum of one million dollars. To my brother-in-law, Floyd Barnett, I leave a matching sum of one million dollars. These monies are to compensate Kathleen for putting up with me, and to compensate Floyd for putting up with Kathleen.''

''Hear, hear,'' Floyd said. Kathleen shot him a stormy glare. Floyd smiled at her warmly.

Mac looked up at the group. ''Before I read this last section, please remember that these decisions were Buck's, not mine. This will is legal and binding and cannot be broken. All right, here we go.''

Hollis clutched her hands in her lap as she looked at Mac Winston.

''To my daughter, Hollis, I leave the house of Gauntlet Run and all its furnishings. I leave her one vehicle of her choosing. I also leave her Gauntlet Run land in the form of twenty feet surrounding the house. This bequeath is made with the stipulation that Hollis must remain living in the house for six months after my death.''

''What?'' Hollis whispered.

''I also leave her the sum of five million dollars with no conditions attached. However, if Hollis vacates the building before the six month period is over, the house and all its furnishings will become the property of Cutter McKenzie.''

''What?'' Hollis shrieked, jumping to her feet.

''Hollis, sit down,'' Mac said. She sank back into the chair, a stunned expression on her face. ''To Cutter McKenzie, I leave the land of Gauntlet Run, including all buildings, livestock, and equipment, with the provision that he must continue in his role of foreman for six months after my death. If he should leave before that time, all land, livestock, and equipment will revert to Hollis Champion Ramirez. I also leave Cutter McKenzie the sum of five million dollars with no conditions attached.''

''I don't believe this,'' Hollis said, shaking her head.

''If both Hollis and Cutter,'' Mac read on, ''conform to these stipulations, each may at the end of the six months negotiate with the other to buy that person's share. Each must give the other first option to buy before placing any portion of Gauntlet Run on the open market. It should be noted that if either Hollis or Cutter plans to be away from Gauntlet Run for longer than twenty-four hours, he or she must clear those plans with the other so as not to break the rules of this directive.''

Hollis shook her head, bewildered.

"Though it may not seem so," Mac read, "I am of sound mind. I also love those of you present, who are listening to Mac read my last will and testament. Let it not be said that Buck Champion left this earth quietly. God bless you all. I love you all. Signed, William Buchanan Champion.''

This was a nightmare, Hollis thought frantically. She would wake up and discover that this was all just a bad dream.

"Any questions?" Mac said.

It was true, Hollis thought, pressing her hand to her forehead. This was crazy! She had to think this through, but her mind was whirling.

"Leave it to Buck to create a hoopla," Kathleen said, laughing. "I, for one, am delighted to know that Hollis will be with us for at least six months. And it's reassuring that you'll be in charge of Gauntlet Run, Cutter. I must say that you and Hollis appear a bit shell-shocked.''

Cutter pushed himself away from the shelf, then ran his hand down his face. "That's a pretty accurate description of how I feel," he said, shaking his head. "I'm not sure this has totally sunk in.''

Hollis got to her feet and spun around to face him. "Are you trying to insinuate you knew nothing about this?''

"Believe me, Mrs. Ramirez," he said none too quietly, "if I had, I would have done everything possible to talk Buck out of it. The last thing I want to do is live under the same roof with you for six months.''

"Here they go again," Kathleen said, throwing up her hands.

"You seem to forget, Mr. McKenzie," Hollis said, planting her hands on her hips, "this is *my* roof. It will be a cold day in hot places before you live under it."

"Oh, really?" he said, narrowing his eyes. "Then I suggest you stay out of *my* barn and away from *my* horses."

"You…are…despicable." Hollis turned to Mac. "Mac, I won't stand for this ludicrous plan. I'm contesting the will."

"It's legal and binding." Mac was grinning. "There's not a thing you can do. Of course, you could just pack up and go back to Mexico City."

"Good idea," Cutter said.

Hollis glared at him. "You'd like that, wouldn't you? Then all of Gauntlet Run would be yours. Well, not on your life, buster. I want you off this land."

"I'm not going anywhere," Cutter said.

"In six months you will," Hollis promised him. "I'm going to buy you out, McKenzie. This is Champion land."

"Then you're definitely staying, Hollis?" Kathleen said. "That's wonderful."

"Yes, I'm staying. No. No, I'm not. I refuse to allow my father to push my buttons. But if I leave … Oh, I don't know what I'm going to do. Mac, why did Buck do this? What did he say to you when he dictated the provisions of the will?"

"That's confidential, Hollis." Mac couldn't keep the grin off his face.

"I have to check on my roast," Mattie said, hurrying toward the door. "Goodness! Such goings-on."

"I wonder," Kathleen said, tapping her fingertip against her chin, "if Buck was doing a bit of matchmaking."

"What?" Hollis and Cutter said in unison.

"Well, Buck's objections to Hollis marrying Raymond Ramirez were that they were too young, *and* the fact that Hollis would be leaving Gauntlet Run. Buck had always pictured his son-in-law taking over this place someday. He was livid when Hollis didn't act accordingly. It was obvious how much Buck admired and respected Cutter. I can see Buck's deliciously devious mind concocting a plan whereby Hollis and Cutter would be forced to live at Gauntlet Run together. He'd be counting on the two of you falling in love and living happily ever after here on the ranch."

"Oh, boy," Hollis said, rolling her eyes heavenward.

"Interesting," Cutter said, chuckling. "Very interesting."

"Well," Mac said, getting to his feet, "I must be on my way. My secretary will see that each of you receives a copy of the will. I'm to be notified if either Hollis or Cutter breaks the rules of the provisions of the will so that ownership can be deeded to the other person. I'll be in touch."

"I see you out, Mac," Floyd offered.

"I can't remember if I told Mattie that Floyd and I are staying for dinner before we drive back into Houston," Kathleen said, following Floyd and Mac from the room.

A silence fell over the library, and Hollis walked across the room to stare unseeing at a row of books on a shelf. She wrapped her arms around her elbows and drew a deep, steadying breath.

Damn that Buck Champion, she fumed. He was controlling her even from the grave. She knew there had been people watching her in the past seven years, detectives who reported to Buck. She'd even confronted one in the marketplace in Mexico and he'd admitted it. She'd thought Buck's death had meant the loss of a father but the gaining of her freedom at long last. But he was manipulating her even in death.

What should she do? Hollis thought frantically. Beat Buck at his own game? Walk out of there tomorrow, leave Gauntlet Run to Cutter, and never look back? No! Cutter McKenzie had no right to this house, this land. Cutter would see her as a woman defeated and give her that maddening smug smile of his as he crowed over his victory. No, she wouldn't leave. She'd fight for Gauntlet Run. And, by God, she'd win!

How much validity was there in Kathleen's theory? Hollis wondered. Had Buck actually thought that Hollis and Cutter would fall head over heels in love with each other? How absurd. Well, at least Buck wouldn't have the satisfaction of *that* happening, if it *had* been his plan. It would have served Buck right if she'd returned for his funeral already married to someone else. But Buck knew every move she made, of course. Oh, how she wished he were there so she could give him a piece of her mind.

"Hollis," Cutter said, coming up behind her.

She turned to look up at him, a determined tilt to her chin. "Yes?"

"I honestly didn't know anything about this. I hope you believe that," he said, his voice low.

"Yes, I suppose I do," she said, sighing. "Buck liked the dramatic too much to have let anyone in on this fiasco. He loved being in the spotlight. To just die quietly would never have satisfied him. This way, the ramifications of his death will be felt for a long time. Oh, yes, Buck planned this very carefully. Control, Mr. McKenzie. That was his forte."

"You sound so bitter," Cutter said, shaking his head.

"And justly so. There are things you don't know."

"Did it ever occur to you that there are things that *you* don't know?" he said, his jaw tightening. "You haven't been here in seven years. Are you so sure you really know who Buck Champion was?"

"Oh, believe me, I know who he was. He's the man who forced me to choose between Raymond and him. Buck didn't think for one minute that I'd have the courage to defy him."

"But you did. You snuck off in the night with your lover and went to Mexico."

"Ah, I see he shared all the little details with you."

"We talked a great deal about many things, Hollis. I've been here for six years, remember?"

"And you became the son he never had," she said sarcastically. "How touching. And now what? You're supposed to woo and win his naughty daughter? Is that part of your payoff?"

"Stop it," he said through clenched teeth.

"You did very well for a six-year investment, Mr. McKenzie. You've got the Gauntlet Run land and a pile of money. Well, I've got news for you. You're not getting this house or me."

Cutter's hands shot out and he gripped her by the upper arms. "Lady," he grated, "I wouldn't touch you with a ten-foot pole. You've got hate flowing in your veins like a disease. I wouldn't run the risk of being contaminated."

"Then perhaps you'd better leave here as quickly as possible." Her green eyes were narrowed in anger. "Go, McKenzie. Get off of Champion land."

"Not a chance, honey," he said. She could see his pulse throbbing at his temple. "I've got six years of my life, my sweat and backbreaking labor, invested in this land. I'm not walking away from it."

"And I was born here! Gauntlet Run is mine."

"What do you plan to do? Paint a picture of it? You don't know the meaning of the word work."

"Get your hands off me." Her tone was icy. "And don't ever touch me again."

"Damn you," Cutter growled, then brought his mouth down hard on hers.

He slid his arm around Hollis's waist, his other hand moving to the back of her head to hold her tightly as he hauled her up against his hard body, his mouth ravishing hers. Hollis struggled to break free, but instantly knew she was no match for Cutter's strength. Instead, she went still in his arms, telling herself to pretend he wasn't there, counting on his male ego to suffer from her lack of response.

But then the kiss became gentler, became soft, sensuous, coaxing. The heat from Cutter's massive body seemed to weave into Hollis, bringing to life fingers of desire that traveled throughout her. Her breasts were crushed against the hard wall of his chest in a pain that was suddenly sweet. Of their own volition, it seemed, her lips parted to receive his insistent tongue, and her arms lifted to circle his neck. She filled her senses with the taste of him, the feel and aroma of Cutter McKenzie. Their tongues met, dueled, danced, and passions soared.

He was evoking long-forgotten wants and needs within her. Never before had she experienced a kiss like this. She felt alive. So feminine and alive. She wondered what it would be like to feel those steely muscles with her hands, instead of through layers of clothes. What ecstasy it would be to have that masculinity and power directed at her, filling her, consuming her, carrying her away from reality and reason.

Cutter lifted his head a fraction of an inch to draw a ragged breath. "Hollis." His voice was gritty with passion. "I want you."

Cutter's words seemed to slam against Hollis's mind and she stiffened in his arms. "What are you doing?" she said, her voice unsteady. "What am *I* doing?" She backed away until she thudded against the bookshelf.

"We were—" Cutter drew in a deep breath "—sharing a kiss. A helluva kiss, I might add."

"Wrong. That was basic lust in the form of a kiss," she said tightly.

"Basic lust?" He grinned at her. "Oh, come now, Hollis, surely a blue-blooded Champion doesn't engage in anything so plebeian as lust. Don't you want to dress it up a little? Call it desire or passion? Chemistry? Yeah, that's good. Chemistry."

"Get . . . out."

"You do that snooty routine very well," he said, nodding. "You get all squinty-eyed and stick your pretty little nose in the air."

"Out!" Hollis shrieked.

"Oh, I'm going. After all, I need to keep tabs on what's happening on *my* land. But don't kid yourself, Hollis. You responded to that kiss, were an equal partner in that delightful exchange. In another few minutes, who knows where we would've been. Think about it." He turned and strode out of the room.

Hollis moved on trembling legs to the leather chair and sat down, pressing her hands to her flushed cheeks. What had she done? Everything Cutter had said was true. It was insane! She detested the man.

Calm down, Hollis ordered herself. Yes, all right, she admitted, her behavior had been disgusting, but she was under a great deal of stress. Her life was being disrupted; she was emotionally drained. It was understandable that she might do something out of character. And kissing Cutter McKenzie like that was definitely out of character.

That man could kiss, though, she admitted. Of course, he'd no doubt had a great deal of practice. And he probably wasn't used to stopping at just kissing, either.

With a sigh, Hollis leaned her head back and closed her eyes. What an incredible day, she mused. "Oh, Daddy," she whispered, "you never did know when to quit, when to let go. You've really made a mess of things this time, Buck Champion."

* * *

Cutter managed to leave the house without coming across anyone, then slowed his step when he reached the plush back lawn. He walked to the enormous swimming pool and leaned against a nearby tree trunk as he stared into the crystal-clear water.

Hollis, his mind echoed. Hollis Champion Ramirez. He hadn't meant to kiss her, but what a kiss it had been. There was a helluva lot of passion beneath Hollis's cool exterior. And a lot of bitterness.

Oh, they were stubborn, those Champions. Buck had been one of the toughest men Cutter had ever met—tough and stubborn. But when it came to Hollis, Buck was vulnerable. Cutter had heard about Hollis for six years, seen the hurt, the pain, in Buck's eyes when he'd spoken of his absent daughter. Cutter had come to despise the spoiled rich kid who was putting her father through such agony.

But now? Cutter asked himself. Hollis had suffered, too. The vulnerability he'd sensed in Buck was there in Hollis. Seven years, wasted. Seven years of a standoff, with neither willing to make the first move.

And now Buck was dead.

Cutter ran his hand down his face and shook his head. Buck shouldn't have died. If only he'd listened to the doctors, had slowed down. But Buck lived the way he wanted to, right to the end. Hell, he was still doing it from his grave: pushing buttons, directing traffic, controlling people's lives. His will was proof of that.

The will, Cutter mused. Incredible. He had five million dollars. What would he ever do with five million dollars? He didn't want or need the money. It was this land he loved, Gauntlet Run. And Buck knew that, knew how much this place had come to mean to him—and Cutter wouldn't give it up without a fight.

Was Kathleen right? Cutter wondered. Had Buck set up this harebrained scheme to bring Cutter and Hollis together? Hell, they'd probably end up shooting each other.

"Buck," Cutter said aloud, "you're a real pain. You know that? This is one helluva mess you've gotten me into."

"Hey, Cutter," a man yelled, "Jesse says we've got a fence down on the west end. I'm heading out there with some of the boys."

"I'll go with you," Cutter called. "I could use the exercise." And he hoped it would help him get rid of the ache in his gut for Hollis Champion Ramirez.

Kathleen poked her head in the library. "Hello?"

"Come in, Kathleen," Hollis answered. "I'm alone."

"Where's Cutter?" Kathleen sat in a chair opposite Hollis.

"I don't know," Hollis said quietly. "He left."

"Did you reach any kind of agreement?"

"All we seem to agree upon is that we don't like each other."

"Which doesn't make sense," Kathleen said. "You hardly know each other. I don't think either one of you is being fair. Well, that's not the issue at the moment. Gauntlet Run is."

"Yes," Hollis said, closing her eyes and squeezing the bridge of her nose to try to ease her headache. "I know."

"And?" Kathleen prompted her.

Hollis looked at her aunt. "I'm staying, Kathleen. I refuse to forfeit this house and see it fall into Cutter McKenzie's hands. I can survive anything for six months, then I'll buy Cutter out. Money can be very persuasive. I'll make him an offer that he'd be a fool to pass up."

"You get more like Buck every day," Kathleen said, laughing. "Feisty and stubborn. Floyd and I will be so glad to have you back. You've always been like a daughter to me, and I've missed you terribly. What about your house in Mexico City?"

"I'll need to go down there and get some of my things. I'll ask the Ramirezes to sell or lease the house for me, I guess. This is going to be hard on them. We've been very close."

"They're lovely people. Do remember, Hollis, that according to Buck's will, you have to clear your travel plans with Cutter if you're going to be gone longer than twenty-four hours."

"Damn."

"Well, I'd hate to see you lose by default. Look at the bright side. You can put a crimp in Cutter's love life. I can hardly picture him asking your permission to go off for a weekend with a woman."

"I couldn't care less about Cutter's love life."

"Well, you must admit, dear, he is one very sexy man."

"I hadn't noticed," Hollis said, examining her fingernails.

"Oh, I see." Kathleen laughed softly. "Then you're the only one who hasn't. Even Mattie said that Cutter sure knew how to fill out a pair of jeans and a western shirt."

"That's disgusting."

"Delicious is a better word. Seriously, Hollis, Cutter is a fine man. If you gave him half a chance, you'd discover that for yourself. You two have been at each other's throats from the moment you met."

With time out for a mind-boggling kiss, Hollis thought dryly. "What are you suggesting? That Cutter and I fall madly in love to satisfy Buck's plan?"

"We're only guessing that that's what Buck intended, although I'm fairly certain that was the motive behind the provisions in his will. But, no, I'm only saying that you and Cutter got off on the wrong foot somehow, and I wish you'd both start over. You do have to live under the same roof, you know."

"We certainly do not. This is my house, and Cutter McKenzie isn't spending one more night in it."

"You're kidding. Surely you wouldn't put him out of the room he's slept in for the past six years."

"Of course I would. He has no rights within these walls."

"I'd be careful if I were you, Hollis. You'd best remember that you have no rights beyond twenty feet outside of this house."

"So?"

"So, I know how much you like to ride. Cutter owns the horses and the barn they're stabled in. And the saddles, the—"

"I get the point." Hollis got to her feet. "How could Buck do this to me?"

"Maybe he did it *for* you, dear," Kathleen said, smiling gently. "He was a very complex man. I've never claimed to fully understand him. I loved him, but I didn't always like him."

"Amen to that," Hollis said, leaning against the edge of the desk. "People worshiped him because he unselfishly devoted his energies and money to those in need. But what about *my* needs? He never had time for me, his own daughter. And selfish? He couldn't stand the thought that I wanted to be with Raymond."

"You were very young, Hollis."

"Don't make excuses for Buck, Kathleen. He wouldn't have let me go graciously if I'd been thirty. And now he's got me under his thumb again. I have no choice but to stay. I refuse to see Gauntlet Run go to Cutter McKenzie."

"So be it. The next six months should be very interesting."

"Explosive would be closer to the mark," Hollis said, smiling slightly. "Cutter and I do have a way of setting each other off."

"Ladies," Floyd announced at the door, "the cocktail hour is upon us. May I have the honor of your company?"

"Yes, you lucky devil," Kathleen said, getting to her feet, "you may. Is Cutter with you?"

"No, he sent word in that he's mending fences with the hands. Mattie will keep a plate of dinner set aside for him."

"He's mending fences?" Hollis said, frowning. "What on earth for? He's the one who gives the orders."

"Cutter's always done that," Kathleen replied. "He works right alongside his men."

"That's ridiculous," Hollis scoffed.

"No, Hollis," Floyd said, "that's a man who loves this land. He's put body and soul into Gauntlet Run. You'd best be aware of that. He won't give it up without a fight."

"Neither will I, Floyd," Hollis said.

Chapter 3

At midnight, Hollis gave up her attempt to sleep and moved off of the bed. Pushing her feet into soft slippers, she put on the satin robe that matched her lavender nightgown. Her hair tumbled down her back in a raven cascade as she left the bedroom and made her way down the hall.

The storm clouds that had disappeared over the horizon at dusk had crept back under the cloak of darkness, and rain beat against the roof in a driving cadence, accompanied by thunder and lightning.

Hollis hesitated in the living-room doorway, remembering the huge crackling fire that Floyd had built earlier that evening. Now the embers were cold, the room unwelcoming. Kathleen and Floyd had left at ten to return to Houston, Kathleen promising to call Hollis the next day. There had been no sign of Cutter McKenzie.

Deciding a glass of warm milk might soothe her jangled nerves and allow her to sleep, Hollis headed for the kitchen. She regretted her long afternoon nap, longing for sleep so that she could obtain respite from the jumble in her mind. At a crash of thunder, Hollis shivered and quickened her step.

When she entered the large yellow and orange room, she flicked on the switches, which brought the area alive with light. Hollis blinked against the sudden glare and turned half of them off to leave the room in a soft semidarkness. As she reached into the refrigerator for the milk, her glance fell on a foil-covered plate on the shelf. A note was taped to it, and she recognized Mattie's sprawling handwriting: *Cutter. Take the foil off. Micro for two minutes. There's cobbler for dessert.*

Hollis took the milk carton from the refrigerator, then looked up at the ceiling as though she could see through it to the storm raging overhead. As she poured milk into a pan and set it on the stove, she frowned.

Surely Cutter wasn't still out on the range, she thought. Didn't he have enough sense to come in out of the rain? Yes, she knew the importance of keeping the fences intact, and there were special lanterns for working at night, but it didn't require the foreman to be in attendance. Maybe Cutter had been too tired to eat when he'd come in and was sound asleep at that very moment. Or perhaps he'd stayed in the bunkhouse with the rest of the men. Or... Oh, who cared? But it was so cold and wet out there and... Forget it. It made no difference to her whatsoever whether Cutter was sloshing through the mud.

Hollis took a mug from the cupboard, set it on the counter, then poured the warm milk into the mug. A tremendous crash of thunder reverberated directly overhead, and she started in surprise, splashing most of the liquid across the countertop. The pan fell from her hand and landed noisily in the milky puddle.

Hollis stepped back as a chilling tremor swept through her. It was the last straw in an excruciatingly emotional day. She cupped her hands around her elbows and watched as the milk dripped onto the floor in a steady rhythm. She couldn't move or hardly breathe as her entire body began to tremble. Her throat ached with unshed tears and a moan escaped from her lips.

"Oh, Daddy," she whispered, covering her face with her hands, "why did you have to die?"

And then she began to weep. Hollis's grief and confusion, along with a sense of utter loneliness, coursed through her in rippling waves of agony. Tears streamed down her face and along her throat, her sobs coming in loud, gulping gasps.

Suddenly Hollis felt large, warm hands on her shoulders. With a gentle motion she was turned so that her face was nestled against a bare chest that was covered with curly dark hair and partially concealed by an open shirt. Blindly, Hollis gripped the material of the shirt in her fists as her head was pressed against the taut skin. She felt another hand splayed on her back.

Not thinking, only feeling, she cried from her heart and from her soul. She leaned farther into her haven, seeking its warmth and strength. He took his hand from her head and circled her body with his strong arms, pulling her closer, closer, into a comforting cocoon.

A collage of pictures danced before Hollis's eyes—memories, ghosts of times past, never to be reclaimed. She saw her mother as a shadowy figure, then Raymond and her father. Gone. They were all gone. And whenever they left her, there was always...

"Rain," Hollis said on a wobbly breath. "It always...rains on the day of the funeral. My mother—I remember—I wore a blue organdy dress and—then Raymond...so much rain everywhere. And now Buck, my daddy, and it rained, and rained, and—why? Why did they leave me? Why did it have to rain?"

Cutter tightened his grip on the fragile figure within the circle of his arms. He resisted the urge to run the silken cascade of her ebony hair through his fingers, and simply held her. The sound of her sobs beat against him like physical blows. Despite his size and the strength he knew he possessed, he was inept, unable to lessen her pain. She felt like a broken bird, frightened, trembling in his arms.

"It has to stop," Hollis whispered as her tears continued to flow. "The rain. Please make it stop."

"Shh, you're all right," Cutter said quietly. "The rain can't hurt you, Hollis. I'm holding you, and you're safe."

"But the rain—"

"Is like your tears. It's cleansing, needed. The thing to remember is that the sun always shines after a rainstorm. Everything will look fresh, new. You'll see."

"No," Hollis insisted, nearly choking on a sob.

"Yes. Trust me, Hollis. Everything is going to be all right. Cry for as long as you need to, and I'll just hold you."

The softly spoken, soothing words sifted through Hollis's mind, her heart and her soul, pulling her back from a faraway place. Her senses, numbed by the flow of tears, awakened, bringing into focus what somehow hadn't been there before. Smells: soap, fresh and clean, and an aroma of something purely male. Against the smooth, wet skin of her cheek, she could feel the swirl of chest hair and the tight layer of muscle beneath. Heat from large hands seemed to burn through the satin of her robe and nightgown, creating a tingling sensation within her. She could taste the salt of her own tears, tears she hadn't meant to shed as evidence of a grief she resented. And, God help her, she'd sought solace in the arms of Cutter McKenzie.

Hollis stiffened and attempted to pull away, only to feel the steel bands of Cutter's arms unyielding in their hold. She looked up at him, her breath catching in her throat as she saw the tenderness in his blue eyes. There was no amusement mocking her, none of the arrogant smugness—only gentleness, which beckoned to her, bade her to stay.

But as Hollis gazed into the eyes of Cutter McKenzie, something changed. The pools radiated a new message, one of desire. She became acutely aware of her nakedness beneath her satin nightgown and robe, of the rugged length of the body against which she was pressed so intimately. She felt the tightening of his muscles, saw his head dip toward hers, and knew he was going to kiss her.

No! her mind screamed. She had to get away from this man.

But her body seemed frozen in place as her heartbeat echoed in her ears. Cutter's lips skimmed her cheek as he kissed away her tears, and Hollis shivered from the light, sensuous foray. He kissed her throat, then the other cheek—kisses feather-light, tantalizing in their gentleness—and a soft moan escaped Hollis's lips. She had no strength to move, pull away, run. She could only feel, and she was awash with desire.

He claimed her mouth with lips soft and warm, undemanding, gentle, tasting her slowly, slowly, until she went nearly limp in his arms.

''Cutter,'' she whispered.

He wove his fingers into her hair to hold her head. With her hands, still clutching his shirt, she pulled him to her. She wanted, needed, to feel the power of his kiss, the maleness of it, needed to taste him, savor the raw masculinity and heat emanating from his body.

Cutter's mind warred with his body as he gazed into Hollis's eyes. He felt the silken strands of her hair, now knew the soft curves of her body that were pressed against him. His muscles ached with the restraint imposed on them as he fought the urge to take full possession of her mouth, meet her tongue, drink of her sweetness. Hollis seemed to be silently pleading with him to kiss her, meet her man to woman, but she was upset, vulnerable, had cried tears long overdo to be shed. He should leave her alone now, let her sleep, view tomorrow fresh, when the rain had stopped. But, damn, he wanted to kiss this woman.

"Cutter," Hollis said with a sob, "I . . . Please."

"Ah, hell," he grated, then his mouth melted over hers.

For Hollis there was no rain, or memories filled with sorrow. There were only the taste and feel of Cutter McKenzie. His tongue delved deep into her mouth in a rhythmic motion that created a matching, pulsing heat in the secret darkness of her womanhood. Her breasts grew heavy, and she ached for the touch of Cutter's hands. She returned his kiss in fevered abandon, wanting, taking, all that he would give her. Desire swirled within her and she welcomed it, allowed it to fill the chilling void of loneliness.

Cutter dropped one hand to Hollis's back, then moved lower to the slope of her buttocks, nestling her to him, his arousal strong against her. The satin material of her robe slipped away from her body, and he shifted his hands to the silky warmth of the nightgown beneath that clung to her soft curves. His hands roamed in a journey of exquisite discovery, over her back, to the slope of her hips, up to cup the sides of her breasts. Blood pounded in his veins, and the flame of passion licked throughout him. Never, *never*, had he wanted a woman as much as he did Hollis. He burned with the need of her, his body coiled with tension, as he struggled for control. He had to stop. He had to! Now!

"Hollis," he said, tearing his mouth from hers. "No. This isn't the time. You're not thinking clearly." He gripped her upper arms and set her gently away from him as he drew a ragged breath. "Hollis?"

Hollis weaved unsteadily on her feet as a wave of dizziness swept over her, then blinked as if coming out of a trance. She stared at Cutter for a long moment, then her eyes widened as her mind cleared.

She took a step backward. "I can't believe this."

"You needed to cry," Cutter said quietly. "There's no shame in that."

"And you were so eager to comfort me, weren't you?" she snapped, her eyes flashing.

A muscle jumped along Cutter's jaw. "Don't do it, Hollis," he said, his voice low. "Don't accuse me of taking advantage of you, because you know it isn't true. I called a halt to what we shared. If I hadn't, we could have ended up right here on the kitchen floor."

"How dare you say such a crude thing."

"Great," Cutter said, crossing his arms before his chest. "Do your high-and-mighty routine. I don't give a damn. But we both know that kiss was equally shared." He ran his hands through his hair in frustration. "The hell with it. I'm tired and hungry, and I have no intention of standing here rehashing the whole thing." He strode past her, yanked open the refrigerator and took out the foil-covered plate.

Hollis's stomach churned with her anger. How was she going to get out of that kitchen with her dignity intact? What Cutter had said was true, and she knew it. But she had also been upset and so couldn't be held responsible for her actions. Cutter had taken advantage of... No, he hadn't, she amended. He'd offered her comfort with his quiet strength, held her while she'd wept her endless tears. *She* had been the one to nearly plead with him to kiss, really kiss, her. She found her behavior loathsome. But she realized that she'd never before experienced such a kiss.

Cutter removed the plate from the micro, poured himself a glass of milk and settled in a chair at the table. Hollis flickered her gaze over him and noted the faded jeans stretching across his muscled thighs, remembered the feeling of his bare chest. She knew those arms, those lips, which kissed with practiced expertise. She knew his taste and aroma, and the incredible power in his massive body. She now knew the smoky hue of his blue eyes when they spoke of his desire and had felt the evidence of that desire pressing against her.

And she knew that during that rush of passion, she had wanted Cutter McKenzie.

Hollis spun around and grabbed a roll of paper towels. She cleaned up her mess from earlier, keeping her eyes averted from Cutter. But she still felt his presence in the room, as though he were hovering over her, not allowing the desire within her to diminish. She had to get out of that kitchen.

"Good night," she said, lifting her chin as she started toward to the door.

"Good night," Cutter replied. "I'll try not to disturb you when I come to bed."

Hollis stopped and turned to look at him. "I beg your pardon?"

"My room is next to yours."

"With all the bedrooms available here, I find that unacceptable."

Cutter shrugged. "So move into another bedroom. Makes no difference to me."

"*You* will be the one moving, Mr. McKenzie. This is my house, remember?"

"You bet, darlin'." He grinned at her. "You can shuffle me anywhere that suits you. Just remember to check with me before you go riding so I can decide which horse you may use and where you can go on the land—my land."

"Cutter," she said, smiling sweetly, "go to hell."

Cutter roared with laughter, the rich, throaty sound following Hollis as she swept from the room, hoping her exit had exhibited a flare of haughty disdain.

Cutter shook his head, a grin still on his face as he redirected his attention to his plate. But the smile faded as he replayed in his mind what had transpired between them. Emotions new and foreign had churned within him when he'd held Hollis in his arms while she cried. He'd registered a fierce sense of protectiveness and possessiveness toward her, a determination to stand between her and anything that might hurt her.

Strange sentiments for him, Cutter mused as he finished eating. All his life he'd traveled lightly, regarding not only the material but the emotional. Each time he'd moved on to a new ranch, he'd allowed no women to become overly important to him. Until now. Until Hollis.

"Forget it," he said, carrying his plate to the sink. Hell, she'd been crying her heart out. He'd have to be made of stone not to have responded to those tears. But the kiss? Oh, man, what a kiss. Yes, there was indeed a helluva lot of passion beneath the cool exterior of Hollis Champion Ramirez. And he wanted her. As he turned off the lights and left the kitchen he wondered what Buck would think of that.

Cutter stopped outside of Hollis's closed bedroom door and envisioned her in bed, her hair spread out over the pillow. Heat spread through the lower regions of his body, and he strode to his door beyond and closed it behind him.

Hollis lay staring up into the darkness and gasped as she heard Cutter's door slam. He was banging around over there like a bull in a china shop. How rude. Tomorrow she would definitely have his things moved to another wing of the house. But if she exerted her power within these walls, would Cutter restrict her activities on the land, draw boundary lines as to where she could ride? He probably would, the rat.

"Darn it, Buck," she said, flopping onto her stomach, "why did you do this to me? It isn't funny, Daddy. It really isn't."

As the rain slackened and drummed a quiet rhythm on the roof, at last Hollis slept.

Sprawled in his bed, Cutter laced his hands under his

head as he stared up at a ceiling he couldn't see in the
darkness. He was bone-weary from the extra hours spent
in the rain mending fences. He had to get some sleep or
tomorrow would be a grueling day. The work never ended
on Gauntlet Run.

Gauntlet Run. The land was his. Land that he'd come
to love with an intensity he'd never dreamed possible.

Two years, he mused. Always he'd stayed in one place
only two years, then moved on, not looking back. But
Gauntlet Run had been different. It had pulled at his soul
from the beginning, giving him something he'd never had
before: a sense of belonging, of having found a home when
he hadn't even known he'd been searching for one.

Buck Champion had been tough and intelligent, and
Cutter had liked the overbearing man from the moment
they'd met.

Buck had tested him, and Cutter had known and welcomed the challenge. Respect had grown, then blossomed
into friendship. The two men would sit in front of the fire,
sipping brandy and talking of many things. It was during
those quiet times that Cutter learned of Hollis and the circumstances that had driven her away from Gauntlet Run.
Only once had Cutter suggested that Buck contact his
daughter and repair the damage. Buck had roared in anger, declaring that Hollis was the one who must come to
him. Cutter had never broached the subject again, and he
would listen in silence when Buck stared into the flames
and spoke of the ache in his heart for his absent daughter.

Well, Hollis was back, Cutter thought dryly. Leave it to
Buck to figure out a way to be in control even after his
death. Foolish was the man who tried to second-guess
Buck Champion. Hell, Buck had left the land of Gauntlet
Run to his foreman! It was crazy. Buck had known how
Cutter felt about Gauntlet Run, but it was still crazy. One
thing was for sure, though. Cutter wanted Buck Champi-
on's daughter, but he sure didn't want to marry her. If that

had been the scheme behind Buck's screwball will, it wasn't going to work!

"Can't win 'em all, Buck," Cutter said, punching his pillow.

A few minutes later, he was deeply asleep.

Sunlight streamed in the window, bathing the bedroom in a warm glow. Hollis opened her eyes, then stretched leisurely, waiting for the fogginess of sleep to fade. She sat bolt upright when the events of the previous day and night came rushing back.

She groaned and flopped back against the pillow. That damnable Cutter McKenzie. Oh, why had she cried in his arms like a child? And why had she responded to his kisses? She was so furious with herself she could scream. She'd given Cutter an edge, weapons to use against her in the battle ahead. No doubt he viewed her now as a weepy, weak female. And, worse yet, as a woman susceptible to his masculine charms. "Ha!" She flung back the blankets and stomped into the bathroom to take a shower.

Under the spray of the hot water, Hollis admitted that she had responded to Cutter's kisses. But she'd been distraught, tired. As for the tears... Well, they'd just snuck up on her when she'd obviously reached the end of her rope. What was done was done.

But, she decided, as she dried herself with a fluffy towel, this was a new day, a fresh start. When Cutter tried to take advantage of her earlier weaknesses, she'd put him in his place, laid the ground rules for the future.

"Six months," Hollis mumbled. "Six lousy months with that man." But she'd stick it out. Gauntlet Run would be hers.

Hollis rummaged through the closet and found faded jeans she hadn't worn in seven years, along with a red flannel shirt and a pair of riding boots. As she dressed in the old clothes, memories assaulted her, but she pushed

them from her mind. She braided her hair into a single
plait, then headed for the kitchen.

It was after nine o'clock, and as the foreman of Gauntlet Run, Cutter would have been out since dawn. Thank
goodness for small favors, she thought dryly. She didn't
need a run-in with Mr. McKenzie before she'd had her
coffee.

Mattie was cleaning vegetables in the sink and smiled
when Hollis entered the kitchen.

"Good morning, sleepyhead," Mattie greeted her.
"Ready for breakfast?"

"I'll just have coffee," Hollis said, pouring herself a
mugful from the pot on the stove.

"That's no breakfast. How about some bacon and
eggs?"

"No, thanks," Hollis said, then gave Mattie a peck on
the cheek. "You've been trying to fatten me up since I was
in high school."

"You've been too skinny since then," Mattie said,
shaking her head. "Look at you in those old clothes of
yours. You haven't gained an ounce since you left here."

"Delicious coffee," Hollis said, smiling as she sat down
at the table.

"It's good to see you in this kitchen," Mattie said. "It's
been so long, Hollis, so many years."

Hollis cradled the mug in her hands and looked out the
window at the sprawling land.

"I know," she said quietly. "Life takes strange twists
and turns sometimes."

"Buck missed you terribly," Mattie said.

"There's no point in discussing it now. Buck got his way
in the end. I'm back and I'm staying. In six months, I'll
buy out Cutter McKenzie and all of Gauntlet Run will be
mine."

"Oh, is that so?" Mattie walked to the table and sat down opposite Hollis. "And just what do you know about running a spread like this?"

"I'll hire a foreman."

"They don't come any better than Cutter. He's a good, decent man, too, Hollis. You act as though you're at war with him."

"Not by my choosing, Mattie. Buck set up the provisions of the will, not me. Cutter and I are being manipulated by Buck, and one of us has to go. It won't be me."

"Or you could both stay," Mattie suggested.

"Impossible," Hollis said, shaking her head.

"You're as stubborn as your father." Mattie shook her head, then went back to the sink. "You and Cutter could run this place together, maybe even—"

"Don't say it. Don't even hint at Cutter and me falling madly in love. That was Buck's cute little scheme when he wrote his will, and it isn't going to happen."

"Mmm," Mattie said noncommittally, vigorously scrubbing a carrot.

Hollis drained her mug, then set it on the counter. When she saw Mattie's stern expression, she smiled and gave the housekeeper another kiss on the cheek.

"You haven't changed a bit," Hollis said, "and I love you dearly. I'm going to go call the Ramirezes and tell them what's happened. Then I'll book a seat on a flight to Mexico City. I have to go down there and take care of some things."

Mattie turned to look at her. "Were you happy there, Hollis?"

"I led a very quiet life, Mattie. I painted, was involved in several charities, had a small circle of friends. It was pleasant."

"But were you happy?"

"Well, yes, of course I was happy. I have to make some calls," Hollis said, crossing the room. "I'll see you later."

"Mmm," Mattie said, returning to her chore.

Happy? Hollis pondered as she walked down the hall. How did a person define happiness? She'd been content in Mexico, neither depressed nor euphoric, simply there, living a serene life that she took one day at a time. She hadn't fantasized about the future but had waited until tomorrow became today, then dealt with it. Happy? She supposed she'd been happy. She hadn't ever given it much thought, she now realized.

With a shrug, Hollis entered Buck's office and settled into the large chair behind the desk. She ran her hands along the padded arms, envisioning her father sitting there. She'd never sat in his chair, nor been pulled into Buck's lap here for a hug. Oh, the power he'd wielded from his throne. He'd issued commands that had touched countless lives. And Buck had been sitting in that chair when he'd forced Hollis to choose between Raymond and Gauntlet Run, between Raymond and Buck Champion.

The chilling scene of seven years before began to replay in Hollis's mental vision, and she shivered as her father's hateful words echoed in her mind.

"No," she said, reaching for the telephone. "I won't relive it again."

A short time later, Hollis was speaking with Maria Ramirez, explaining the provisions of Buck's will and Hollis's plans to stay on at Gauntlet Run. Hollis paused, waiting for Raymond's mother to express dismay at the startling turn of events.

"I see," Maria said. "I admire your father for his cleverness. You'll be home, where you belong, on Gauntlet Run."

"I thought you'd be upset that I was leaving Mexico City," Hollis said, frowning.

"Of course I am. I love you like my own daughter, and I'll miss you terribly. But you don't belong here, living the life of a widowed matron. You're young, with your entire future before you. Yes, your returning to Texas is good."

"I ... I had no idea you felt this way."

"Oh, Hollis," Maria said, sighing, "it wouldn't have served a purpose for me to speak up. You're a strong-willed young woman. A part of me was so grateful to have you here, but my heart was heavy, because I knew it was wrong for you. You should've gone home after Raymond died."

"No, Maria, my place was there, with you and Carlos. My memories of Raymond were there, too."

"Hollis, listen to me. Raymond was my son, and I loved him. But I know he was immature, spoiled, knew nothing about responsibility. That was my fault. I pampered him. Carlos was trying to teach him about the business holdings we have, but Raymond was bored by it all."

"He didn't know what he wanted to do," Hollis said, a frantic edge to her voice. "He was trying to discover who he was. He needed support, encouragement, and I gave him that."

"Yes, you did, just as I always had. Oh, my darling Hollis, don't you see? Raymond needed you like a boy needs a mother, and in return he gave you what Buck Champion never did: time and attention."

"Raymond loved me," Hollis insisted, her eyes filling with tears.

"Of course he did—in his own way. But it wasn't at the level of maturity that it should've been. Raymond used you to make his way forward. You used him to fill the emptiness within you. What you and Raymond had together wasn't wrong, but it wasn't real. You have yet to discover love with a complete man, Hollis. A man you can go to as a complete woman."

"Why are you saying all this to me now?" Hollis asked, blinking away her tears.

"It's long overdue. Thanks to your father's foresight, you're back where you belong, with the chance to live again, not just exist. I'll go over to your house and start packing some of your things. Let us know when you'll be arriving."

"Maria, I don't know what to say."

"No words are necessary. It's time for thought, for looking deep into your heart. I love you, Hollis. You deserve to be happy."

"Happy," she repeated. "That seems to be the word of the day."

"It's an emotion you have yet to receive, experience to the fullest. It was never going to happen for you with the life you were leading here. Now you have a chance—there, on Gauntlet Run."

"I..."

"Goodbye, my daughter."

"Goodbye, Maria," Hollis said, then slowly replaced the receiver, her mind whirling. She pressed her fingertips to her throbbing temples, leaned back in the chair and closed her eyes.

Why hadn't Maria just left the past alone? she moaned silently. Why had she dredged it all up now? Five years. It had been five years since Raymond had died—killed while driving his sports car too fast, as always not caring about the ramifications of his actions, just wanting to have an exciting time. Like a little boy.

"He needed me," Hollis whispered. And she'd needed him, his attention, devotion. What had Maria been saying? That Hollis and Raymond's marriage had been an emotional sham? No! They'd loved each other, they'd... Or had they only used each other? "I don't know," Hollis said, covering her face with her hands.

"Hollis?"

Hollis dropped her hands and snapped her head up to stare at Cutter, who stood in front of the desk, a deep frown on his face.

"Are you all right?" he asked.

"Yes, of course," she said coolly. "Was there something you wanted?"

"Papers from the desk. I have a horse buyer from Austin due within the hour to pick up his colt."

"You use this desk?" Hollis said, getting slowly to her feet.

"Buck and I shared it. Left-hand drawers are mine."

"I was never allowed... Was there anything you and Buck didn't share?"

"We never trod on each other's turf when it came to women," he said, a lazy grin creeping into his face.

"I'm sorry I asked," she said, glaring at him as she came around the desk. "I'll leave you to find your papers. I can use the phone in my room to call the airline."

"Oh?" Cutter said, shoving his Stetson to the back of his head with his thumb. "Leaving, are you?"

Hollis crossed her arms over her breasts. "I'm simply going to Mexico City to make arrangements for my house and ship some of my belongings here."

"I see," he said. He sat on the edge of the desk and crossed one ankle over the other as he stretched his long legs out in front of him. "How long are you planning on being away?"

"I'm not sure."

He grinned. "Longer than twenty-four hours?"

"Yes, of course."

"Hollis, Hollis," he said, shaking his head. "Have you forgotten the provisions of Buck's will so quickly? You have to clear your plans with me if you're going to be gone for more than twenty-four hours. Unless, of course, you prefer to forfeit."

"I certainly do not intend to forfeit, but any idiot knows I have personal matters to attend to in Mexico City before I can move in here."

Cutter chuckled. "Well, this idiot needs details of said trip. What's the program? You bid all your lovers a sad adieu?"

A sharp retort was on the tip of her tongue, but then she smiled. "Yes, as a matter of fact that *will* be part of my agenda. It would be so unkind to just disappear after they've been so...special to me."

Cutter narrowed his eyes. "I don't believe you."

"Why? Because Buck's detectives didn't turn in reports indicating I was involved with any men other than casual dating? My dear Mr. McKenzie, I've been aware of my watchdogs for years. I became very adept at leaving false trails."

"I still don't believe you've had a string of lovers, Hollis," Cutter said gruffly. "Knock off the worldly-and-wise act. It doesn't become you."

"Act?" she said pleasantly. "Now, just how do you know it's an act? After all, Cutter, you really don't know me very well."

"Don't I?" he said, his voice low. "I think I do."

"Based on what? Things my father told you about a daughter he hadn't seen or spoken to in seven years?"

Cutter took off his Stetson, then resettled it on his head and pulled the brim low onto his forehead, casting shadows over his face.

"No," he said, pushing himself away from the desk to tower over her. "I admit I had some preconceived opinions regarding you, but I realize now that wasn't quite fair."

"How big of you," she said dryly.

"I know you, Hollis, because I held you when you cried tears that were honest and real. I know you because you've responded to my kisses, then were shocked and embarrassed that you had. Oh, yes, Mrs. Ramirez, I know you. The more important question is . . . do *you*? Do you know who you are, what you really want?"

"That," she said tightly, "is none of your damn business." She wheeled around and started toward the door. "I will inform you as to when I'm leaving for Mexico City. Bear in mind, Mr. McKenzie, that I *will* be coming back."

Cutter grinned as Hollis slammed the door after her. "I'm counting on it, darlin'. Oh, yes, ma'am, I'll be looking forward to it."

Chapter 4

One week later, Hollis gazed out of the plane window at the Texas land below. It looked like an enormous patchwork quilt. As the pilot made the landing approach, she could make out the skyline of Houston in the distance. Hollis had seen this view countless times, but today it was different, for it represented a tremendous change in her life. She was home to stay.

Home, Hollis thought. Texas. Gauntlet Run.

A surge of excitement swept through her, startling her with its intensity. The week in Mexico City had been hectic, involving much more than Hollis had realized would be necessary in order to leave her previous life behind. She'd sorted, packed, then shipped her belongings, and had given full boxes to charities. Papers had to be signed to transfer her funds to a Houston bank, and her house and furniture put up for sale. She'd given Carlos Ramirez her power of attorney to sell her house and to oversee the investments she had inherited from Raymond.

The Ramirezes had given Hollis a huge farewell party, which was attended by over two hundred people. Hollis had felt disoriented at the festive affair, forcing a smile as everyone wished her well in her new adventure. She'd felt like a baby bird being pushed from the nest before she was ready to try her wings, and fought the urge to shout above the din that she would stay in Mexico City, where it was safe.

Maria Ramirez had sensed Hollis's sudden panic and ushered her into the quiet library, where Hollis had run into Maria's arms.

"Maria, I don't want—"

"Hush," Maria had said, setting Hollis gently on a chair. "You're frightened, and that's understandable. But your fears mustn't keep you from growing, changing. You're going home, Hollis."

"Home? Gauntlet Run is a house, not a home. For a house to be a home, there must be love and laughter within the walls. There're only ghosts and cold memories at Gauntlet Run."

"Then it's up to you to change all that," Maria had said. "Unless, of course, you'd rather turn it over to that Cutter McKenzie."

"No!" Hollis had said, getting to her feet. "Never. It's mine, and the land will be mine, too."

"Ah, that's better." Maria had smiled. "Your eyes are dancing with fire and determination. You're going to be fine, my daughter. You'll learn to look to the future, have hopes and dreams."

"Oh, Maria, I'm going to miss you and Carlos so much."

"And we'll miss you. But this is good, Hollis, your going home. God be with you."

The sound of the changing speed of the plane's engines brought Hollis out of her reverie, and she checked to make sure her seat belt was securely fastened. Her thoughts skittered to Raymond and she saw him laughing, the wind tousling his silky dark hair. In Mexico, Hollis had gone alone to Raymond's grave and stood staring at the massive marble headstone.

The words Maria had spoken on the telephone sifted through Hollis's heart and mind. How young they'd been, she and Raymond, Hollis mused. So full of life and what they'd been so sure was love. Had they really known what love was? Did it matter? No, not really. Each had met the other's needs, filled voids that had been empty. What they'd shared had been special, rare, like rich gifts offered and received.

It had been with a sense of peace and greater understanding that Hollis had bidden Raymond a last, silent farewell, then walked away from the cemetery.

The plane bumped onto the runway and the tingle of excitement swept through Hollis once again. She was being ridiculous, she told herself. There was nothing exciting about returning to a war zone. The battle lines had been drawn, marked at precisely twenty feet beyond the house on Gauntlet Run. And the adversary was Cutter McKenzie.

Cutter, Hollis thought. He had crept into her thoughts with annoying regularity while she'd been in Mexico. She knew it was understandable, for his name had come up often as she'd explained the provisions of her father's will to her friends.

But, Hollis mentally rambled on, there was no reason for the appearance of Cutter in her nightly dreams. There he'd been: tall, strong, tanned, with that heart-stopping smile. She'd had the most disturbing dream the previous night. Cutter had emerged from the depths of a fog wearing only his low-slung, tight jeans. He'd held out his arms, and Hollis had stepped forward clad in a sheer, filmy gown. She'd rushed into his embrace and his lips had captured hers.

"For Pete's sake," Hollis mumbled as the remembrance caused desire to swirl within her. There would be no more kisses shared with Mr. McKenzie, she told herself firmly. She was on solid emotional ground again, in control of herself. She was starting her life over on Gauntlet Run and in Houston, and it didn't include falling prey to the masculine magnetism of a sexy cowboy. No, sir, there would be no more leaping into Cutter McKenzie's arms. "And that," Hollis said decisively, "is that."

Cutter leaned against the wall in the airport, his Stetson pulled low on his forehead. A shapely woman walked by and looked him over, head to toe, a coy smile forming on her lips.

"Ma'am," Cutter said, touching his fingers to the brim of his hat.

"Too bad I've got a plane to catch," she said over her shoulder. "Maybe next time, cowboy."

Cutter chuckled. Ah, women, he thought. They checked him out like beef on the hoof, then sent the signal: "ready and willing." He treated them right when he was with them, gave what they wanted, took what they offered and walked away without a backward glance. Neat and tidy, no one got hurt.

A young couple strolled by, arms entwined around each other. The man lowered his head to whisper something in the woman's ear, and she laughed, then smiled up at him adoringly.

Cutter frowned slightly as the pair disappeared into the milling crowd. What would it be like, he wondered, to love, really love, just one woman, have a lifelong commitment to cherish, protect, be someone's best friend? Was he capable of making a woman happy day after day, capable of sharing his innermost thoughts? No, probably not. He'd been alone too long to change now.

He shook his head. Where were these off-the-wall thoughts coming from?

A door across the busy corridor was opened and a few moments later, people began to file through it.

And then there she was.

Hollis.

Cutter straightened and watched her, his blue eyes missing no detail as they swept over her. Her hair was coiled at the nape of her neck, the way she'd worn it the day of Buck's funeral. Her dress was the color of burgundy and hugged her lush breasts and the gentle slope of her hips before falling to midcalf, accentuating her shapely legs.

Cutter's mind skittered to the night in the kitchen when he'd nestled Hollis to him, her body clad only in thin layers of lavender satin. His mind replayed the kiss they had shared, and heat shot across his loins—just as it had every night since Hollis had left for Mexico City.

"Damn," he said, his pleasant mood shattered. He strode forward, weaving through the crowd to stand in front of Hollis. "Hollis," he said gruffly, touching the rim of his Stetson with his fingertips. "Come on, let's get your luggage."

"Cutter," she said, looking up at him in surprise, "what are you doing here? I phoned Kathleen and asked her to meet me."

"She had to fill in for someone at the hospital gift shop, so she called me. Let's go."

"Oh. Well, I—"

"I've got a ranch to run." He turned and started to walk away. "I don't have time to stand around and chat."

"Well, excuse me," Hollis snapped, following after him. "You could have sent someone else in—one of the hands."

"Right," he said, stopping so she could catch up with him. "There's not one man on that ranch who was there when you were living on Gauntlet Run. Are you in the habit of going off with strange men?"

"No, of course not." She was glaring at him now. "But he'd be driving a Gauntlet Run vehicle, with the insignia on the door."

"Wonderful," Cutter muttered. "You'd be all the way to the parking lot before you realized the guy was a phony."

"Cutter, for heaven's sake, quit being so dramatic. I'm perfectly capable of taking care of myself."

Cutter shot her a dark look that clearly indicated his doubt of her statement, then checked the monitor to see which carousel held the luggage from her flight.

"What color?" he asked. "And how many?"

"Powder blue. There are two pieces. I shipped most of my things."

"Ah, yes, your fancy paintbrushes, right?"

"Mr. McKenzie," Hollis said tightly, "I don't know why you're in such a lousy mood, but I'll thank you not to take it out on me."

Cutter opened his mouth, then snapped it closed again. Hollis was right, he admitted. *She* hadn't followed him into his bed every night for the past week; it had been only the image of her in his mental view. It wasn't really her fault that he had an ache in his gut and a driving need to haul her into his arms and kiss her senseless. He was acting like a teenager. And Miss Snooty Britches wasn't going to know he'd given her even a fleeting thought while she'd been gone!

Cutter shoved his Stetson to the back of his head with his thumb and smiled down at Hollis. A smile, he knew from experience, that could smooth ruffled female feathers.

"You're absolutely right, darlin'," he drawled. "I surely do apologize for being so all-fired ornery. You won't hear another cross word from this cowboy's lips, ma'am."

"Cutter," Hollis said, batting her eyelashes at him, "stuff it."

Cutter chuckled, then reached for the luggage Hollis pointed to. She watched the gray western shirt pull tightly across his back and the fascinating play of muscles beneath the material as he accomplished his task. She swallowed heavily.

Darn him, Hollis fumed. He could turn on the charm at will and conjure up his hundred-watt smile. Well, she was totally unaffected by his blatant sexuality. But, oh, heavens, if he ever knew about her dreams of the past week, she'd die. Absolutely die.

"Do you have your claim ticket?" Cutter asked after straightening and facing her again.

"Of course, and my clearance from customs," she said, pulling papers from her purse. "Shall we go?"

"Yes, ma'am," he said, still smiling. "Whatever you say, ma'am."

Hollis rolled her eyes heavenward, then started off at a brisk pace.

"Hollis," Cutter called after her.

"Now what?" She spun around.

"You're going the wrong way. I'm parked on the other side of the terminal."

Hollis narrowed her eyes and retraced her steps, giving Cutter a withering look in the process.

"Mercy," he said, falling in step beside her, "you certainly are in a lousy mood yourself, Miss Hollis. I would be truly grateful if you didn't take it out on my fragile hide."

Hollis couldn't help it.... She laughed. She looked up at Cutter, and he matched her smile with a genuine one of his own.

"We sound like squabbling kids," she said.

"Yeah, I guess we do. Let's start over. How was your trip?"

"Fine. Tiring, but I got a lot accomplished."

Cutter nodded, then waited as Hollis showed the security guard the necessary documents. Outside, the air was clear and cool, and Hollis filled her lungs with the freshness. They walked in silence across the parking lot. Hollis noticed that Cutter toted the heavy suitcases as though they were empty.

Several women passed them, and Hollis saw the appreciative glances they gave Cutter. Oh, yes, she reaffirmed in her mind, he was something, a cut above the rest. He had an aura about him that was unique: an unspoken message of authoritativeness and masculinity. She could easily picture Cutter and her father admiring each other. Buck Champion, too, had had that special magnetism that had set him apart from other men.

Just how alike were Cutter and Buck? Hollis wondered. Did Cutter possess that need to control? His role as foreman of Gauntlet Run was evidence of his intelligence and leadership ability, but there was a tremendous difference between leaders and dictators. Hollis had seen Buck's staff scurry after him like servants following the king, and it had repulsed her.

What kind of man was Cutter? she mused. Floyd had said Cutter worked next to his men. Out of love for the land, or a perverse need to control all those under his command? Was Cutter McKenzie nothing more than a carbon copy of Buck Champion?

Hollis was pulled from her vaguely disturbing thoughts as they came upon the late-model station wagon with the Gauntlet Run insignia on the door. She slipped into the passenger side while Cutter placed her luggage in the back. He drove out of the parking lot and merged into the busy traffic.

"Is everything all right at Gauntlet Run?" Hollis asked, glancing over at Cutter.

"The house is fine," he said with a shrug. "Mattie runs it like a drill sergeant. She finally agreed to have extra help a few years ago, and she keeps everyone hopping."

"She's an amazing woman. And the ranch itself—is everything running smoothly?"

"Why do you ask?" He looked at her quickly, then redirected his attention to the traffic.

"Because I'm interested. All of Gauntlet Run is important to me, Cutter."

"You didn't have any problem staying away from it for seven years," he pointed out, frowning.

"Please," she said, sighing, "let's not get into that again. The fact remains that I'm home now, and I intend to stay."

"Fine." He yanked his Stetson further forward. "Concentrate on *your* house, and don't mess with *my* land."

"I was just making conversation. Forget I mentioned it." She turned and began to look out the side window.

"Hollis, I'm sorry," Cutter said quietly. "It's been a helluva week. The fence we put back up that night of the storm went down again. It didn't make sense to me, and I took a closer look. The wire had been cut."

"What?" Hollis said, snapping her head around. "Someone cut the fence? Why? Were they after the cattle?"

"Damn right," Cutter said, a muscle jumping along his jaw. "We lost thirty head of prime beef. Over the next ridge, we found tire marks from a large truck. Gauntlet Run has been hit by cattle rustlers."

"Has this ever happened before?" Hollis said, her eyes wide.

"No. Damn," Cutter said, smacking his palm against the steering wheel. "Why now? It's common knowledge that I've been managing Gauntlet Run for the past six years. Buck's death shouldn't make the ranch appear suddenly vulnerable, easy pickings for those vermin."

"What did the sheriff say?"

"Gauntlet Run is the only ranch that's been hit."

"Maybe it was an isolated incident, Cutter," Hollis suggested. "They came in, went out with a truckload of cattle, and that's the end of it."

"We'll see. Man, I'd like to get my hands on those guys. No one has the right to touch what's mine. No one."

Hollis shivered slightly as she heard the low, menacing tone to Cutter's voice. The tension emanating from his massive body was nearly palpable in the close quarters of the car. Her gaze was riveted on his rugged profile and the tight set to his jaw. She couldn't see his eyes clearly, but knew they would be like icy blue chips.

For the first time, Hollis realized what passion Cutter felt for Gauntlet Run. Such emotional intensity, the depths of which would probably match that which he felt for a woman. Was there a special woman in his life? she wondered. She didn't think so. Mattie had hinted that Cutter had a long string of female companions.

What would it be like to have that possessiveness, that raw evidence of caring, directed at her? To be the focal point of Cutter's existence? To hear him declare his intention to protect her as he intended to protect Gauntlet Run? What absurd thoughts. Totally absurd.

"I hope there's no further trouble, Cutter," she said sincerely.

"Yeah, all the hands hope it was a one-shot deal. All we can do now is wait and see. There's no point in putting everyone on double shifts to patrol if this is the end of it. We'll take our chances for now."

"Did the sheriff agree with you?"

"*I* make the decisions for Gauntlet Run, Hollis."

"All right, Cutter," she said wearily. "I don't want to argue with you. I realize you're upset about the rustlers, but I am, too. You're obviously holding against me the fact that I was gone for seven years. What you seem to be forgetting is that I was born on Gauntlet Run and lived there for twenty years before I married Raymond. I hate thinking that rustlers violated that land.''

Cutter nodded slightly but made no comment. Damn, he fumed. He'd had no intention of telling Hollis about the missing cattle. He'd made a firm decision that anything happening on the land at Gauntlet Run was none of her business. He had no desire to give the slightest impression that he was reporting in any way to Buck's daughter.

So, big mouth? he asked himself. Now she knew all about the rustlers before she even got back to the ranch! Why had he told her? Hell, he didn't know. Her ongoing declarations of loving that land didn't wash. Oh, sure, she'd no doubt ridden horseback across Gauntlet Run— but then turned the sweaty horse over to a hand to be tended to. She'd attended the fancy parties Buck had produced around the pool, reaped all the financial rewards of being a Champion.

But love the land? Oh, yeah, a person could appreciate the beauty and tranquility of it by standing alone and drinking in the sight of a sunrise or filling one's lungs with the rich, earthy scents. But to have the land become a part of himself a person had to work, sink his hands in the soil, push his body and mind to the limit and then beyond. He had to sweat and ache from backbreaking labor, feel the rush of joy when witnessing the birth of a calf or colt, and register the knife-sharp twist of pain when an injured horse had to be destroyed.

Hollis knew none of these things, Cutter mentally went on. She'd been Buck's pampered little princess, kept among the expensive trappings in the big, fancy house. No, he hadn't meant to tell her what had happened on the land beyond her ivory tower. But it could be worse, he thought dryly. He could have blurted out how she'd consumed his thoughts and nightly dreams for the past week!

Cutter glanced quickly at Hollis with the irrational thought that perhaps she was reading his mind at that very moment. She had leaned her head back on the top of the seat and closed her eyes, exposing the creamy skin of her slender throat.

Concentrate on driving, Cutter told himself firmly. But, oh, damn, Hollis was a beautiful woman. When he'd kissed her, he hadn't wanted to stop. And the emotions he'd felt while holding her—protectiveness, possessiveness—were still fresh in his mind, despite the fact that she'd been gone for a week. Well, now she was back, and new rules were called for. He would stay clear of Hollis Champion Ramirez.

The remainder of the drive to Gauntlet Run was made in silence. When Cutter stopped the car in front of the house, Hollis lifted her head and blinked.

"I'm sorry," she said. "I must have dozed off. I wasn't very good company. I appreciate your picking me up, Cutter."

"No problem," he said, opening the door. "I'll get your luggage."

In the entry hall, Cutter set the suitcases on the floor, then touched his fingertips to the rim of his Stetson. "I'll see you at dinner in a few hours."

"Yes, fine. Thank you."

Their eyes met and held for what Hollis wasn't sure was seconds or minutes, then Cutter went out the door and closed it quietly behind him. Hollis stood staring at the hand-carved wood, suddenly aware of the silence of the enormous house, of the chill within its walls.

It was as though Cutter had taken the warmth with him, she thought. His vibrant masculinity seemed to bring things alive, create a current of sexuality that wove from him into her.

"Oh, how silly," Hollis scoffed at herself.

"Hollis," Mattie said, bustling down the hall, "you're back. How was your trip?"

"Hectic, but productive," she said, hugging the housekeeper. "Have any of the things I shipped arrived yet?"

"No. You look tired. Would you like to nap before dinner?"

"No, I'll never sleep tonight if I do. I'll change my clothes and relax for a while, then go to bed early tonight."

"After you eat a big dinner. I intend to fatten you up a bit."

"Don't you dare," Hollis said, laughing. "None of my clothes will fit."

"Then buy new ones." She eyed Hollis's luggage. "Do you want me to unpack those for you?"

"No, I'll take care of them."

"I'm so glad you're home to stay, Hollis."

"Yes. Yes, so am I," she said, picking up the suitcases.

A moment later, Hollis was scrutinizing her bedroom with a critical eye. She'd redecorate it, she decided. Get rid of the frills of her childhood. Actually, she could redo Buck's master suite to her taste and move in there. She was, after all, the mistress of Gauntlet Run. Doing so would also remove her from the wing inhabited by Cutter McKenzie. First thing tomorrow, she'd explore the master suite—a set of rooms, she realized, that she hadn't entered since she was a little girl.

Hollis unpacked, took a quick shower, then dressed in pleated gray wool slacks and a raspberry-colored silk blouse. She brushed her hair, braided it, then coiled the plait into a figure eight at the back of her head. The telephone rang but stopped when Hollis glanced at it. A moment later a buzzing noise sounded by the phone, indicating that Mattie had answered it and the call was for Hollis.

"Hello?"

"Hollis, it's Kathleen. Oh, goodness, I'm sorry I couldn't meet your plane."

"That's all right, Kathleen. I'm safely deposited here at Gauntlet Run. How are you?"

"Fine. Busy, per usual, but fine. Why do I say yes to so many of these volunteer committees? Oh, well, I'm going to recruit you, you know."

Hollis laughed. "Not right away. I'm going to do some redecorating around here."

"Really? How marvelous. I can't even remember when there have been changes in that house. That's a wonderful idea, Hollis. Where do you plan to start?"

"I thought I'd redo Buck's master suite for myself."

"Oh. Well, I suppose you could but..." Kathleen paused.

"But what?"

"It occurs to me that if you redo those rooms with a feminine flair, you'll have to turn right around and do it again if a man is going to take up occupancy with you."

"A man? Kathleen, for heaven's sake, what an absurd thing to say."

"I don't think Cutter McKenzie is absurd," Kathleen said, laughing. "I think he's delicious."

"Cutter! Listen to me, Kathleen. Cutter McKenzie is not coming within a hundred feet of my bedroom. And furthermore, in six months he'll be gone from Gauntlet Run."

"Don't be so sure of yourself, Hollis. Cutter isn't going to just fade into the sunset in six months. And as far as him being in your bed, the more I think about Buck's devious plan to get you and Cutter together, the more I like it. You two would make a wonderful couple."

"You have a choice, Kathleen," Hollis said, narrowing her eyes. "Change the subject, or I'm hanging up."

"You're no fun."

"How's Floyd? Please notice that we're changing the subject."

"I noticed. Floyd is in San Francisco putting together some big fancy deal. He's been gone since the day after you left for Mexico City."

"When is he due back?"

"He isn't sure. He called me last night and said they'd hit a snag. It'll be several more days, I guess."

"Well, I'll call you tomorrow and we'll make plans to have dinner in Houston," Hollis said.

"Dinner? That would mean Cutter would have to eat alone."

"So?"

"Let's meet for lunch."

"Kathleen, you'd better put your matchmaking schemes to rest right now. I am not—nor will I ever be—interested in Cutter McKenzie." She tried to sound more confident of this than she felt. "Is that clear?"

"Perfectly, dear. I must go. I'll talk to you tomorrow. 'Bye for now, and welcome home."

"'Bye," Hollis said, then replaced the receiver. Wonderful. Kathleen apparently planned to pick up where Buck's will had left off. Well, no thank you, she thought, shaking her head. She'd meant what she'd said. She was not interested in Cutter—not in his kiss or touch or incredible blue eyes. His mile-wide shoulders, dazzling smile, and strong but gentle hands were of no importance to her. And the sooner Kathleen accepted that, the better off everyone would be.

"Fine," Hollis said, getting to her feet. And once she figured out a way to keep Cutter from invading her dreams at night, everything would be under control.

In the barn, Cutter ran his hand along the belly of a mare that was due to deliver what should prove to be a topnotch colt.

"How's it going, Butterfly?" Cutter said. "'Bout ready to bring this baby into the world?"

"She looks good," a man said.

Cutter glanced up, then redirected his attention to the horse. "Yep, she does, Jesse," he said. "Everything okay here?"

"Yep."

Jesse Thatcher was a lean, tightly muscled, short man in his early fifties. Cutter had hired him more than three years earlier, and Jesse was now the second in command, Cutter's right-hand man. He made no bones about the fact that he liked horses better than he did people.

"You get her highness picked up from the airport?" Jesse said.

Cutter chuckled. "She wouldn't appreciate being called that."

"Well, hell, Cutter, she's got no business moving back in here like she's so all-fired important. Where was she when her daddy was alive? Off playing jet-setter in Mexico, that's where. Why didn't she just stay there?"

"I told you about Buck's will, Jesse, and you gave me your word it wouldn't go any further than the two of us. But you know she has a right to be in that house. She'll be riding, too, I imagine."

"She'll want her horse saddled for her, I suppose," Jesse said with a snort of disgust. "We don't have time for prima donnas around here, Cutter. I never met this Hollis, and I can't say I'm anxious to make her acquaintance."

"There's no reason for you to have to have any dealings with her," Cutter said.

"I don't intend to give her the time of day." Jesse pulled his Stetson forward. "Gauntlet Run should be yours, Cutter—all of it."

As he strode away, Cutter watched, a deep frown on his face. He'd never seen Jesse like that, and it was disturbing. The other ranch hands had been easily assured of their job security despite Buck's death, but Cutter had felt Jesse deserved to know the whole story. He'd worked hard for

Cutter over the past years, and Cutter considered him a friend as well as a first-rate second in command.

"I don't need any more hassles right now, Butterfly," Cutter said, stroking the horse. "You just concentrate on getting that baby here safe and sound."

Butterfly swished her tail as though indicating she was in complete agreement, and Cutter smiled, then left the stall. He stopped in the center of the aisle to survey the huge building. It was neat and clean, and Cutter knew that the tack room beyond was in equally precise order.

Or so it had been until Hollis's arrival, he mused, walking toward the barn door. Hollis wouldn't be put into a slot and stay there with her mouth shut. She'd be out in that barn, riding those horses across Gauntlet Run, tempting his cowboys with her lush figure. Hell, tempting *him*! As if cattle rustlers weren't enough of a problem, he also had Hollis Champion Ramirez to contend with!

"Hell," he muttered.

Cutter stopped by a workbench and picked up a length of barbed wire, the strip he'd shown to the sheriff to prove that the fence had been cut. The sheriff had had plaster molds of the tire tracks taken, which, in Cutter's opinion, was a waste of time. The thieves would have to be caught red-handed, Cutter decided. And, he was prepared to do just that if they struck Gauntlet Run again.

"Cutter," yelled a man from farther back in the barn.

"Yeah?"

"Phone," the man called.

"Got it," Cutter hollered, lifting the receiver off an extension by the door. "McKenzie."

"Cutter, this is Sheriff Dunbar."

"Yeah?"

"We found your cattle."

Every muscle in Cutter's body tensed. "Where?"

"In a canyon 'bout a hundred miles from here. We got an anonymous tip. Cutter, they're dead, every one—shot through the head and left there."

"What in hell for? That was prime beef. They could have doctored the brand and gotten top dollar for them. Do you think the rustlers panicked?"

"No, I don't. Nobody was on their trail, and that canyon had been carefully chosen so no one would hear the gunfire. Apparently they did exactly what they set out to do. It might even've been them that tipped us off."

"Why?" Cutter said, running his hand over the back of his neck.

"Well," the sheriff said, sighing, "if Buck was still alive, I'd say it was somebody who had a grudge against him, which would be a mighty long list. Buck Champion stepped on more than one set of toes in his day. I assume his daughter inherited Gauntlet Run, so I'll have to talk to her, see if she has any idea who might be angry at her."

"No, wait," Cutter said. "I'll talk to her and get back to you."

"It's my place to investigate—"

"Sheriff, you agreed to let me call the shots on this. I'll speak with Hollis. She's been through a lot lately, you know. Let me decide when the best time is to approach her. Judging from what you said, I guess the general assumption is that Buck left all of Gauntlet Run to Hollis."

"Well, yeah. Everyone knows they haven't been exactly chummy in the past seven years, but she's still a Champion. Personally, I always felt Buck was closer to you than he'd ever been to Hollis—I don't think Buck knew what to do with a daughter. Would've made more sense to me to leave Gauntlet Run to you. But seeing how rumor has it that Hollis is home to stay, I figure the ranch is hers."

"You couldn't get her out of that house with a stick of dynamite, Sheriff," Cutter said. "I'll talk to her and get back to you as fast as I can."

"You do that, because I'm at a dead end. There's not a mite of evidence in that canyon except a bunch of dead cattle."

"I'll call you," he said, then replaced the receiver. What in the hell was going on? "Easy, McKenzie," he muttered, running his hand over his face. He had to think this through. The stealing, then killing of the cattle, was not a money-making endeavor. It was a message to...to who? Not Buck. Everyone in the country knew Buck was dead. Only a handful of people knew that those cattle had actually belonged to Cutter. The sheriff was right. The useless destruction of that valuable beef had been a missive directed at Hollis.

But who could Hollis possibly have angered to the point of doing something like this? Could it be someone who'd hated Buck but had been too intimidated by the powerful man to act? Or someone who had admired Buck and resented Hollis's returning after seven years and inheriting Buck's empire? One thing was for damn sure. Whoever had done this was sick, really sick.

"Hey, Cutter," Jesse said, coming up beside him, "you look like you could break somebody in two."

"The sheriff called," Cutter said gruffly. "They found the cattle—shot in the head in a canyon a hundred miles from here. Those rustlers didn't intend to change the brand and sell them."

"Damn it," Jesse roared, smacking his fist into his other palm. "Damn her to hell and back."

"What are you talking about?" Cutter said, frowning.

"Hollis. Who wants you off this land, Cutter?"

"She wasn't even here, Jesse. Besides, there wasn't time for her to—"

"Come on. Money can buy anything. I'm telling you, Cutter, she did this."

"You don't know that," Cutter said, his voice rising. "You keep your mouth shut about this, Jesse. You could start a lot of trouble making accusations you can't back up. Just slow down and let me handle this."

"You watch your back, Cutter," Jesse said. "That's Buck Champion's daughter you're dealing with. Yeah, okay, I'll keep my mouth closed for now, but my eyes will be wide open. I work for *you*, Cutter. I never felt any loyalty to Buck Champion, and I sure as hell don't have any toward his kid." He stomped off.

The sheriff's words, then Jesse's, drummed against Cutter's mind with a painful, throbbing cadence. With long, heavy strides, he started toward the house.

Chapter 5

When Cutter entered the house, he heard Mattie humming in the pantry. He moved quietly, suddenly not wishing to see the housekeeper, or Hollis either, for that matter. He needed time to cool his inner fury and sort through the confusion in his mind. A few minutes later, he was standing in his shower, allowing the hot water to beat against his body.

Slow down, he told himself. Angry accusations hurled without thinking would get him nowhere. *One step at a time* was the key here. Was Hollis capable of planning such a devious act? Damn it, no!

Sure, she resented the provisions of Buck's will and Cutter's hold on the land of Gauntlet Run, but he knew she wouldn't stoop to something like this.

Cutter stepped from the shower and dried off. Not Hollis, he repeated in his mind. Jesse didn't know her, so had hit on the first person who had something to gain by Cutter's getting fed up at Gauntlet Run and eager to move on. No, Jesse didn't know Hollis the way Cutter did.

"Oh, yeah?" Cutter muttered as he pulled on his jeans. Did he himself really know Hollis Champion Ramirez? Yes, damn it, he did! He'd held her when she'd cried, felt her respond totally to his kiss and touch. He sensed the vulnerability in her, the gentle, sometimes frightened woman beneath the cool veneer.

No, Cutter decided, as he put on a blue western shirt, it had to be someone with a grudge against *her*, as everyone believed that Gauntlet Run was hers.

Cutter combed his hair, pulled on his boots, started toward the door, then stopped. He returned to the bed, sat on the edge and frowned. He rested his elbows on his knees and made a steeple of his fingers, thinking.

Jesse had pronounced Hollis guilty in an instant, Cutter realized. And Cutter had declared her innocent just as quickly. Both conclusions had been formed during emotional outbursts, with no examination of facts. It dawned on Cutter that he wanted—he needed—Hollis to be innocent of any wrongdoing.

Cutter ran his hand through his hair. This wasn't like him, not at all. His judgment was being clouded by emerald eyes and a lush body that molded to his as though custom-made for him, by the remembrance of her honeyed lips moving beneath his.

No, this wasn't like him, Cutter thought dryly, but then neither was being haunted in his dreams by the image of a woman, of having an ache coiled in his gut from the driving desire to bury himself within her and make her his. All of her. Not just her body, but her heart, soul, her emotions.

What in the hell was she doing to him?

Cutter slapped his thighs and pushed himself to his feet. He wasn't accomplishing anything by hiding in his room, he decided. Unless going slowly out of his mind counted. Man, he didn't need this hassle!

Cutter strode down the hall, then to the doorway of the living room. And stopped. His blood pounded as he viewed the scene before him. Hollis sat in a high-backed chair before the hearth, her stockinged feet tucked next to her. Her elbow rested on the tufted arm of the chair, and her chin was cupped in her hand as she stared into the roaring fire. The flames were the only light in the darkening room and cast a warm glow over her.

She was so beautiful, he thought. She looked so alone sitting there, so fragile. He wanted to hold her, kiss her, see the sparkle of a smile dance through her eyes.

And he wanted to talk to her, really talk, find out all there was to know about Hollis Champion Ramirez. What was her favorite color? Did she like ice cream? Did she sing in the shower? There were no details too small, too mundane. He wanted to know them all.

He was . . . Damn it, was he falling in love with Hollis? Was old love-'em-and-leave-'em McKenzie going down for the count? How in the hell could this happen? Even more, what was he going to do about it? Talk about a hassle. This was a beaut!

Cutter shook his head, then a smile crept onto his lips. Love, he mused. Son of a gun. It didn't sound so bad. In fact, he rather liked the idea now that it was sinking in. Gauntlet Run had offered him a haven, a home, and now maybe love. With Hollis, who was a part of Gauntlet Run. Together, they could maintain the excellence of the land.

Oh, really? Cutter thought. He was sure getting ahead of himself. Hollis wasn't exactly declaring her undying love for *him*. More often than not, she was ready to strangle him. He had a rough road to go here, but he'd always met challenges head-on.

Cutter went forward, clearing his throat to warn Hollis of his presence. She turned her head, and their eyes met as Cutter emerged from the shadows to stand next to her chair.

"Hello, Hollis," he said, his voice low.

"Cutter," she said, nodding slightly, her eyes riveted on his. She'd been gazing into the fire, Hollis thought wildly, thinking about him, and now here he was as though she'd conjured him up. She'd been reliving yet again being in Cutter's arms, feeling the rugged length of his body, tasting his lips on hers. Desire had swirled unchecked within her, and her breasts had begun to ache for his magical touch. And now, here he stood in all his magnificent, masculine glory.

"You're in early," she remarked, tearing her gaze from his to stare back into the flames.

"Would you like a drink before dinner?" he asked.

"Sherry, please."

Cutter went to the bar and returned with two glasses. Hollis accepted hers but kept her eyes averted from Cutter's, willing her heart to stop its racing cadence. He settled into the chair next to her and stretched his legs out in front, crossing them at the ankle. Hollis's gaze flickered over his muscular thighs under the soft denim of his jeans, then she directed her attention to her drink.

"Sheriff Dunbar called," Cutter said quietly.

"Oh?" She snapped her head up to look at him. "Does he have any lead on the cattle?"

"He found them. They're all dead, Hollis. Shot in the head."

"What?" She sat bolt upright. "That's insane! That was valuable beef. Does the sheriff think the rustlers lost their nerve at the last minute?"

"No, it looks as though it was planned to go exactly as it did. The cattle weren't taken to be sold."

"But why would anyone do such a thing? It's such a waste, and it's cruel, senseless."

"Oh, there was a reason for it," he said, then took a swig of liquor. "Trick is to figure it out. It's a little late to be settling old scores with Buck, so as far as everyone is concerned, Gauntlet Run is yours. The sheriff feels it could have been planned by someone who has a grudge against you."

"Me? That's crazy. I imagine there are people who resent me simply because I'm a Champion, but I don't view them as enemies."

"There are no jilted lovers with an ax to grind?" Cutter said.

"We've covered that ground, Cutter. I have no idea who would do this. Besides, that cattle was yours."

"Very few people know that." He leaned forward and rested his elbows on his knees as he looked directly at her. "If the sheriff was aware of that fact, he might view this differently. He'd wonder who *my* enemies are or who might benefit from my having problems here."

"Benefit?"

"You know, push me to the point where I give up and sell out."

Hollis quickly got to her feet, nearly spilling her drink. "You're talking about me," she said angrily. "I can't believe you're actually insinuating that I could be behind the slaughtering of that cattle. You have gall! How dare you even think such a thing. If I were a man, I'd break your jaw."

Cutter slouched back in his chair and looked up at her with hooded eyes, no readable expression on his face. Seconds ticked by.

"Well?" Hollis finally demanded. "Say something, McKenzie."

He smiled, a lazy, sensual smile that caused Hollis's pulse to race. "Darlin', the fact that you're a woman, definitely a woman, is one of the greatest joys of this cowboy's life."

"Don't change the subject." Hollis plunked her glass on the end table, then planted her hands on her hips. "Do you or do you not think I was involved in having those cattle stolen and killed?'' He couldn't think that of her, could he? It was suddenly very important to her that he didn't believe she was capable of such a thing. ''Well?'' she said, her voice trembling slightly.

Cutter got to his feet and set his glass on the mantel. He stared into the flames of the roaring fire. Hollis was beautiful, he thought. Her eyes were fierce, and she had that stubborn tilt to her Champion chin. And he'd seen it—the flicker of pain in her eyes when she'd asked whether he thought she was guilty of the cattle deaths.

He should be suspicious of her, Cutter realized. She had a solid motive for wanting to cause him problems on Gauntlet Run. A motive and the money to back it up. She was a Champion, with the same drive and determination as Buck. Yes, he should be suspicious and wary and not trust her.

''Cutter?''

He turned slowly to face her, his heart thundering as he saw the pain in her eyes she was unable to hide.

''Do you think I did this awful thing?'' Her voice was a near-whisper.

''No,'' he said, smiling at her. ''No, Hollis, I don't.'' He opened his arms to her. ''Come here.''

And she went. Not thinking of the right or wrong of it, she went into the strong, safe circle of Cutter's embrace and leaned her head on his chest. She heard the steady beat of his heart, inhaled his soapy aroma, which was combined with his own special scent, felt the hard wall of his body and the steely muscles in his arms.

''Thank you,'' she said softly. ''I couldn't bear it if you thought I had done such a deplorable thing.''

Cutter tightened his hold on her, inhaling her feminine fragrance as he nestled her closer to him, fitting her softness to his rugged contours. Why did it matter to her what he thought? he wondered. Did she care about him as a man? Or was she merely afraid of what he might do if he decided she was the guilty party? Why had she moved into his arms so willingly? And why in the hell didn't he have the answers to his questions?

Hollis tilted her head back to look up at him. "I guess we have to try to figure out who was behind the stealing of the cattle."

"Yeah," he said, gazing into her eyes, "we need to do that."

"It's . . . it's rather frightening, Cutter, because if everyone believes that Buck left all of Gauntlet Run to me, then this was a personal attack against me."

"No one is going to hurt you, Hollis." His voice was harsh. "No one."

"But—"

"No one," he repeated, then brought his mouth down hard on hers.

In the next instant, the kiss became gentler as Cutter's tongue delved into the sweet darkness of Hollis's mouth—exploring, tasting, seeking and finding her tongue. A wondrous trembling of desire began once again deep within Hollis and burned throughout her like the flame in the hearth.

Somewhere in the far recesses of Hollis's passion-laden mind she registered the fact that Cutter's declaration—that no one would hurt her—had been spoken in the same dark, fierce tone he had used when stating he protected what was his.

This was where she belonged: in Cutter's arms, sharing Cutter's kiss. *This* was coming home. She was alive like never before, rejoicing in her own femininity, savoring the sensations rocketing through her.

Oh, dear heaven, was she falling in love with Cutter McKenzie?

Hollis stiffened in his arms and he lifted his head to look at her questioningly, his blue eyes smoky with desire.

"Don't pull away from me, Hollis," he said, his voice gritty. "You want to be here, in my arms. You know you do."

Hollis couldn't move, or hardly breathe. She suddenly felt frightened and confused, bombarded by emotions that tumbled together in a maze in her mind. She wanted to run or hide, yet dreaded the thought of leaving the safety and warmth of Cutter's arms. She was a breath away from laughing or crying, but she didn't know which. She couldn't, shouldn't, fall in love with this man, but feared it was too late to turn back her emotional clock.

"Ah, damn," Cutter said with a groan, "don't look so sad."

His mouth melted over hers and a sob caught in Hollis's throat. She sank her fingers into the night darkness of his hair and pressed his mouth harder onto hers, feeling, only feeling, not thinking, not caring about anything but the taste, the power, the essence of Cutter. His manhood was hard against her, declaring his want of her, and she rejoiced in the knowledge.

The kiss went on and on, and passions soared.

Cutter's hands roamed seductively over Hollis's slender body, down to her buttocks, up to cup the sides of her breasts, which ached for his touch. Their breathing was labored as their hearts thundered.

"Hollis." Cutter drew a ragged breath. "I want you. And you want me. We're going to be so good together. So damn good. Let me love you." It was going to be fantastic, like nothing he'd experienced before. "Hollis?"

"Yes, I want you." She heard the thread of breathlessness in her voice. "But I can't do this, Cutter." No! If she made love with Cutter she'd be lost. This was Cutter, who had Gauntlet Run, who had what was hers and what she intended to get back. She had to find the strength to step away, be strong, not fall prey to his vibrant masculinity.

Not fall prey to her own heart. "No," she said, moving out of his arms.

"Why?" he said, his voice low. "Why are you denying us when it's what we both want? What are you afraid of, Hollis?"

"Nothing." She busied herself by putting on her shoes.

"Are you afraid of me? Or yourself?"

"There's nothing complicated about this," she said, leaning back against the soft leather of her chair. "I simply have no intention of going to bed with you."

Cutter chuckled. "Did you inform your body of that fact? It seems to have different plans."

"I admit I'm susceptible to your kiss. However, I have no desire to pursue it further," she said coolly.

"I don't believe you."

"Of course, you don't. Your male ego couldn't stand the strain. I'm sure you're used to having any woman you decide you want. Well, take me off your list, Cutter. I'm not available."

Cutter's jaw tightened, and he narrowed his eyes. "Then how do you explain what just happened here?"

"Lust. Chemistry. Whatever," she said, waving her hand breezily in the air. And fear. The fear that she was already in love with him, and she did *not* want to be in love with him.

Damn her. Cutter turned to the fire and braced his hands on the mantel. She was going into her high-and-mighty routine again. Damn, he hated it when she ran hot, then cold. It was driving him nuts! She wanted him, all right. Every inch of her luscious body had announced it loud and clear. He could seduce her, he knew. But he wasn't going to.

He couldn't be sure why. All he knew was that when they made love for the first time, he wanted it to be by mutual consent. He'd pleasure Hollis, meet her needs first, before he sought his own gratification. But he couldn't run roughshod over her sense of reason. He had to know—he had to!—that she had gone to him willingly.

He'd wait. With an ache in his gut and blood pounding in his veins, he'd wait. Hell.

Cutter picked up his glass, then settled back into the chair, staring into the amber liquid.

"Are you sure you can't think of anyone who might have a grudge against you?" he said, striving for a casual tone to his voice.

"What?" Hollis said, frowning. What? They were back to discussing the cattle? He certainly turned off in a hurry. Heavens, listen to her. She'd informed him she had no intention of sleeping with him, and now was pouting because he wasn't pursuing her.

"Enemies, Hollis. You know, the bad guys in the black hats."

"I've told you, Cutter, I can't imagine anyone who despises me that much."

"What about someone who hated Buck but was too afraid to make a move against him while he was alive?"

"That's sick."

"What was done to that cattle was sick. Well, I'll tell the sheriff that you couldn't point the finger at anyone."

"Are you going to inform Sheriff Dunbar about the will?"

"No," Cutter said, then drained his glass.

"Why not?"

"I don't feel he needs to know."

"Then you honestly believe I had nothing to do with this?"

"I believe you," he said, looking directly at her. "Why does it matter so much to you?"

Because she loved him, damn it all, Hollis fumed. How—when—she'd fallen in love with Cutter, she didn't know, but it had happened and she was furious at herself. This was the man she wanted off of Gauntlet Run, not the one she wished to spend the rest of her life with. Oh, she really would enjoy popping him in the chops.

"No one likes to be unjustly accused, Cutter," she said. "Our living together here at Gauntlet Run under forced circumstances is difficult enough without you thinking I'm some sort of thief in the night."

"Our living together?" He was grinning at her. "Are we doing that? Did I miss something?"

"You know what I mean. We wouldn't be here if it weren't for Buck's will."

"Oh, really? Which one of us would be long gone? If you'd inherited all of Gauntlet Run, would you have sent me packing?" Cutter said. Why did he get the feeling he wasn't going to like her answer? he asked himself.

"I... There's no point in discussing it, because that's not how Buck set up his will," she said. Send Cutter packing? she pondered. Never see him again? Never be held, kissed, touched by Cutter McKenzie? Oh, what a bleak, lonely picture that painted in her mind. To her, now, Gauntlet Run included Cutter. But how did he see it? What if... What if Cutter's slow, steady seduction of her was part of a master plan to win her over, gain her trust, even her love, so that he could have it all, all of Gauntlet Run!

"Hollis?" Cutter said, frowning. "What's wrong? You look like you just saw a ghost."

"What? Oh, I was just thinking. Tell me, Cutter, if you had inherited this house, would you have insisted that *I* leave?"

Hell, no, he thought fiercely. It dawned on him that he was trying to figure out a way to get her to stay there. This was becoming complicated. Very complicated.

"Well?" Hollis said.

"What? Oh, like you said, there's no point in discussing it, is there? What's done is done."

"Dinner is on the table," Mattie announced from the doorway.

"Best news I've had all day," Cutter said, getting to his feet. He extended his hand to Hollis. "Ma'am."

Hollis placed her hand in Cutter's and allowed him to pull her to her feet. Their eyes met, and Cutter didn't release her hand. A sensual current seemed to weave between them as crackling as a downed electric wire. As if pulled by invisible silken threads, each leaned toward the other. Mattie's muffled laughter broke the eerie spell.

"Oh!" Hollis said quickly, snatching her hand from Cutter's. "Dinner. Yes. I certainly am hungry." She hurried toward the housekeeper. "We mustn't let the food get cold."

"No rush," Mattie said, beaming. "Microwaves were invented in case a person gets delayed on the way to the table. There's just no telling what might delay someone. Could be any number of things."

Cutter chuckled.

Mattie's smile grew even bigger.

Hollis frowned.

In the dining room, Hollis slid onto her chair and made a major production of filling her plate, totally ignoring Cutter.

"Are you going to eat all that?" he said finally, grinning at her when she glanced up at him.

"Of course. You have more than this on your plate," she pointed out.

"But I'm a man with a man's appetite. A big appetite," he said, his voice low. "It takes a lot to satisfy me."

Cutter wasn't talking about food, Hollis realized. He knew it, she knew it, and he knew she knew it.

"Your cheeks are flushed," Cutter said, all innocence. "Is it too hot in here for you?"

"You're cute," she said, glaring at him. "Just too cute for words. Your innuendos are boring, Cutter."

"I'm just inquiring as to your comfort. That's a gentlemanly thing to do."

"And I suppose your mother tried her best to raise you to be a gentleman."

Cutter's smile faded. "No. I never knew my mother. She died when I was a few months old."

"I'm sorry," Hollis said softly. "I didn't know. What about your father?"

Cutter shrugged. "He raised me as well as could be expected, I guess. He was a drifter, a ranch hand. Usually the wife of one of the cowboys was willing to make extra money by watching me."

"What about school?"

"It was hit and miss. I managed to graduate from high school, but I was older than the other students. But ranching? Ranching I learned firsthand from the time I could walk."

"Where is your father now?"

"Dead. I was fifteen."

"Oh, Cutter."

"I did all right. I was big for my age, could do a man's share of work. I've never gone hungry."

"Are you like your father? A drifter?" Hollis said, a knot tightening in her stomach.

"I was," he said, nodding. "I never stayed anywhere for longer than two years. I'd get restless, edgy, have to move on. Until Gauntlet Run. This place staked its claim on me, Hollis. Maybe it was the land itself, or a combination of it, and the fact that it was time for me to settle down. I don't know. What I do know is that this is home to me. The only home I've ever had." And Hollis was there, he mentally tacked on.

"Buck knew, didn't he? He knew how much Gauntlet Run meant to you."

"He knew. I think that made it easier for him to turn over the authority to me. He trusted me, pure and simple."

"But for him not to have total control of Gauntlet Run," Hollis said, shaking her head. "I can't picture Buck relinquishing his hold."

"He was very busy and had endless demands on his time and energy."

"And by his own choosing," Hollis said, lifting her chin. "He did what he wanted to do for those who were important to him."

"Meaning you weren't important to him?" Cutter said, frowning. "You're wrong."

"I don't think so. He fitted me in around the edges of his life."

"Hollis, Buck didn't know what to say to a daughter, what to do with you. He loved you. He missed you terribly when you left here. It was his foolish, stubborn pride—and yours—that kept the two of you apart all those years."

"My stubborn pride? Buck's the one that gave me a choice, Cutter."

"I know that, but Raymond's been dead for a long time. Damn it, Hollis. Why didn't you attempt to mend the breach between you and Buck?"

"I was no longer welcome here," she said, her voice rising.

"Damn," Cutter muttered. "You and Buck Champion had to have been the two most stubborn people on the face of the earth. Buck wouldn't budge even when the doctors told him—"

"Cutter," said a man from the doorway.

"Yeah, Jesse?"

"Butterfly is in labor."

"I'll be right there," Cutter said, getting to his feet.

"Ma'am," Jesse said. Though she could tell he tried to cover it, Hollis couldn't help but notice the look he gave her before he turned and walked away.

"That man doesn't like me," Hollis said, an incredulous expression on her face. "I don't even know him."

"Don't worry about it," Cutter said as he strode toward the door.

"Cutter, wait. What were you about to say about my father and the doctors?"

"Later, Hollis."

"No," she said, getting to her feet. "Tell me now. It won't take long. Had my father been ill for a long time?"

Cutter ran his hand over the back of his neck. "Yeah, he was in rough shape. It was his heart. The doctors told him to take it easy, but Buck just lived his life the way he wanted to—until it killed him. There's another thing you two had in common: choices. Choices that had far-reaching effects. I've got to get to the barn. I doubt if I'll be back in tonight. Sleep well, Hollis."

As Cutter hurried out of the room, Hollis sank back onto her chair. She pressed trembling hands to her cheeks, her mind whirling from the impact of Cutter's words. Choices, she mentally repeated. Buck had deliberately disregarded his doctor's orders? Had made a choice that had ultimately killed him? Had kept his decision a secret from Hollis?

"Dear God," Hollis whispered. But, she reasoned, she understood. Buck wouldn't have been happy living his life any differently. To cut back, not to operate at maximum effort, would have frustrated and depressed him. To have had his daughter know of his weakness would have humiliated him. Yes, she understood why her father had done it his way right up until his moment of death.

And even beyond death, she thought wryly. The will was evidence of her father's reluctance to ever let go. He trusted Cutter, wanted him to stay on Gauntlet Run. He wanted Hollis there, too, where he felt she belonged, but he'd been too stubborn to ask her to return to his side.

He trusted Cutter McKenzie, Hollis repeated again, tracing a line on the tablecloth with her spoon. But did *she*? She loved him—she admitted it—but did she trust him? Trust and love should go hand in hand, but everything was complicated at Gauntlet Run, so confusing. Buck Champion would go to any extreme, take whatever steps he'd deemed necessary to achieve a goal. Would Cutter? Would Cutter go so far as to fake affection, lavish attention, hold, kiss, touch her, to gain what he wanted, to get Gauntlet Run?

She knew so little about the ways of men, Hollis realized. She'd never known a man like Cutter, other than to say he had the determination and drive of her father. Cutter was exciting and frightening to her at the same time. He'd awakened desire within her that had slumbered long and deep. Her heart hummed at the mere sight of him, and her senses had an awareness like never before. Oh, yes, she was in love with him. And she had absolutely no idea how he felt about her.

Was she Cutter's pawn now? Hollis wondered dismally. Just as she'd been her father's? Could Cutter see the desire in her eyes, feel it in her response to his kiss and touch? Was he laughing at her, mentally patting himself on the back as he worked toward making her putty in his hands?

"Damn it," Hollis said, smacking the table with her hand. Why, why, why had she fallen in love with that man, a man who could very well be playing a game with her emotions so he could possess all of Gauntlet Run?

Tears stung Hollis's eyes, and she blinked them angrily away. She couldn't turn off her heart, but she could certainly keep her mouth shut. She would not, she told herself firmly, allow Cutter to know she had fallen head over heels in love with him. She'd observe, listen, pay attention. She had to know the truth about Cutter, know why he was lavishing his attention on her. Know if he really cared for her or merely regarded her as a means to an end. If her heart was to be shattered into a million pieces by Cutter McKenzie, at least he would never know it. Her pride would remain intact.

"Hollis," Mattie said, coming into the room, "have you finished eating?"

"What? Oh, yes, thank you. It was delicious, Mattie."

"Well, I see that Cutter ate most of his dinner this time before he went to the barn. I swear, that boy would starve before he'd put off seeing to the needs of those horses. Guess we'll have a new baby before the night is over. Butterfly is a beautiful horse. She should produce a fine colt. I'll make up a bunch of sandwiches later and send them down to the barn. Cutter won't come in until that baby is born."

"He's obviously very dedicated to Gauntlet Run," Hollis said quietly. "He considers this land his home."

"That he does, and Gauntlet Run is lucky to have him. Buck knew that. You'd admit it, too, if you weren't so stubborn, my girl."

"Stubborn. That seems to be a favorite word used in reference to a Champion."

"It fits. Lordy, does it ever fit," Mattie said, smiling and shaking her head.

"Mattie, did you know that Buck's heart was giving him problems long before he had the attack that killed him?"

"Land's sake," Mattie said, sitting down. "I had no idea Buck wasn't up to par. He certainly didn't slow down any. His heart attack was a tremendous shock to me. One minute he was with us and the next... Who told you Buck was sick?"

"Cutter."

"Yes, Cutter would have known. They were close, Buck and Cutter."

"Like father and son," Hollis said, a slight edge to her voice.

"Oh, Hollis," Mattie said, shaking her head, "don't resent what Buck shared with Cutter. Cutter was here, and you weren't, honey. Besides, they were men with a mutual love for Gauntlet Run. It stands to reason they would have a special relationship. But . . . Well, it wasn't always a bed of roses."

"What do you mean?"

"It's hard to explain. Buck lost something within him when your mother died: his gentleness, his ability to act from his heart as well as his head. A part of him was empty, cold. But Cutter isn't like that, Hollis. Oh, he's strong and has a temper—drive and determination, too. I'd hate to be the one who crossed Cutter or betrayed his trust. But the gentleness is there in that boy, the warmth, the caring. Yes, he and Buck were a lot alike, but in the final accounting, there are major differences between them. Does that make sense?"

"Yes, I think so," Hollis said, fiddling with her spoon again. "I feel as though I'm trying to piece together a very complicated puzzle."

"Sometimes," Mattie said, getting to her feet, "things are much simpler than we think. Folks make a lot of misery for themselves by muddling up what is as plain as the nose on their face. Me? I just take things as they come. Don't go looking for trouble, Hollis. It will find you on its own if there's any to be had."

"But people have to protect themselves, Mattie."

"By building walls around their hearts? That's how I see Buck. He was devastated when your mother died. He built walls so high they kept all the sunshine from reaching his heart and soul. He was a powerful, dynamic man, but he was lonely. Empty and lonely. Be careful with walls, Hollis, honey."

"Yes. Yes, I will. I'm very tired, Mattie. It's been a long day, and I think I'll go to bed."

"That's fine. You do look tired. A good night's sleep will do wonders. Good night, honey."

"Good night, Mattie."

A short time later Hollis lay in bed, willing her body to relax and willing the voices in her mind to cease their in-

sistent chatter. So much had happened so quickly, and she
was exhausted, emotionally and physically drained. With
a weary sigh of relief that the day was at last at an end, she
gave way to the somnolence that drifted over her.

Hours later, Hollis woke from a deep sleep, suddenly
wide awake. She glanced at the clock and saw that it was
just after two a.m. Had it been Cutter entering his bedroom that had awakened her? She wondered if everything
was all right with Butterfly.

Hollis swept back the blankets and reached for her satin
robe. Leaving the bedroom, she saw that Cutter's door was
ajar, just as it had been earlier. She approached it cautiously, then hesitated outside.

"Cutter?" she said in a loud whisper. She moved closer
and pushed the door farther open. "Cutter?" The moon-
light streaming in through the window of the dark room
clearly illuminated the neatly made bed. Obviously Cutter
hadn't come in from the barn.

Hollis returned to her room and closed the door, registering a sudden restlessness as she paced the floor. Was the
birth of a horse supposed to take this long? She'd never
seen Butterfly, but she hated the thought of any animal
being in pain. Cutter had been in the barn for hours. He
could probably use some coffee. Maybe she could even be
of help.

She dressed in jeans and a green flannel shirt, pulled on
her boots, then quickly wove her hair into two thick braids
so it wouldn't get in the way. She reached in the closet for
a gray windbreaker, then went into the kitchen and made
coffee to put into a thermos. With a surge of tingling excitement, she left the house and hurried toward the barn.

Chapter 6

Seven years.

It had been seven years since Hollis had stepped foot in that barn, and as she entered the huge building, memories washed over her. She stood perfectly still as vivid pictures from her childhood danced in her mental vision.

It was to that very spot that Buck had led her by the hand on her sixth birthday. Keeping her promise to squeeze her eyes tightly closed, she had held on to Buck's strong hand.

"Okay, princess," her father had said at last. "Open your eyes and see your birthday present."

Quivering with excitement, Hollis had slowly lifted her lashes, then her eyes had widened. Standing before her was the most beautiful pony she had ever seen.

"Oh, Daddy," she had whispered. "Is it really mine? Forever?"

"Forever," Buck had said. "Go on and say hello."

"Thank you, thank you, thank you," Hollis had said, throwing her arms around her father's waist.

He had lifted her high in the air and she'd squealed in delight. Then he'd placed her on the pony's back and Hollis had sat straight and proud in the saddle.

"You'll ride like a Champion," he had said. "You'll love and respect your horse and the land of Gauntlet Run that you explore together. You'll never forget to feed her or groom her. Promise?"

"Oh, yes, I promise, Daddy," she'd said solemnly.

"That's my girl. I know you'll make me proud. What are you going to name your pony?"

"Forever. Her name is Forever, because that's how long you said she could be mine."

Her father had roared with laughter. "Forever it is, then. Happy birthday to you and Forever."

"I love you, Daddy."

"I love you, too, baby. Now! I'll get my horse and we'll go riding together."

"Just you and me?" Hollis had said, her eyes dancing.

"Just the two of us," he'd said, smiling at her.

"And Forever."

"Yes, ma'am," he'd said, laughing. "Forever is part of the family now."

"Forever and ever and ever," Hollis had whispered as Buck went to saddle his horse.

Hollis pulled herself back from the past and drew a shuddering breath, realizing that tears had spilled onto her cheeks. She hastily brushed them away.

"Hollis?" Cutter said from across the large expanse. He walked toward her, covering the distance rapidly with his long-legged stride. "What's wrong?" He gripped her upper arms, a deep frown on his face.

"Nothing," she said, managing a weak smile.

Cutter trailed his thumbs over her cheeks in a soft, caressing motion that caused Hollis's heart to race.

"Tears?" he said. "Talk to me, Hollis."

"It's nothing, really. Some memories snuck up on me, that's all. Buck gave me a pony for my sixth birthday and... Well, never mind."

"Forever," Cutter said, nodding. He continued his foray over her soft skin with his fingers.

"You know about Forever?" Her surprise was evident in her voice.

"Yeah, I do. I'd forgotten about it until now. Buck and I sat in front of the fire one night, and he told me he'd never forgotten the joy on your face when you opened your eyes and saw that pony. For the next three years, you and Forever were inseparable. The minute you came home from school you were out here in the barn. In the summers, Buck said, if he saw one of you, he saw both."

"And then... then," Hollis said, her voice trembling, "Forever was running in the pasture after a rainstorm. The ground was soft and she stumbled. Oh, God, Cutter, I'll never forget the scream, that horrible scream that she made. Buck told me to go to the house, but I refused. One of the hands picked me up and carried me, and I kicked and cried all the way, yelling at him that Forever needed me. Buck shot her. He got a rifle and he shot her."

"He had no choice, Hollis," Cutter said gently. "You know that. He told me it was one of the most heartbreaking things he'd ever had to do."

"But he told *me* nothing," Hollis said, her voice rising. "He pretended that Forever had never existed."

"He didn't know what to say to you! He'd stand outside your bedroom door at night hearing you cry yourself to sleep, and he didn't know how to comfort you. He left you alone because he didn't know what else to do."

"I thought he didn't care, that it meant nothing to him."

"Oh, no. His heart was aching for you, Hollis. I could hear the pain in his voice as he told me the story all those years later. He said that after what happened to Forever, you refused to have your own horse again. You rode constantly but didn't become attached to any special one."

"I couldn't. I'd lost my mother, then Forever and... No, I haven't had my own horse since then."

"Maybe you'll change your mind now that you have all the facts. Buck was torn apart by what happened. Every time you refused his offer of a new horse it hit him hard, reminded him he hadn't come through for you when you needed him."

"I don't know what to say," Hollis said, her voice hushed.

"Just think about it, okay? Now then, why are you out here in the middle of the night?"

"I realized you hadn't come in, and I was concerned that something was wrong with Butterfly." She held up the forgotten thermos.

"You checked my bedroom?" He smiled and dropped his hands from her face. "Damn, I'm never in the right place at the right time."

"I was thinking of Butterfly, not you, Mr. McKenzie," Hollis said, frowning up at him.

"She's doing fine. These things take time, you know."

"No, I don't know. Buck never wanted me underfoot when a horse was giving birth, and I was shooed away. But maybe I could do something to help."

"Do you want to stay?" He took the thermos and poured himself a cup of coffee.

"Yes. Yes, I do, but Butterfly doesn't know me. Maybe I'd make her nervous. Or maybe I'll faint dead out on my face. Twenty years on Gauntlet Run and I've never seen a litter of kittens born."

Cutter chuckled. "It's time you broadened your horizons. I don't think Butterfly will mind. She's one of the calmest first-time mothers I've ever seen. I've just been sitting there telling her my boring life history. She'll probably hurry that baby along so I'll shut up and leave her alone.''

Cutter smiled to himself. It was a good thing he'd seen Hollis out of the corner of his eye, or she might have heard the ridiculous monologue he'd been delivering to Butterfly. There he'd sat, telling the horse that ole Cutter Mc-Kenzie was in love with Hollis Champion Ramirez. He'd even gone so far as to ask the animal how to go about getting Hollis to fall in love with him! He was definitely cracking up.

"It certainly is quiet in here," Hollis said, bringing Cutter from his reverie. "Sort of spooky."

"I sent Jesse and the other hands on to bed. I can buzz Jesse on the intercom if Butterfly gets in trouble, but I don't think that'll happen. I enjoy the barn when it's like this. There's a peacefulness here, a rightness, a . . . I guess that doesn't make much sense."

"Yes, it does," Hollis said, looking up at him. "Especially on a night when a birth, a miracle, is going to take place."

Cutter smiled at her warmly and put his arm around her shoulders. "Let's go check on the mother," he said, pulling Hollis close to his side.

Butterfly had been moved to a double stall in the rear of the barn. Cutter and Hollis walked down the aisle into the darkness between the light at the front of the building and the one glowing above Butterfly's stall. Hollis could hardly see where she was going, and instinctively moved closer to Cutter. She inhaled his aroma of soap and hay, and the heady scent of his masculinity. She savored the strength of his hard body and allowed his heat to flow into her. There was an aura of leashed power surrounding Cutter, of authoritativeness and strength, and Hollis felt feminine, fragile and protected at his side.

Dear heaven, how she loved this man.

Why did it have to be so complicated? she asked herself. Why was it all shrouded in doubts, fears, unknowns? She just wanted to love and be loved in return by Cutter McKenzie.

Cutter led Hollis to the edge of the stall, then dropped his arm from her shoulders to hunker down next to the panting horse.

"Hey, Butterfly," he said in a soothing tone as he stroked her nose, "I brought you some company. There's a lovely lady here to share your special time. Sound good? You bet."

As Cutter spoke to the horse, Hollis smiled. Her gaze flickered over the material of Cutter's shirt, which strained across his back and shoulders. She saw the muscles of his thighs bunching beneath the soft denim of his jeans and the ebony glow of his thick hair. And she saw his hands. Hands that were big and strong and callused. Tanned hands, with long fingers that were caressing Butterfly with infinite gentleness. Hands that had touched Hollis and ignited a raging flame of desire within her. She felt a warm flush of heat on her cheeks and averted her eyes from him.

"Here we go," Cutter said suddenly. "This is it. Easy, girl. You're doing fine, just fine."

Butterfly whinnied and lifted her head as the bulging weight within her shifted and a rush of fluid poured forth. And then the colt.

"Oh!" Hollis gasped. "Oh, my gosh. Oh, Cutter. Look! The baby! It's beautiful."

"Damn right it is," he said, excitement evident in his voice.

He shifted his attention to the colt, making sure its breathing passages were clear, then moved out of Butterfly's way to allow the horse to tend to the foal. Cutter quickly disposed of the soiled hay, replaced it with fresh, then went to wash his hands. Hollis never took her eyes off the mother and baby.

Cutter returned to Hollis's side, watching the expression of wonder on her face. He resisted the urge to lift her braids and pull her gently to him to cover her mouth with his, meet her tongue, crush her lush breasts to his chest.

"Unbelievable," Hollis whispered, her gaze riveted on the animals.

"Yes," he said, looking only at her.

"Thank you for letting me stay."

"I'm glad you were here to share it with me," he said, his voice low.

Hollis turned her head slowly to look up at Cutter, her breath catching in her throat as she saw the raw desire evident in the blue depths of his eyes. He cradled her face in his hands, then slowly lowered his lips to hers, flicking his tongue over her bottom lip in gentle insistence. Hollis complied, parting her lips as she put her arms around his neck. The barn, its pungent aromas, the animals, all disappeared, and for Hollis there was only the sensations evoked by Cutter.

Cutter slid one hand to Hollis's back, the other to her buttocks to nestle her close to his body—his body, which ached with wanting her as blood pounded through his veins. His tongue met hers, and the soft purr coming from her throat ignited his passion further. The kiss deepened, became frenzied, urgent, as though they couldn't get enough of each other.

Cutter's muscles trembled as he strove for control, pulling himself back to the here and now, remembering where he was and what he was doing. He wanted to carry Hollis to a stall laden with fresh, fragrant hay and slowly remove her clothes, kissing every inch of her as her nakedness came into his view. He wanted to touch and kiss her until she was clinging to him, calling to him to come to her.

But not here, Cutter's mind raged. Not in the barn. Not where Hollis might later see herself having succumbed to

her passion and engaged in a cheap tumble in the hay. It
had to be perfect for her, and he had to know she truly
wanted him as he did her.

"Hollis," he said, lifting his head, "no more."

Hollis gazed up at him through half-closed eyes, saw the
perspiration on his brow, felt the shudder rip through his
coiled, restrained body. He wanted her—she knew he
did—and, oh, how she wanted him. Nothing else mattered, not the doubts, fears, confusion. Only Cutter, and
what they could share.

"I'll…" Cutter started, then cleared his throat roughly.
"I'll walk you back to the house."

"Aren't you coming in?" she said a bit breathlessly.

"No, not right now. I have a few things to finish up
here," he said, lifting one of her braids in his hand.
"You'd better get some sleep."

He was rejecting her, Hollis thought frantically. He
wanted her. He did! But he was sending her to her room,
alone, like a child. Why?

"Cutter?" she said, searching his face for an answer.

Cutter looked into the emerald depths of Hollis's eyes,
saw the hurt and confusion there mingled with the smoky
hue of her lingering desire. He dropped her braid and took
a step backward, staring at the ceiling for a long moment
before he looked at her again.

"I want you, Hollis," he said, his voice gritty. "I want
to take you back into the house and into my bed, but this
isn't the time or the night. Trust me a little here."

Trust him, Hollis's mind echoed. How she wanted to
add the ingredient of trust to her ever-growing love for
him. He was forcing her to think, be reasonable and rational, and she didn't want to. He was making her come
back from the rosy place of only feeling, tasting, touching
him. And, damn him, he was right. She'd been hazy with
desire, need, want, not thinking clearly. She would've
made love with Cutter, and then what? What would she

have felt in the light of a new day? Love him? Oh, yes. Trust him? She didn't know. She just didn't know.

"I'll see you in," Cutter said quietly.

"That isn't necessary."

"I said I'll see you in," he repeated, narrowing his eyes. "Don't argue with me. Not right now."

Hollis opened her mouth, then snapped it closed, deciding this was not a terrific time to get sassy. Cutter McKenzie was pushed to the limit of his sexual control, and the tight set to his jaw told her he was not in a pleasant mood. She glanced quickly at Butterfly and the foal, smiled gently, then started toward the door. Cutter fell in step beside her.

Outside the barn, they filled their lungs with the crisp night air. Neither spoke. At the back door, Cutter stopped.

"I'll see you in the morning," he said.

"It *is* morning."

"Yeah, I suppose it is. Well, whatever. Good night, Hollis."

The moon sent a silvery glow over Cutter as Hollis gazed up at him, making him appear even bigger, more massive. She shivered.

"I would have made love with you in the barn, Cutter," she said, hardly above a whisper.

"I know," he said, shoving his hands into the back pockets of his jeans. "But when we make love, Hollis— and we will—I have to be sure you're aware of what you're doing, what you want. That's very important to me. Go in the house now."

He cared, her heart sang. He really cared!

"Damn it," he said gruffly, "don't look at me like that, or I'll forget every noble intention I have. Go!"

"Good night, Cutter," she said smiling, "and thank you."

Cutter watched as Hollis disappeared into the house, then, with an earthy expletive, he spun on his heel and strode back to the barn.

In her bedroom, Hollis shed her clothes and slid naked beneath the sheets, pulling the warm blankets up to her chin. Oh, how she loved that Cutter McKenzie, she mused sleepily. And he had feelings for her, too. If he didn't, he would've taken what she'd so blatantly offered him in the barn. *When* they made love, he had said. Not *if*, but *when*. But he needed to know she was thinking clearly, that she knew exactly what she was doing. That was dear and sweet and wonderful.

And the trust? she asked herself. She needed desperately to believe that Cutter wanted her for herself, with no thought of Gauntlet Run. But she didn't know that, not for sure. Oh, she just couldn't think anymore tonight. Not tonight.

Hollis burrowed deeper under the blankets, closed her eyes and slept.

The next sensation Hollis registered was the sound of someone pounding on her bedroom door. She struggled to sit up, blinking against the bright sunlight flooding the room, and clutched the sheet to her bare breasts.

"Yes?" she said. "Who is it?"

Cutter stormed into the room, his face dark with rage. He tossed a newspaper onto her lap and glowered down at her.

"Why?" His voice was low and menacing.

"Why what?" she said, shaking her head slightly. "What are you talking about?"

"Front page," he said, pointing to the paper. "A quote from Mac Winston outlining the provisions of Buck's will and stating that a family member had decided to make the will public knowledge. What in the hell do you think you're doing, Hollis?''

"Me!" she shrieked, nearly dropping the sheet.

"Who else? It sure as hell wasn't me. No one else is involved enough to give a damn. The big hoopla in Houston will be over the provisions regarding us and Gauntlet Run. Why did you do it?"

"I didn't! I haven't spoken to Mac since the day of Buck's funeral."

"Bull!"

"Call him. Pick up that phone and call him this very instant. That never occurred to you, did it? You were too busy deciding I was guilty. Go on—call him. My phone numbers are in that leather-bound book."

"Damn right I'll call him." Cutter flipped open the book, then punched out the numbers.

"Fine," Hollis said, tucking the sheet more tightly over her breasts. "I'll be waiting for your apology."

Cutter glared at her, then ran his hand over the back of his neck as he waited for the ringing to start on the other end of the line. When the secretary answered, he identified himself and asked to be put through to Mac.

"Cutter, good morning," Mac said cheerfully. "What can I do for you today?"

"You can tell me," Cutter said, through clenched teeth, "whichever famous family member authorized you to release the provisions of Buck's will to the press."

"What?"

"Come on, Mac, you heard me. Whose screwball idea was this?"

"Cutter, have you been drinking?"

"What in the hell is that supposed to mean?" Cutter roared. Hollis cringed.

"*You* called me yesterday and said to release the story," Mac said.

"What?" Cutter said, sinking onto the edge of Hollis's bed. She quickly scooted her legs out of his way, her gaze riveted on his face.

"It was you, Cutter. I know your voice. I talked to you yesterday as clearly as I'm speaking with you now."

"Listen to me, Mac. I didn't call you yesterday. That was not my voice you heard."

"Someone phoned Mac and said they were you?" Hollis said. "Why?"

"Shh," Cutter said, glaring at her again.

"I'll be damned," Mac said. "I could have sworn.... Whoever it was did a damn good impersonation of you, Cutter. I'm sorry about this. You— Well, the man on the phone—gave me precise instructions to let it be known that the land of Gauntlet Run was yours and the house was Hollis's, providing neither of you forfeits. I was merely following your—his instructions. Damn."

"It's not your fault," Cutter said. "You had no reason to doubt that you were speaking with me."

"This doesn't make sense," Mac said. "Who would do such a crazy thing?"

"I don't know," Cutter said. "If you get any more calls from me, phone me back and verify what I said. Okay?"

"Yes, of course. This is like a bad movie. I really am sorry."

"Don't blame yourself. I'll keep in touch. 'Bye, Mac." Cutter slowly replaced the receiver. "Damn it to hell."

"Cutter?" Hollis said. "Did I understand that right? Someone called Mac and pretended to be you?"

"Yeah." He got to his feet and began to pace the floor. "I'm sorry I jumped to conclusions about you, Hollis. That wasn't fair."

"You're forgiven. Why would someone do this? Who would want our business publicly known? Who could impersonate your voice that well?"

"I don't know—to all of the above," he said, heading for the door, "but I'm sure as hell going to find out. Somehow." He stopped, turning to look at her. "By the way, you're beautiful when you first wake up. I like your nightgown, too."

"I'm not wearing one." She could feel the warm flush on her cheeks.

"That's what I like about it," he said, giving her a lazy grin.

"You certainly change gears quickly, Mr. McKenzie," she said, poking her nose in the air. "There's a weirdo out there wreaking havoc with our private lives, remember?"

"And," he said, still grinning, "there's a beautiful, desirable woman in this room, naked beneath the sheets, wreaking havoc with my libido. See ya." He strode from the room, closing the door behind him.

"See ya," she whispered, a warm smile on her lips. "Oh!" she said an instant later, snapping out of her rosy glow. She snatched up the newspaper and quickly scanned the print.

Incredible, she thought. Clever. "Impersonated Cutter's voice," Hollis mused aloud. She flipped back the blankets and headed for the shower.

After dressing in navy wool slacks and a pale blue cashmere sweater, Hollis blow-dried and brushed her hair. In the kitchen, she found a note from Mattie saying that the housekeeper had gone into Houston with one of the ranch hands for household supplies. Hollis poured herself a cup of coffee and sat down at the table, gazing out the window at the lush land of Gauntlet Run.

Cutter, Hollis's mind whispered. He was never far from her thoughts, and her body was continually a breath away from being consumed by tingling desire. But to love and not be loved in return was incredibly sad. To love and not fully trust the man of her heart caused an inner chill of misery. And now there was the mystery, the frightening aura of suspense hanging over Gauntlet Run.

"Tangled webs, Buck," Hollis said softly, "and you probably would have enjoyed the challenge of every minute of it." Buck, she mused. And Forever, her precious pony. She'd spent all those years believing that Buck didn't care, that he'd been unaffected when Forever had had to be destroyed. But now Hollis knew differently, knew that Buck had been cut to the quick by her brokenhearted pain. How strange it seemed that the articulate, dynamic Buck Champion, who could hold the multitudes riveted in place with his spoken word, had not known how to comfort a grief-stricken child.

How strange.

And how very, very human.

Hollis sighed. It was a deep sigh, a sigh from her soul as she wondered how often Buck hadn't been able to tell her things that were in his heart. Had he seen Raymond Ramirez for the immature young man that he was? Had it been sorrow more than rage that had caused Buck to force Hollis into the choice that had driven her away?

Stubborn pride, Hollis's mind echoed. How would that pride affect her relationship with Cutter?

"There he is again," Hollis muttered.

She replayed in her mind the scene in the barn the previous night, saw Cutter's strong, gentle hands stroking Butterfly, heard the soothing quality to his deep, rich voice. He had placed such reverence on the foal's birth, and Hollis knew it would be the same for every birth. Cutter was a man of the land, treasured its bounty and treated its offerings as rare gifts. As had been Buck Champion, Cutter McKenzie was Gauntlet Run. And she loved him.

Hollis got to her feet and washed out her mug. Enough heavy thinking for now, she decided. She'd go to the master suite and start formulating her decorating plans. What had Kathleen said? If Hollis worked with too much of a feminine flair, it would have to be redone if a man took up residence with her in those rooms. Kathleen was being absurd.

"Oh, really?" Hollis said under her breath as she went down the hall. Facts were facts. Hollis Champion Ramirez was in love with Cutter McKenzie. She wanted him in her bed, in her life, in her future. She wanted him to love her in kind, be real and honest and everything she hoped he was. "How nice," she said dryly. She could remember wanting to go to sleep, wake up and find that Forever was still alive, that the death of her pony had been only a nightmare. But there had been nowhere to hide from the truth.

The truth. How was she to know the truth about Cutter? Did he want *her*, or Gauntlet Run?

"Don't think," she said aloud, quickening her step. "Not now."

Outside Buck's rooms, Hollis hesitated. Then, squaring her shoulders and lifting her chin, she turned the knob, opened the door and entered.

In the barn, Cutter leaned against the wall of the stall and watched Butterfly's foal greedily suckle the mother's sweet milk.

"Fine, fine animal," Jesse said, coming to Cutter's side.

"Sure is," Cutter said, nodding. "And Butterfly came through it like she'd been on a Sunday picnic."

"You know how to breed 'em, Cutter. You've got a sixth sense about horses. I respect that."

"Thanks, Jesse."

"Cutter, what's with the story in the paper? The boys were really buzzing about it this morning. I told them to just get to work and mind their own business. Thing is, that story makes it the business of everyone in Houston. Hell, the whole damn country!"

"I know," Cutter said, sighing. "Are you ready for this? Someone phoned the lawyer, impersonating me. Mac Winston honestly thought he was talking to *me*! On the instructions from the man who sounded like me, Mac released the story to the press."

"Are you joshing me?"

"I wish I were."

"It's tied into the killing of the cattle, Cutter. I'd bet my boots on it. Do you think Hollis had anything to do with it?"

"She had nothing to do with that joker who pretended to be me," Cutter said, his jaw tightening.

"What makes you so sure she's innocent?"

"What makes you think she might be guilty?" Cutter roared. Butterfly jerked, causing the colt to teeter on its wobbly legs. "Come into the tack room. We're getting Butterfly tensed up."

In the large room at the end of the aisle, Cutter leaned against a bench. He pulled off his Stetson, raked his fingers through his thick hair, then tugged the hat back into place. He crossed his arms over his broad chest.

"I don't understand you, Jesse," he said, frowning. "You've never been one to pass judgment on someone you don't even know."

"She doesn't belong here, Cutter,"

"Hollis is a Champion! She's Buck's daughter. Of course she belongs here. More than I do, if you really think about it."

"You've sweated for this land, Cutter, worked harder than anyone here. Don't you see what that newspaper article is going to do?"

"Why don't you tell me, Jesse?" Cutter said narrowing his eyes.

"It'll be all over the state that Cutter McKenzie was hit by rustlers. Not Buck or Hollis Champion, but you. You've earned a fine reputation in Texas. If you start looking like an easy mark, some are going to think you were just hanging on to Buck's shirttails all those years. You've worked too hard for me to stand by and watch that happen."

"I appreciate your concern," Cutter said. "I'd like you to go check on the hands on the south ridge and make sure they're moving that group of cattle to the other pasture like I said."

The two men stared at each other with a long, hard look with no words spoken, then Jesse spun on his heel and stalked from the room.

"Damn," Cutter said. His fury erupted, and he smashed his fist into the wall. "Wonderful," he moaned, clutching his hand. "Just wonderful."

Hollis stood still as a statue, her heart pounding as tears misted her eyes. She had entered the living room of Buck's master suite and wandered through the groupings of dark, massive furniture. One set was in front of a large, stone fireplace much like the one in the living room. She had been no more than seven or eight years old the last time she'd been in these rooms, and they appeared foreign to her, as though she'd never really seen them at all.

She moved into the bedroom beyond, glancing at the king-sized bed with the hand-carved wooden headboard. There was another grouping of soft, leather chairs, an upright chest of drawers, and a long, low dresser that stretched along one wall. It was to that piece of furniture that she was drawn, and she stood before it, hardly able to breathe.

Photographs of every shape and size in frames of a wide variety.

Pictures of her.

Her entire life was there before her, from infancy to the present. With a gasp, she recognized a snapshot of herself taken just weeks before at the orphanage in Mexico City where she had spent many hours a week playing with the children. In the photo, she was laughing as she held a small girl in her arms. She remembered that day, the yellow dress she'd worn, the hugs exchanged with the child, who was celebrating her fourth birthday.

Buck's detectives had been instructed to take pictures of her, Hollis thought incredulously. It was all there—the seven years she'd been away from Gauntlet Run.

"Oh, Daddy," she whispered, tears spilling onto her cheeks, "you did love me. You did miss me. Oh, God, Daddy, what did we do to each other?"

With a trembling hand, Hollis reached for the single framed picture of her mother and gazed at it with misty vision. She set the frame gently back in place, then brushed the wetness from her cheeks.

She hadn't really known Buck Champion at all, Hollis realized. She'd seen only the surface of the man—the power, the driving need to accomplish all he'd set out to do. She'd viewed him as a father who was too busy, too preoccupied, to meet the needs of his lonely daughter. But there had been more, much more, to Buck. He'd never recovered from the death of his beloved wife, had not known how to relate to the little girl left in his care.

How he must have suffered, Hollis thought. Those pictures of her were tangible proof of his desire to have her with him through all those years. Their pride had kept them apart. And so, in death, her father had brought her home. Home to Gauntlet Run. Home to Cutter, the man who'd helped fill some of the chilling emptiness within Buck. He'd counted on Hollis's stubborn pride to keep her there to fight for Gauntlet Run. And he'd counted on Hollis to see in Cutter what Buck knew was there.

In the terms of her father's will, what Hollis had previously viewed as manipulation, the urge to control, she now saw as a lonely, loving man's last attempt to right a wrong.

He had done it the only way he could—in death—for in life his pride had held him in an iron grip.

Hollis walked over and sat in the leather chair before the hearth. Buck's plan had worked, she mused. She was there, on Gauntlet Run, and she loved Cutter McKenzie with every fiber in her being.

And now? she asked herself, staring into the cold fireplace. Now her father's role in her and Cutter's lives was over. He'd done what he'd set out to do; Hollis and Cutter were both on Gauntlet Run, and both were determined to stay. Hollis had gone one step further with Buck's fervent wish and fallen in love with Cutter.

And what of Cutter McKenzie? she wondered. Yes, he'd stayed as Buck knew he would. And, yes, Cutter loved Gauntlet Run as Buck knew he did. But what were Cutter's feelings for Hollis? Buck's plan was clever, as were all the projects he put his mind to, but he'd forgotten one major thing: he couldn't control a man's heart; he couldn't manipulate Cutter into falling in love with Hollis.

It was up to her now, Hollis realized, to determine if Cutter's attentions were real and honest or merely part of a scheme to gain Gauntlet Run. A plan that picked up where Buck's will left off. A plan that Hollis was so far following to the letter. But if he was sincere? Then . . .

"Oh," Hollis groaned in frustration, leaning her head back. It was jumbling together in her mind again, confusing her, tormenting her. She had to remember that she, like Buck, had that damnable Champion pride, which would either be her salvation or stand in the way of her finding true happiness and love.

She felt so alone, so desperately alone, Hollis thought dismally. Her life had become so complicated since she'd returned to Gauntlet Run. How serene her existence had been in Mexico City. And empty. Empty, because there had been no Cutter; no feel of his strong arms holding her so tightly, no taste of his kiss, no special aroma that was uniquely his. There had been no awakening of her femininity, nor the sweet pain of simmering desire.

Yes, Hollis admitted, she was glad she was home. She was on the brink of either ecstasy or heartbreak with Cutter McKenzie, but she felt alive as never before.

"Well, Buck," she said aloud, getting to her feet, "you got me here just as you intended, and I've fallen in love with Cutter. Thing is, Daddy, I don't know where it's all going to end."

Hollis's gaze once again swept over the room, lingering for a moment on the pictures on the dresser. She wouldn't redecorate in there right away, she decided. She'd start with another area of the house first, and wait until later to redo the master suite.

She'd wait until she knew whether she'd be sleeping there alone or with Cutter McKenzie.

Chapter 7

When Hollis approached the entryway to the house, she heard the murmur of voices and quickened her step. A ranch hand and a man in a khaki uniform were stacking boxes in the foyer.

"Oh," Hollis said, smiling, "my things have arrived from Mexico."

"Yes, ma'am," the deliveryman said. "I need you to sign this receipt, please."

"Certainly." Hollis scribbled her name on the offered paper. The deliveryman mumbled his thanks and went out of the door.

"Was there anywhere special you wanted this stuff, ma'am?" the ranch hand asked.

"No, just leave it there for now. Thank you for your help."

"Yes, ma'am." He touched his fingers to the brim of his hat, then turned and left.

A tingle of excitement swept through Hollis as her eyes darted from one to the next of the ten boxes. She now had her painting supplies, she realized, plus special knick-knacks from Mexico that would add a new touch to some of the rooms at Gauntlet Run. She'd shipped her favorite books and a portion of her wardrobe. She knew everything that was in those boxes but it still brought on a feeling of Christmas.

A smile securely in place, Hollis checked the shipping labels until she found the box containing her painting supplies. She tugged on the strapping tape and gasped as the flaps popped free at last. Hollis dragged the carton across the foyer and into Buck's library.

For the next hour, Hollis pushed and pulled the heavy furniture in the room, opened the drapes to allow sunlight to pour into the semidark expanse and unpacked her precious supplies. The paints were placed in a glass-front cupboard, the books she'd removed now wiggled into available spaces on the wall shelves. Her easel stood in front of the large window.

"Perfect," she said, gauging the direction of the sun. "Buck's library has just become Hollis's studio."

"Hollis?" Mattie poked her head in the door. "There you are. I saw all the boxes in the... Land's sake, what have you done?"

"Set up my studio," Hollis said, beaming. "I'll need one of the hands to take these two chairs to a spare bedroom. Oh, and that end table and lamp have to go. I may replace some of the heavier, dark pieces with lighter furniture—airy, happy colors. Since this is my studio now, I want it to have just the right mood for me to work."

Mattie frowned as she walked slowly forward, glancing around. "Oh, my," she said, shaking her head, "I don't know about this, Hollis."

"It's marvelous," Hollis went on. "The light from the big window is exactly what I need to paint. It will all look better once I get the extra furniture moved out."

"I'm sure it'll look fine." Mattie was still frowning. "That's not the problem. Cutter uses this library as an office when prospective horse buyers come to Gauntlet Run. Cutter and Buck sort of shared this room to conduct their business. I'm not sure how Cutter is going to feel about this. Where will he meet with his buyers?"

Hollis planted her hands on her hips. "Don't tempt me to tell you where Cutter can go with his almighty horse buyers. Mattie, this is my house, and I can do with it as I see fit. This room is no longer a dark cave for men only. This is a bright, sunny studio, and it's mine. Would you please call down to the barn and see if anyone is free to come up and move these things out?"

"Oh, mercy," Mattie said, hurrying from the room, "the fur is going to fly."

"Well, that's just too bad," Hollis muttered. This was her house, darn it, and she'd only just begun to make changes. Cutter McKenzie could talk to his horse buyers in the barn, where the horses were. "So there." She nodded decisively.

Wonderful, she thought. She sounded like a kid again.

A short time later, a couple of ranch hands appeared, and Hollis directed traffic. The men grunted and groaned, grumbled about doing women's work, but Hollis completely ignored their complaints. The excess furniture was moved to a spare bedroom, then the remaining pieces were arranged. Then arranged again. And then once more before Hollis nodded in approval. The cowboys beat a hasty retreat.

"Oh, mercy," Mattie said from the doorway.

"Mattie, please," Hollis said. "You act as if I'm a naughty child who's going to pay the piper when Cutter discovers what I've done. You seem to be forgetting that this is my house."

"Mmm," Mattie said, frowning. "Well, your lunch is ready. Come eat."

"Is it that late? Goodness, the morning flew by. There was no need for you to rush back from town. You could've spent some time shopping, doing what you wanted to."

"There's nothing in Houston I need," the housekeeper said. "I get the supplies and come straight home. What's missing at Gauntlet Run can't be bought in some fancy store."

"Missing?"

"The sound of children's laughter ringing through this big, empty place," Mattie said. "That and the warm feeling of love that would make this house a home. No, money can't buy those things.... Well, come eat your lunch."

"I'll wash my hands and be right there," Hollis said quietly. Laughter and love, her mind echoed. Oh, yes, Gauntlet Run should be overflowing with the welcoming warmth of love. Was that just a fantasy, a pipe dream? Or maybe, just maybe, were she and Cutter on the brink of discovering a wondrous world together, a true and lasting love? Oh, how she loved him. But there was no escaping from the shadow that hung over her; the doubt, the lack of trust regarding Cutter's intentions toward her. Were his feelings for her growing, or did he only want Gauntlet Run?

With a sigh, Hollis left the room and went to wash her hands. Pushing her distressing thoughts to a dusty corner of her mind, she headed for the kitchen. Outside the door there, she hesitated as she heard Cutter's booming voice.

"Ow! Damn it, Mattie," he said, "just leave it alone. As a nurse, you make a great cook."

"Hush," Mattie scolded. "Don't be such a big baby. What did you say you did to this hand?"

"I didn't say."

Hollis stole into the room. Cutter had his back to her as he and Mattie stood by the sink. Hollis crept forward and peered around Cutter's massive body.

"Oh, Cutter," she gasped, "that hand looks awful."

"Don't sneak up on me," he yelled. Hollis jumped. "My hand is fine, just dandy. Or it was before Florence Nightingale got her paws on it. Ow! Mattie, quit dabbing that junk on it."

"It's an antiseptic," Mattie said. "Your knuckles are skinned raw, and they're swollen. What or who did you hit, Cutter?"

"Hit?" Hollis repeated, her eyes widening. "You hit someone?"

"No!" Cutter said, yanking his hand free of Mattie's grasp. "Can't a man get some lunch around here without being interrogated by the CIA?"

"It's probably too late to put an ice pack on there," Mattie said, reaching for Cutter's hand again, "but it's worth a try."

"Don't touch me," Cutter said, clenching his hand to his chest. "You're a menace."

"And you're acting like a five-year-old," Mattie said, poking him on the arm with her finger.

Hollis laughed.

Cutter shot her a stormy glare.

Mattie threw up her hands in disgust.

Cutter stalked to the table and sat down, tossing his hat onto the chair next to him. Hollis followed him across the room, sat down opposite him and folded her hands primly on top of the table. She smiled pleasantly, swallowing the bubble of laughter that threatened to escape her lips.

"What are you smiling about?" Cutter asked gruffly.

"Nothing," she said with a shrug. "I was just wondering what the other guy looks like."

"I didn't hit anyone!" Cutter roared.

With a thud, Mattie plunked a plate containing three sandwiches and an assortment of fruit in front of Cutter. Hollis's sandwich and fruit were delivered with a gentler touch.

"Thank you," Hollis said.

"It's about time," Cutter said. "I could have starved while you played Dr. Kildare. You've seen me messed up worse than this in the past six years, Mattie. Just lighten up."

"That's right, Cutter McKenzie," Mattie said. "I've been patching together cowboys on Gauntlet Run—you included—for more years than I care to count. But I've always been told what happened. What's next? Jesse shows at my back door dragging the poor fool whose nose you busted? What's the big secret here?"

"Damn it! I hit a wall, okay? A wall, Mattie, that is not going to need your dubious doctoring duties. Got that?"

"Why would someone hit a wall?" Hollis said to her sandwich. "Sounds pretty dumb to me."

"That's it. I've had it." Cutter got to his feet and picked up his plate and glass of milk. "I've got a contract to review in the library. I'll eat in there."

Hollis's eyes widened. "The library? Oh, well, I think maybe you should reconsider that plan. What I mean is..." Her voice trailed off as Cutter strode from the room. "Uh-oh."

"I'm going to go strip the linens from the beds," Mattie said. "All the beds, every one."

"You're deserting me?" Hollis said.

"Darn tootin'. That boy's temper is at the boiling point now. When he takes a gander at the library... Mercy!" She scurried from the room.

"Well, it's my house," Hollis muttered, but she strained her ears for any sound of Cutter. He was approaching the library now, she mentally envisioned. He was pushing open the door. He was—

"Hollis!" Cutter hollered from down the hall.

"Oh, good Lord," Hollis said, her hands flying to her cheeks.

The kitchen door banged open and Cutter entered, slamming his plate and glass onto the table with such force that the milk shot up and out of the glass, drenching the sandwiches. Cutter flattened his hands on the table and leaned forward, his nose no more than an inch from Hollis's. His blue eyes were dark with anger.

"What in the hell do you think you're doing?" he said, a muscle twitching in his jaw. "I can't conduct serious business in a room that looks like a day-care center complete with finger paints."

"Finger paints!" Hollis shrieked. "Those are expensive oils, and that's the finest canvas made, resting on that easel. And furthermore, Mr. McKenzie, that is *my* room, located in *my* house, and I will do with it as I darn well please."

"And where, pray tell, do you expect me to negotiate with my potential customers, then have them sign the necessary papers?"

"In *your* barn!"

"Oh-h-h, I'm warning you." Cutter narrowed his eyes. "You are really pushing me to the limit. Gauntlet Run has a class-act reputation, and I'm not going to stand by and watch you destroy even the smallest part of that. I'll be damned if I'll ask men who've flown here in their private jets to sign papers on the top of a bale of hay. Get your artist junk out of that room!"

"Not on your life, buster. I'll . . ." Hollis glanced down to Cutter's hands, splayed flat on the table. "Oh, Cutter," she said softly, "your hand. Your knuckles are bleeding again."

Cutter straightened and reached for a paper napkin, which he pressed onto his hand. "Don't worry about it. My hand isn't the subject here."

She looked up at him. "Why did you hit the wall?"

"Give it a rest, will you?" he said, going to the sink. He turned on the cold water and flinched as the stinging spray hit his raw knuckles. Damn it, she'd switched gears so fast it had knocked him for a loop. She'd been screaming like a banshee, all spit and fire, feisty as hell. Then? She went soft and feminine, her green eyes filled with concern, her voice a husky whisper as she expressed her dismay at the condition of his bummed-up hand.

And her hair, Cutter's mind rushed on. It was beautiful. He wanted to sink his hands into it, watch the silken ebony strands slide through his fingers. He could envision that raven cascade spread out on a pillow as she lifted her arms to receive him into her embrace. Like a waterfall, that glorious hair would flow over his body, igniting flames of passion that only Hollis could quell. How he wanted her!

"Oh, man," Cutter groaned as heat coiled in the lower regions of his body.

Hollis was instantly on her feet and hurrying to his side. "Cutter? Are you in pain? Should I drive you into Houston to see a doctor?"

"What? Oh, no, the doc can't help me."

"Are you sure it isn't broken?"

"Everything's in working order," he said, flexing his fingers. And some parts of his body, he thought, biting back a smile, were working overtime.

Hollis picked up a towel from the counter. "Here," she said, "let me pat it dry."

Cutter placed his hand in the towel and watched as Hollis carefully dried each finger, then began to gently dry his cut and swollen knuckles. The caressing motions caused him to grit his teeth against the passion rising in his body. He curled his other hand into a tight fist at his side to keep from weaving his fingers through Hollis's hair.

He was a dying man, he moaned inwardly. Hollis smelled so good, and she was so damn close to him. He wanted to pull her closer yet, capture her mouth with his, fit every soft inch of her tightly against him.

"Well, I guess you'll live," Hollis said. She slowly lifted her lashes to look up at him. "Is the wall still standing?"

"It's a tough wall," he said, his voice gritty as his gaze met hers.

"What made you so angry that you hit a wall?" Oh, he was so beautiful, she marveled. She wanted him to kiss her. Now. She wanted him to pull her into his arms and kiss her until she couldn't breathe. He smelled so good, and looked so good.... She wanted him. Now!

"What?" Cutter said, and blinked once slowly.

"The wall," she repeated, hearing the breathlessness in her voice. "Why did you hit it?"

"I...I don't remember. Ah, damn it," he said.

With a groan, Cutter slipped his arm around Hollis's waist, then cupped the back of her head with his good hand. He pulled her up against him, and his mouth melted over hers. His tongue delved between her lips, which parted instantly for the sweet invasion. He leaned against the counter, fitting Hollis to him as he parted his legs slightly to nestle her close to his heated body.

Yes, Hollis's mind whispered. Oh, Cutter, yes!

The heat from his massive frame flowed into her. Her desire soaring, she met his tongue with hers to engage in a seductive duel. She filled her senses with his aroma, with the feel of his steely muscles beneath her hands, which were splayed on his broad back. He was hard against her— tempting, teasing, announcing what could be hers, what would consume her, make her whole, make her Cutter's woman. Her breasts were crushed against his chest and ached for the touch of his callused, yet gentle, hands.

Cutter tore his mouth from Hollis's, then trailed a ribbon of kisses down her throat, his breathing raspy. Impatiently, he sought her mouth again in a searing kiss. His tongue plummeted within in a rhythmic motion that matched the pulsing heat in the dark, secret center of Hollis's womanhood.

A soft purr of pleasure, of want, of need, escaped Hollis's throat.

Cutter sifted his fingers through her silken hair, then moved his hands to her buttocks to press her hard against his aching body.

Sweet heaven, his mind raged, he had to have this woman! He would bury himself so deep within her honeyed warmth and take them both to a place that held no reality or reason. It would be ecstasy. He would kiss and touch every inch of Hollis's ivory skin until she was calling for him. . . .

"Cutter."

Yes, like that, his mind went on. Calling to him in a voice husky with desire. They would be fantastic together, they . . .

"Cutter," Hollis whispered. "Cutter, we're in the kitchen. We can't. . . . Cutter, stop."

Hollis's softly spoken words inched their way into the passion-laden recesses of Cutter's mind as he pulled himself back from the haze of desire that clouded his brain. He lifted his head to gaze at her flushed face.

"What?" he said, shaking his head slightly.

"The kitchen." She drew a steadying breath. "We're in the kitchen."

"Oh, yeah, you're right," he said, gripping her upper arms and moving her gently away from him. "I start kissing you and I can't stop. Damn it, Hollis, I want you. I've never wanted any woman the way I do you. I know that sounds like a line, but it's true. And *you* want *me*."

But she also loved him, she thought. "Yes. Yes, I do." She knew he desired her, lusted for her, but wasn't there more? A tiny seed of love for her that could be nurtured? "I can't deny that, Cutter. I do want you. But . . ."

Hollis paused and stepped farther back, crossing her arms over her breasts in a protective gesture. "But what heading does it come under? Two consenting adults who desire each other, so why not? A quickie? Mutual sexual gratification?"

"Hollis, don't," he said, his jaw tightening. It would be love, damn it, his mind raged. Should he tell her he loved her? Would she believe him or see his declaration as nothing more than a ploy to get her into bed? "There would be nothing cheap or sordid about our making love. It would be fantastic, and no one's business but ours."

"I can't believe I'm having this conversation," she said, shaking her head. "It sounds so cold, so clinical, like we're making an appointment to go to bed together."

"It's not like that at all. I just have to be sure you want this as much as I do. I don't want to be guilty of seducing you, then have you regret what we shared. Ah, damn it, Hollis, this is too special, too important. I don't usually stand around discussing this topic, either, but I don't want to make a mistake. Not with you."

Hollis pressed her fingertips to her suddenly throbbing temples in an attempt to quiet the warring voices in her mind. She didn't know what to do, she realized frantically. The entire situation was beyond her level of sophistication. All she knew was that she loved Cutter McKenzie and wanted to be one with him. He sounded so sincere, so determined that their coming together would hold special meaning. But what did she really know about men like Cutter? How smoothly did the flowery words roll off of his tongue so he ultimately got what he was after? What did he really feel for her, and how closely was it intertwined with his driving need to possess all of Gauntlet Run? Should she listen to her head or her heart?

"Hollis?"

"Cutter, I . . . I have to have some time."

"I understand. I won't rush you." He grinned. "Well, I'll try not to. I seem to forget all my noble intentions when I start kissing you."

"I think we should change the subject." She spun around and walked to the table, her legs trembling.

Cutter sat opposite her at the table, pulling his plate in front of him and picking up a sandwich.

"Wonderful," he muttered. "It's soggy."

"I could make you fresh ones."

"I've had worse," he said, shrugging. "Now, about the library."

"My studio, you mean?" She took a bite of sandwich.

"Give me a break, Hollis. I need to do business in that room. The megabucks boys I deal with are used to a certain protocol, a high level of class on Gauntlet Run. I can't maintain that in the barn, for cripe's sake."

"Well," Hollis said slowly, "I do have the right to set up my studio anywhere I choose."

"I know," he said, frowning. "This is your house. You never let me forget it."

"We could compromise, I suppose."

"Oh?"

"I won't remove the heavy furniture that's in front of the desk. That will give you, say, a masculine area to conduct your high-roller business. I'll keep my studio, per se, on the other side of the room."

"Is that your best offer?"

"Yep," she said, smiling.

"I'll take it. I don't like it, but I'll take it."

"Fine." She got to her feet. "Why don't you come with me now and tell me exactly what you want left in place?"

"Brother," he muttered, then took a big bite of soggy sandwich.

When Hollis and Cutter reached the entryway, she glanced at the remaining boxes by the door and stopped, frowning as she looked at the cartons. Cutter continued walking.

"Coming?" he said, poking his head out of the library doorway.

"This isn't right."

"What's wrong?" He went to her side.

"There were ten boxes delivered, and I opened the one with my painting supplies. There should be only nine left, but there's ten again."

"You must have counted wrong in the first place."

"No, I shipped ten. Cutter, look," she said, pointing. "There's no writing or shipping labels on that box. It wasn't here before."

She started to reach for the plain box.

"No," he said, grabbing her arm, "don't touch it."

"Why not?"

"Hollis, we don't know who put it there or why."

"What do you mean? Cutter, you're frightening me."

"Come into the library."

"But—"

"Now!"

Hollis hurried ahead of Cutter, then stepped out of his way as he strode to the desk and pushed three numbers on the phone.

"Jesse?" he said. "Come up to the house, and bring a lasso. I'll wait for you inside the front door. Oh, and bring a pitchfork, too. I'll explain when you get here."

Cutter slammed the receiver back into place and started toward the door. Hollis was right behind him.

"Stay here," he said.

"No."

Cutter stopped abruptly, and Hollis bumped into him. He spun around and gripped her shoulders.

"I said stay in this room," he said, giving her a small shake.

"And I said no," she said, squinting at him.

"Spare me from stubborn Champions. There are times, lady, when you drive me crazy."

"Too bad. That's my box out there, Cutter, and I want to know what's in it."

Hollis ignored the curse Cutter uttered, and they got to the foyer as Jesse walked through the front door.

"What's up?" Jesse said.

"I'm not sure," Cutter said. "See that box with no markings on it? It just suddenly appeared while Hollis was in the kitchen having lunch. It's not something she shipped from Mexico."

"Maybe it's a surprise from Mattie," Hollis suggested.

"What's a surprise from Mattie?" the housekeeper said, coming up on the group.

"That box," Hollis said, indicating it.

"No, I don't know anything about it," Mattie said. "You didn't ship it? No, there's no markings on it. Where did it come from?"

"That's the question," Cutter said. "Mattie, you and Hollis go in the kitchen."

"No," Hollis said.

"Ah, damn it," Cutter said. "Well, at least move back out of the way, will you?"

"That I'll do," Hollis said, and backed up a few feet. Mattie hurried to join her.

"I'll do this, Jesse. Go on back to the barn," Cutter suggested.

"Nope," Jesse said. "I'm stayin'. We rope it and pull it outside, right?"

"That's the plan. Give me the rope."

"You're talking to the Gold Buckle champion for three years straight in lasso competition. I can control this baby like a willing woman."

"This isn't your problem, Jesse." Cutter sounded a little firmer.

Jesse shot a glare at Hollis. "The way I see it, it's not yours either, Cutter. If you're in, I'm in. Let's get it done."

"Yeah, all right," Cutter agreed reluctantly.

As he carefully moved the other boxes away from the one in the plain paper, Hollis chewed on the inside of her cheek and Mattie twisted the corner of her apron into a tight ball. When the ominous box stood free, Jesse slipped the lasso over it and slowly tightened the knot.

"Easy," Cutter said. "Take it slow and easy, Jesse. Stay as far away from it as you can. I'll hold the back of your belt and guide you out the door."

This was insane, Hollis thought frantically. Did Cutter actually think that box was potentially dangerous, contained a bomb or...a bomb? *Her* box? Who would do such a thing? She had to calm down. There was a logical explanation as to how the box had gotten there, and when they opened it they'd find... Dear heaven, what would they find?

"Easy over the doorjamb," Cutter instructed Jesse. "That's it. Good, good. Bring it on out to the center of the porch, then slip the rope off."

Jesse did so, then Cutter reached inside the house for the pitchfork.

"Stay put," Cutter told Hollis and Mattie.

Hollis went to the open doorway but did not step out onto the porch. "Cutter," she said, "please be careful. I can't imagine that there's anything dangerous in that box, but be careful anyway."

"Quit jawing at him," Jesse said gruffly. "He doesn't need you nagging at him."

"I am *not* nagging," Hollis protested.

"Shut up, people," Cutter said. "You two can argue later."

"Sorry," Hollis said. "But please be careful."

"Hell," Jesse said.

It seemed to Hollis that Cutter was moving in slow motion as he slit the paper on the box with the prongs of the pitchfork, then gingerly lifted the flaps. No one spoke.

"So far, so good," Cutter said.

"Watch yourself now," Jesse said. "There's a wad of newspaper there. It could be attached to a triggering device."

"Cutter, please be—" Hollis whispered.

"Careful," Cutter finished for her. "I plan on it."

The roaring of her own heartbeat echoed in Hollis's ears as she stood staring at the scene before her. Mattie grabbed Hollis's hand and clutched it. Cutter inched the newspaper upward, the sun glaring off the prongs of the pitchfork. Cutter released a long-held breath as the paper came free of the box.

"Whew," Cutter said. "Okay, let's see what the mystery is all about. Hollis, don't you move."

Cutter and Jesse stood over the box for a long moment, then hunkered down on opposite sides as they continued to examine the contents.

"Land's sake," Jesse said.

"What is it?" Hollis said, clutching Mattie's hand between hers.

"Son of a…" Cutter started, shaking his head. "We're dealing with a crazy person, Jesse."

"Cutter?" Hollis said.

Cutter pushed himself to his feet and looked at Hollis. "Call the sheriff, Mattie. Tell him to get out here."

"I want to know what's in that box," Hollis said, coming out onto the porch. "I was the one meant to open it, so I…" She looked inside the box. "Oh, dear God."

"Take it easy, Hollis," Cutter said. "It may be someone's idea of a joke, but we'll have the sheriff check it for fingerprints."

Mattie crept forward and peered into the box. "Heavenly saints," she said.

"Go call Sheriff Dunbar," Cutter said.

"Yes. Yes, I'm going." Mattie hurried into the house.

"Go inside, Hollis," Cutter said. "Don't look at it anymore."

Hollis's gaze was riveted on the contents of the box. "That doll is supposed to represent me." Her voice was trembling. "Long black hair, green eyes. It's even wearing a western shirt and jeans. Oh, Cutter, there's a knife stuck in its heart and blood on the shirt and— Oh, God.''

Cutter came around the box and pulled her into his arms, holding her head against his chest.

"It's just a prank." he said.

"Like shooting thirty head of cattle was a prank?'' Jesse said. "No way, Cutter."

"Someone came right into the house," Hollis said, lifting her head. "They just opened the door and brought that box in. Who would do such a thing? My God, someone is threatening to kill me!"

"Or so it would seem," Jesse said sarcastically. "Funny thing about this is the story about Buck's will hits the paper under false pretenses, then something happens to you, Hollis, to make it seem even to Cutter's cattle being slaughtered."

Hollis looked at him, aghast.

"That's all, Jesse," Cutter said, his anger barely under control. "Lighten up."

Jesse nodded reluctantly, though he still looked at Hollis with hostile eyes.

"Jesse, you stay out here and wait for the sheriff. Bring him into the library when he gets here, but don't touch that box in the meantime."

Cutter put his arm around Hollis's shoulders. "Come inside. Don't say anything. Just come inside."

She glanced at the box, a shiver coursing through her. She moved closer to Cutter's side as he led her inside. In the library, he set her in one of the leather chairs and crouched in front of her.

"Would you like a drink?" he offered.

"No, thank you."

"You're terribly pale."

"Seeing that doll was a gruesome shock. And then Jesse. Cutter, why does he think so poorly of me? He doesn't even know me."

"Don't worry about, Jesse." Cutter said. He patted her knee, then got up and leaned against the desk. "The sheriff is going to ask if you have any idea who would threaten you."

"I don't know," she said, throwing up her hands. "I told you I don't have any enemies that I'm aware of. Do you realize that while we were in the kitchen, someone walked right into this house and set that box with the others?"

"Yeah, but was it a coincidence that the other boxes were delivered first, or timed that way? There're a lot of unanswered questions, Hollis. The fact that there was no name on the box, no markings, says they waited until it could be hidden among the others. There was a better chance that you'd be the one to open it, and be very frightened."

"Then someone is watching?" she said, getting to her feet. "Someone knew my other things had been delivered? Oh, Cutter, that gives me the chills. Who's doing these things? And why?"

"I don't know. Let's wait and see if the sheriff has any brilliant ideas."

If anything, Sheriff Dunbar was thoroughly baffled after being brought up to date on what had happened.

"It's crazy," he told Hollis and Cutter. "Because of the story in the paper, everyone knows the provisions of Buck's will. You both have had trouble, which means it must be coming from the outside. Unless, of course, either the cattle or the doll was a decoy to draw attention away from one of you, make it *appear* you're being harassed."

"Now, wait just a minute," Cutter began.

"I don't believe that, Cutter," the sheriff said, "but there'll be some who will. You both have a hefty motive for wanting to drive the other one off Gauntlet Run."

A lot he knew, Hollis thought. She wanted Cutter McKenzie on Gauntlet Run forever, with her, loving her, truly loving her.

"The rumors are going to fly," the sheriff warned them. "But me? I'm looking further than you two. Who stands to benefit if you both call it quits and leave Gauntlet Run?"

"Anyone," Cutter replied. "The ranch would go on the open market for sale."

The sheriff shook his head. "Sure don't have much to go on. Well, I'll take the doll and the box with me and check for fingerprints. In the meantime, you both be careful. This doll thing could be nothing more than a sick prank, but it's better to be safe than sorry. Keep the doors locked, and pay attention to anyone who might be milling around the ranch. It's a mighty big spread to watch every minute, though. I wish I knew if this incident really is tied in with those cattle being slaughtered."

"There're a lot of things I wish *I* knew," Cutter said, running his hand over the back of his neck.

"Well, I'll keep in touch," Sheriff Dunbar said.

"I'll see you out," Cutter offered.

As the two men left, Hollis got to her feet and wandered around the room, feeling edgy and nervous. She stopped in front of her easel, finding it hard to believe it had been only a matter of hours since she'd registered such a sense of excitement over setting up her studio.

How frightening it all was, she thought, wrapping her arms around herself. This was Gauntlet Run, her home, and someone had violated it, just walked right in and left that box with the despicable doll. Dear heaven, who would do such a thing?

"Hollis?" Cutter said as he came back into the library. "Are you all right?"

"No," she said, managing a weak smile, "I don't think I am. I feel as though I'm in the midst of a nightmare, and

I'll be grateful when the alarm clock goes off and I wake up."

"I wish that were true," he said, walking slowly toward her.

Hollis shook her head in disbelief. "I can't believe Jesse could actually even consider that I would plant that doll among my belongings."

"Hollis, I told you, don't worry about Jesse," Cutter said, resting his large hands on her shoulders. "It's not important what he thinks. What matters here is what *we* believe."

"What do you mean?"

"There's no way to keep all this quiet. Rumors are going to fly fast and furious. I don't care about the gossip mill, Hollis. What counts is that you trust me."

Trust him? Hollis's mind echoed. She loved him, but the trust was still an elusive shadow just beyond her reach. Oh, how she wanted to trust him, believe he cared, really cared for her.

Cutter dropped his hands from her shoulders. "Damn it, you *don't* trust me, do you? Hell, do you think *I* had that doll put among your things?"

"No! No, I don't." She pressed her fingertips to her aching temples. "It's just that so much has happened and... No, you're misunderstanding my silence."

The telephone on the desk rang, and Cutter glanced at it. It was quiet after the second ring.

"Then why don't you explain your silence," he said tightly, crossing his arms over his chest. "You either trust me or you don't. Just give me a simple answer."

"Hollis," Mattie said from the doorway, "I didn't buzz the phone, because I wasn't sure where you were. Kathleen is calling."

"Thank you, Mattie," Hollis said. "I'll pick it up in here."

"All right." Mattie bustled away.

"Cutter, I—"

"Saved by the bell," he interrupted, a sharp edge to his voice. He spun on his heel and strode toward the door.

"Cutter, wait!"

"For what?" he said, stopping to look back at her. "To hear that you don't trust me? No thanks, I'll pass. Ah, the hell with it. I really don't care one way or the other."

"Cutter!" Hollis said, but he disappeared from view. "You don't understand. Oh, damn, the phone." She hurried to the desk and picked up the receiver. "Kathleen?"

"Heavens, were you in the shower?"

"No, I . . ."

"Hollis, what's wrong? Your voice sounds funny."

"Kathleen, could we have dinner together in town tonight?"

"I thought we'd agreed on lunch. It's a bit late for that, though. Sure, we can have dinner. Floyd is still away, and we can chatter like magpies."

"Thank you."

"Hollis, what is it? I know something is wrong."

"I'll tell you when I see you," Hollis said, pressing her hand to her forehead. "I just have to get away from here for a few hours. I have to, Kathleen!"

Chapter 8

Damn, it hurt.

Cutter flicked the reins to urge the horse faster, its pounding hooves seeming to echo the painful message in Cutter's mind.

Hollis didn't trust him.

He muttered an oath as the sleek animal covered the ground of Gauntlet Run. What a fool he'd been, Cutter inwardly raged. He'd been hoping, watching, for any sign that Hollis might be falling in love with him. She responded more each time he took her in his arms. Her body spoke volumes as she molded herself to him; she returned his kisses in total abandon. He'd seen the want, need, raw desire, in her exquisite eyes.

But, he now realized, he'd never seen trust. No trust.

And, ah, damn, it hurt.

Did Hollis really believe he'd had something to do with that doll? How could she think that of him? But he had the motive, and the money to hire someone to take care of it.

Had their shared kisses meant nothing to her? Was she merely experimenting with her newfound freedom now that Buck was dead?

"No," he said, leaning over the horse to gain even more speed. No, damn it, not Hollis. The vulnerability, the warmth, the womanliness that was blossoming under *his* touch and *his* kiss, were real. Hollis was real. And he loved her.

He loved her, his mind repeated. He was in love for the first time in his life, and he expected . . . what? Guarantees that he'd chosen well? That Hollis was all he thought her to be? What a fool he was. Jesse was convinced Hollis was behind the trouble at Gauntlet Run. She, too, had the money and the motive. Cutter shouldn't trust her, according to Jesse. Shouldn't trust her any more than Hollis trusted him.

"Hell," Cutter said, then began to slow the horse. He steered the animal toward a clear, cold creek for a drink and dismounted. "There you go, boy."

Cutter sank onto the ground and rested his back against the trunk of a tree. The sight of the bloodstained doll flickered into view in his mind's eye, and he clenched his jaw. No, he said again in his mind and heart. No, Hollis hadn't planted that doll, nor had she had the cattle slaughtered. Not Hollis. He was going to find out who'd been behind it and have this dark cloud removed from their existence.

But, oh, damn, why didn't she trust him now, without his having to prove his innocence? Why couldn't she love him as he loved her?

Cutter dropped his hat on the ground next to him. He leaned his head back against the trunk of the tree and closed his eyes with a weary sigh, his senses filled with the sounds and scents of Gauntlet Run. He soon drifted off into a light slumber.

* * *

Hollis showered, then dressed in winter-white shark-skin slacks with a green silk blouse. As she sat at her dressing table to twist her hair into a chignon, she stared at her reflection.

She was still pale she realized, fear still evident in her eyes. And sadness was there as well. Cutter was angry with her because she hadn't immediately stated that she trusted him. But he didn't understand! The incident with the doll and her love for him were two different issues. She didn't believe for one moment that Cutter had had that doll put among the other boxes.

But the word trust encompassed all and everything. What Cutter didn't know was that she loved him yet questioned his feelings for her. She couldn't just open her mouth and declare that, so she'd kept silent. But she knew he wouldn't do anything like that. There was someone else out there, watching, waiting. Someone who wanted both Hollis and Cutter to leave Gauntlet Run.

Hollis shivered as she secured the bun with pins at the nape of her neck. She kept reliving that final moment in the library when Cutter had said he didn't care if Hollis trusted him or not. The extent of his anger proved to her that he did care. But she couldn't explain her silence to him without revealing her feelings. She wasn't ready to do that yet.

Hollis got to her feet and began to pace the room. It was too early to go into Houston to meet Kathleen for dinner, but she was driving herself crazy with her own jumbled thoughts. She'd leave now, Hollis decided, and wander through the boutiques, try to make her mind go blank, and simply look at pretty clothes.

She snatched up her jacket, grabbed her purse and went to the kitchen in search of Mattie.

"Mattie," Hollis said, entering the room, "I'm going into Houston. I'm meeting Kathleen later for dinner."

Mattie turned from the sink to look at Hollis. "Does Cutter know?"

"No, but there's no reason for me to tell him. My goodness, Mattie, I'm not accountable to Cutter McKenzie for every move. Having to tell him if I plan to leave Gauntlet Run for twenty-four hours is ridiculous enough. I have no intention of informing him when I plan to go out for the evening."

"Listen to me, Hollis. You have no business making that drive to Houston and back alone. Are you forgetting that horrible doll? Your life could be in danger. There're terrible things happening here." Mattie sniffled and dabbed at her eyes with the corner of her apron.

Hollis hurried to Mattie and grasped the housekeeper's hands. "I know it's frightening, Mattie," Hollis said gently, "but I can't live like a prisoner here, hiding behind locked doors. I need to get away for a few hours, put all this out of my mind for a while. Surely you can understand that."

"I suppose," Mattie said, then sniffled again, "but I really wish you'd tell Cutter where you're going."

"When he comes in for dinner, simply tell him I'm meeting Kathleen in town. I won't be late getting back. I promise."

"I still don't like it."

Hollis kissed her on the cheek. "I'll be fine. Now, quit worrying."

"Mmm," Mattie said, frowning.

Hollis smiled and went out the back door, glancing at the sky. Storm clouds hovered on the horizon as if trying to decide whether to move forward with their cargo of rain or fade into oblivion. As she entered the six-car garage, she swept her gaze over the variety of cars and trucks.

Buck had stated in his will that she was to have one vehicle, she mused. Well, she might as well go first-class.

She took a set of keys from a pegboard on the wall, pressed a button to lift the appropriate door and moments later slid behind the wheel of a steel-gray Mercedes. With a sigh of relief, she drove away from Gauntlet Run.

When Cutter entered the house several hours later, he saw neither Hollis nor Mattie. He went to his room, showered, changed, then wandered into the living room to pour himself a drink.

Well, now what? He'd had all afternoon to decide what to say, how to act, when he saw Hollis at dinner, and he still didn't know what he was going to do. What he *wanted* to do was haul her into his arms, kiss her senseless, then tell her he loved her and that she sure as hell had better trust and believe in him, because she was the only woman he'd ever lost his heart to.

"And that, McKenzie," he said, taking a swallow of liquor, "is really stupid." He knew he couldn't get Hollis to love and trust him by screaming in her face. It would take... *He* didn't know what it would take. He'd never been up against anything like this before. And to top it off, there was a weirdo out there, a potentially dangerous person, who slaughtered cattle and had created that doll.

The man, woman—the sicko, Cutter amended—was smart. The rustling of the cattle had been done with ease, the secluded canyon carefully selected. The placing of the box containing the doll had called for precision timing. This person was clever, no doubt about it. But who in the hell was it? If Cutter and Hollis both left Gauntlet Run, there was no one waiting in the wings to snatch it up. Buck's will made it clear that the ranch went on the open market at that point. It was already established that the culprit was an insider, so it wouldn't help him or her for money men from across the country, the world, to be bidding on it. Driving Cutter and Hollis away just didn't make sense!

Thunder rumbled through the heavens, jarring Cutter from his tangled thoughts. He glanced at the ceiling, recalling the night in the kitchen when he'd held Hollis in his arms while she cried, while she sobbed out her misery and told him of how she'd come to associate rain with death.

He'd held her so close, Cutter mused, and she'd been heaven itself as he'd nestled her to him, inhaling her fresh, feminine aroma, feeling her soft curves beneath her satin gown. He'd wanted her then; he wanted her now.

"Cutter," Mattie said from the doorway.

He jerked in surprise as he pulled his thoughts back to reality. "What!"

"I didn't mean to startle you."

"I was thinking about something, that's all. Is dinner ready? Where's Hollis?"

"Yes, dinner is ready, but Hollis... Well, you see, she decided she needed... That is, she..."

"Mattie," he said, plunking his glass on the bar with a thud, "where is Hollis?"

"She went into town to have dinner with Kathleen," Mattie said in a rush. "I tried to talk her out of it, but she wouldn't listen. She left real early, said she had to get away from Gauntlet Run for a while."

"Damn it," Cutter muttered under his breath, striding across the room. To Mattie he said, "Is she nuts? That's a long, empty stretch of road. She has no business being out there alone."

"I know," Mattie said, wringing her hands. "I told her to tell you she was going."

"I can imagine her reaction to that," Cutter said gruffly. "Spare me the direct quote."

"What are you going to do?"

"There's nothing I *can* do. But when she gets back, my dear Mattie, I will have a few well-chosen words to deliver to Hollis Champion Ramirez. Pretending nothing is wrong isn't going to make this whole thing go away. Even Sheriff Dunbar warned us to be careful."

"That reminds me. He called about an hour ago, Cutter. He said to tell you there were no fingerprints on the doll or box."

"Figures," Cutter said, dragging a restless hand through his hair. "The person behind this is too smart to make a mistake like leaving fingerprints. Hollis is being very foolish. I thought she realized the serious implications of what has happened. We can't just shrug this stuff off as pranks."

"I think she knows that," Mattie said. "She looked very upset. I can see if she wanted a few hours away, but I wish she hadn't gone alone. You could've driven in with her, Cutter."

"No," he said quietly, "she wouldn't have agreed to that. She ... she doesn't trust me, Mattie. She's considering the possibility that I arranged to have that doll delivered."

"That's nuts," Mattie said, her hands planted on her hips. "Hollis was upset, that's all. She's not thinking clearly. When she calms down, she'll come to her senses."

"Will she? I have the motive and the money to pull it off. I asked her if she trusted me, and she just stared at me. What she said with her silence was like a punch in the gut."

A smile crept onto Mattie's lips. "It matters to you what Hollis believes, does it?"

"It matters." He paused. "Well, no man likes to be thought poorly of by anyone."

Mattie laughed. "I see."

"What do you see?" he said, glaring at her. "And what's that silly grin for?"

"Nothing. Come eat your dinner. Hollis isn't going to get back any sooner if you starve. Once I get the kitchen cleaned up, I'm going to hide in my room. The fur is going to fly when Hollis comes in that door."

"It sure is. She isn't using the brains she was born with going off alone like that, and I plan to make it clear that it isn't to happen again until this mess is solved."

"Oh, mercy," Mattie said, "they'll hear the two of you hollering in the next county."

"If that's what it takes," Cutter said, nodding, "so be it. Bring on the food, Mattie. I'm going to need my strength to take on Miss Stubborn Champion."

In the exclusive candlelit restaurant where Hollis and Kathleen were dining, silence had fallen at their small table. Hollis had told Kathleen of the man who'd called Mac Winston, impersonating Cutter's voice, of the slaughtered cattle and of the hideous doll.

Now, Hollis realized, she had no desire to go further, to speak of her feelings and inner turmoil regarding Cutter McKenzie. As close as she'd always been to her aunt, Hollis wasn't ready to tell about her love for a man who'd never declared his love in kind. A man who'd staked a claim on Hollis's heart but whom she didn't totally trust with regard to his attention to her. No, she didn't wish to bare her soul about such things, and so she kept silent.

"Well?" Kathleen said, leaning slightly forward. "That sounded like the grim headlines of the six o'clock news. What's the inside scoop? What's Cutter saying about all of this?"

"He says that there will be a lot of rumors going around," Hollis said, fiddling with her napkin. "You know, some people will say that Cutter is behind it and is trying to drive me off of Gauntlet Run, and vice versa."

"Oh, yes, the gossip mongers will have a field day with this. But you both know it's someone from the outside." Kathleen paused and frowned at Hollis. "You do believe that Cutter had nothing to do with that doll, don't you?"

"Of course."

"Thank God for that much. The way you two have been squabbling, I wasn't sure what you might be thinking."

"He said it's important that we trust each other. Yes, trust . . . each other."

"It certainly is," Kathleen said, nodding. "This is scary, isn't it? The idea of someone walking right into the house and placing that box with the others gives me the willies. I'd bet an extra dessert the sheriff won't find any fingerprints on the doll or box. This person is too clever for that. Darn it, who could it be? You and Cutter are the only ones with motives. If you both leave, Gauntlet Run is up for grabs."

"I know," Hollis said, sighing. "Thank goodness that Sheriff Dunbar doesn't believe it's either of us. He certainly doesn't have any clues as to who it is, though. Let's change the subject, all right? I wanted to come into town tonight to get away from it all for a while."

"Of course, sweetie. This hasn't been much of a welcome home for you, has it? Tell me what you had shipped from Mexico. Where are you going to set up your studio at Gauntlet Run?"

To Hollis's amazement, she found herself chatting while her mind was elsewhere: centered on Cutter. Kathleen laughed in delight as Hollis told the story of the battle over the library. Hollis smiled in all the right places, while her heart ached at the vision in her mind of Cutter's face when he'd stalked from the room.

Cutter now believed, Hollis knew, that she doubted his innocence in regard to the doll, and that wasn't true. What could she say to prove to him that she hadn't thought for one minute that he'd done such a horrible thing? What could she say without revealing her love for him?

"Floyd is buying up property on Mars," Kathleen was saying. "The Martians are finally ready to dicker."

"That's nice," Hollis remarked absently.

Kathleen laughed. "Okay, I give up. You're not with me, Hollis."

"I'm sorry. I guess I'm more exhausted than I realized. It's been a draining day. I know I haven't been very good company."

"And that's understandable."

"I think I'll go on home, Kathleen. Things will look better after a good night's sleep. Or at least that's what Mattie always says," she said, laughing a little.

"And she's right." Kathleen signaled to the waiter. "Dinner is my treat. Next one's on you."

Outside, the thunder continued to rumble.

"I hope you get home before it rains," Kathleen said. "Drive carefully, Hollis. That long stretch of road gets very dark."

"I've driven it a thousand times. Good night, Kathleen." She gave her aunt a quick hug. "I'll talk to you soon."

"You'd better. I want to know everything that's going on at Gauntlet Run. This is one of those situations that is exciting as long as it's happening to someone else. The way it stands, it's just downright creepy. 'Bye."

"Good night, Kathleen."

As Hollis drove through the heavy Houston traffic, she prided herself on the fact that she was relaxed, wasn't a bit nervous about being alone. But as she left the lighted city and drove along the county road, she tightened her grip on the steering wheel and found herself glancing more often in the rearview mirror. The continuing rumble of thunder jangled her nerves further, and a tension headache began to throb at the base of her head.

Suddenly, bright headlights appeared in the rearview mirror, causing Hollis to gasp in alarm. She squinted against the glare, trying to concentrate on the road ahead. Glancing in the mirror, she saw that the headlights were getting closer, and she gave her car more gas. The other automobile followed suit, and her heart began to beat wildly against her ribs. She was aware of the metallic taste of fear in her mouth.

"Oh, Cutter," Hollis whispered. "Oh, Cutter, I'm so frightened. I need you, Cutter. Please."

The approaching vehicle flooded the interior of Hollis's car with bright light. She choked back a sob and tried desperately to follow the curves of the winding road. Her high beams shone on the first fences of Gauntlet Run, and she put her foot down on the gas pedal harder yet.

Suddenly, the vehicle whipped along side of her, and Hollis glanced at it in wide-eyed horror. It was a pickup, the bed filled with teenage boys waving bottles in the air. The truck shot forward, and the boys hooted and hollered, saluting Hollis with their bottles. They disappeared around a bend in the road.

"Kids," Hollis said numbly as she reduced her speed. "It was only kids out joyriding."

With what seemed to be her last ounce of energy, Hollis drove the remaining distance to Gauntlet Run and parked the car in the garage. On trembling legs she entered the house and went through the kitchen. As she walked down the hallway, Cutter stepped out of the living room.

"I want to talk to you," he said, his voice gruff.

"Not now, Cutter," she said wearily.

"Yes, now. Come into the living room."

The last whispers of fear still tingling within Hollis were replaced by a burst of anger.

"I said not now," she said, her voice rising. "I don't report in to you, Cutter McKenzie. I'm going to my room, and if you don't like it, that's too bad." She turned and started down the corridor.

Cutter closed the distance between them quickly. He grabbed Hollis's arm and spun her around to face him.

"You're going to listen to me," he said, "whether it suits your mood or not. You had no business going into town alone. This isn't a game we're playing here, Hollis."

"I know that!" she fairly shrieked. "I was just frightened out of my mind because I was being followed. It was nothing more than a truck full of teenagers sowing some wild oats. I hate this. Isn't there anyplace safe, Cutter?"

"Ah, man." He pulled her close and wrapped his arms around her. "You're shaking all over. I'm sorry, Hollis. I shouldn't have hollered, but I was so damn worried about you making that drive alone. Are you sure it was just kids who followed you?"

"Yes," she said, leaning her head on his chest. She inhaled his special aroma, felt the power in his hard body. This was her haven, she thought. Here, in Cutter's arms.

"Promise me you won't go off alone again," he said quietly. "Not until this mess is cleared up."

"I promise."

"There were no fingerprints on the box or the doll," he told her. "The person is clever and we'll have to stay alert."

"Yes. Cutter?" She tilted her head back to look up at him.

"Yeah?"

"I know you didn't have anything to do with that doll."

With a throaty moan, he brought his mouth down hard on hers. Hollis went nearly limp against him, circling his neck with her arms and clinging to him for support. He moved his hands over the rich material of her jacket, then slipped them inside to caress her silk-covered back. They were strong hands, Hollis thought, rough but gentle hands. A coil of need swept through her as her breasts were crushed against the hard wall of his chest in a sweet pain. She gasped as she felt his hands slide over the slope of her buttocks and he fitted her to his rugged contours.

"Hollis," Cutter murmured brokenly, his mouth against her throat, "it means so much to know that you trust me."

Trust him? Hollis's mind questioned in a hazy blur of desire. About the doll, yes. But trust him totally as a man? She didn't want to think about that now, not now. She'd been so frightened on the road, so alone, but there, in Cutter's arms, she was safe, protected against all harm. She wanted only to feel, give way to the heated passion churning within her. She wanted, she needed, Cutter McKenzie.

A soft sob caught in her throat as she reached for the top snap on Cutter's shirt with trembling fingers.

"Hollis." His voice was gentle as he caught her hands with his. "No."

"Cutter?" She looked up at him, confusion evident on her face.

"You're exhausted. You've had a grueling, frightening day. You know I want you, but this isn't the time. Not tonight." He stepped back slowly, bringing each of her palms to his lips for a light kiss that sent shivers coursing through her. "Go to bed."

Cutter's voice was so husky, his smile so tender, that Hollis nearly moved back into his embrace. But a wave of fatigue swept through her and she nodded.

"Yes, you're right," she said with a sigh. "Good night, Cutter." She turned and walked down the hall.

Cutter drew a deep breath and let it out slowly. He went back into the living room, poured himself a stiff drink, and downed it in a single swallow.

Hours later, a loud clap of thunder woke Cutter, and he groaned as he rolled over in bed and glanced at the clock.

Wonderful, he thought. It was two in the morning and he'd just dozed off when the thunder woke him. Now, he supposed, Hollis's image would taunt him again. He could see her so clearly in his mental vision, hear her laughter, remember her aroma and taste as vividly as if she were there, in his arms. She was Hollis, and he loved her.

Rain began to pelt against the window. Thunder rolled, lightning flashed, and a wild wind whipped the torrent of rain into a frenzy.

Rain, he thought suddenly, sitting bolt upward. Hollis. She'd had a terrifying day. What if the rain and the memories it evoked were more than she could take? What if she were crying?

Cutter tossed back the blankets and strode naked across the room to grab his jeans off a chair. He yanked them on, then stepped into the hall, hesitating when he arrived at Hollis's closed bedroom door. He knocked, then leaned closer to listen for a reply. Hearing nothing over the noise of the raging storm, he turned the knob and pushed the door slowly open. Lightning crackled at that moment, casting an eerie luminescence over the room.

Hollis was standing by the window, staring out at the rain.

Cutter closed the door and walked to where she stood, clad in a satin nightgown with tiny straps. He lifted his hands to place them on her shoulders, then changed his mind and dropped his hands to his sides.

"Hollis?" he said. "Are you all right? I was concerned that the rain might upset you." He paused. "Hollis?"

"I'm all right." Her voice was a near whisper. "It's time I conquered my fear of rain. It's time to bury the past and look to the future. Yes, Cutter, I'm fine."

He touched her, unable to resist a moment longer. He moved close behind her, laying his hands on her shoulders, easing her against him, inhaling her aroma, fitting her soft curves to his taut length. She leaned her head back on his chest, closing her eyes, savoring the feel and scent of him, the strength of his hands and body.

Heat, Hollis thought dreamily. Such heat emanated from Cutter's half-naked body. It flowed into her, warming the chill of loneliness and fear, fanning the ember of desire to a roaring flame. Male heat. Cutter's heat. Even through the thick curtain of her hair, she could feel the crisp, curly fur on his chest.

And she wanted him.

Tonight she had overcome her phobia of the rain. She had grown, moved forward into another place.

And she wanted to go further.

She wanted to become one with the man she loved.

Nothing mattered but the moment, Hollis decided in her heart and mind. She'd pay no heed to the niggling voices of doubt, nor to the insistent question of Cutter's feelings for her. Not tonight. Not in this moment of splendor and wanting, and such incredible heat.

She turned slowly in his arms and felt him tense as though he were preparing himself for the words that would send him away. She slid her hands up his magnificent chest and tangled her fingers in the moist hair, hearing him suck in his breath as she discovered his flat nipples beneath her palms.

"Hollis, don't." His voice was raspy. "If I don't leave now, it will be too late."

"Don't leave," she said softly. "I want you so much. Make love to me. Please."

"Are you sure? I couldn't handle it if you were sorry later. I have to know this is really what you want."

"It is," she said. Because she loved him. "I promise you, Cutter, I won't regret tonight." She would always love him. "You want me, don't you?"

"I want you," he said. And he loved her. "I ache with wanting you."

Hollis placed her hands on his face and drew his lips down to hers, meeting his tongue with hers. His hands moved to the straps of her gown, and she shifted her arms to allow him to slip the material free. The satin gown slid to the floor in a soft pool of color. Lightning flashed and

Cutter's gaze flickered over her naked body as she stood before him.

"Beautiful," he said, his voice thick with passion. "So beautiful."

He filled his hands with the lush fullness of her breasts, bowing his head to pay homage to the womanly offering. Exquisite sensations swept through Hollis, and she closed her eyes to savor each. As Cutter's mouth worked its magic on one breast, his thumb teased the nipple of the other. He suckled rhythmically, his tongue adding sweet torture as a matching pulse thrummed deep within her.

"Cutter," she gasped, her legs beginning to tremble.

He lifted her into his arms, his mouth claiming hers in a searing kiss before he carried her to the bed. He laid her on the cool sheets, then slipped off his jeans. The flashing lights of the storm outlined his body, and Hollis gazed at him in wonder, seeing all that he was and all that he would bring to her. He stretched out next to her and rested on his forearm, his other hand splayed on her flat stomach.

"Are you frightened?" he asked.

"No, not of you."

"I'll try not to rush you, Hollis, but my control is on the edge. I feel as though I've waited an eternity for this moment."

"So do I. Come to me, Cutter McKenzie. We've waited long enough."

"Ah, Hollis," he said with a moan, then his lips melted over hers.

It was ecstasy.

It was as tempestuous as the storm beyond the window, and as gentle as a spring shower. It was lips and hands touching, exploring, discovering mysteries. It was a body tanned and tightly muscled, and one as soft as ivory velvet. Hearts beat a cadence as wild as the thunder, and their breathing became labored as passions soared.

Cutter's lips sought Hollis's breast once more, drawing the sweet flesh deep into his mouth as his hand slid to the apex of her thighs. A groan rumbled up from his chest as his fingers discovered the warm moisture of her, the evidence that told him her want of him matched his driving need of her.

"Cutter," she gasped.

He lifted his head from her breast, his breathing rough. "Soon." He captured her mouth, plummeting his tongue within.

The stroking of his tongue over hers matched the exquisite rhythm of his fingers, which were creating shattering sensations of pleasure within Hollis. She gripped his shoulders as a sob caught in her throat.

"Oh, Cutter, please!"

"Yes. Yes, my Hollis."

He moved over her and eased into her, drawing on his last ounce of self-control to hold himself back, to be certain she had time to adjust to this new invasion. He gritted his teeth, his muscles trembling from the forced restraint.

Even in her hazy mist of passion, Hollis realized what Cutter was doing, and her heart nearly burst with love for him. She could feel him inside her, making her whole, complete. But, oh, she wanted more. The heat, the fire raging within her, had to be quelled before it became pain.

"Cutter, please!"

"Easy. Slow and easy," he said, his voice raspy. "I don't want to hurt you. I can't, I won't, hurt you."

A desperation seized Hollis, a need greater than anything she'd ever experienced. With strength she hadn't known she possessed, she lifted her hips and arched her back.

"Hollis, no!"

"Love me, Cutter. Love me."

His control snapped. He drove deep within her with a thrust that stole the breath from her body. The tempo was urgent, frenzied, and Hollis matched it beat for beat as they became one entity. Sensations gathered within Hollis, pulling her further away from reality and closer to the place she sought.

"Cutter!"

"Yes! Now! Go with it, Hollis. Take it all."

She seemed to splinter into a million pieces that scattered into oblivion as spasms of ecstasy swept through her. She clung to Cutter, then heard him call her name as he shuddered above her, his strength passing from him to her. He collapsed against her, spent, sated, his body glistening with moisture.

Moments passed as their breathing quieted. The storm continued to rage outside as a sense of peace settled over the room. Cutter pushed himself up to rest on his arms.

"Hollis?"

She slowly lifted her lashes as a soft smile formed on her lips. "Beautiful," she whispered. "We were so beautiful together, Cutter."

"Yes. Yes, we were. I hope I didn't hurt you."

"No, you didn't."

He started to ease himself away.

"No," she cried, circling his broad back with her arms, "don't go. You feel so good inside me, so very good."

He smiled. "I'm also very heavy." His smile faded. "Hollis, what we just shared was special. It was... I'm not very good at flowery speeches. I just want you to know how much this meant to me." Damn it, he wanted to tell her that he loved her, but the timing was wrong. She might view it as nothing more than something blurted out in the aftermath of fantastic lovemaking. He'd wait. Again. Hell. "You're not sorry, are you?"

"No. I'll never regret this night, Cutter. I'll cherish it."

He kissed her. It started as a light, fleeting kiss, then deepened an instant later as she opened to him, receiving his tongue, meeting it with hers. Her hold on his back tightened as if she would never again let him go. And within her honeyed warmth, he began to stir with renewed desire. Cutter lifted his head.

"Can you feel what you do to me?" he said, looking directly into her eyes.

"Yes. Yes, it's heavenly."

"You won't think so when you can't walk tomorrow."

"I'll risk it," she said, lifting her hips seductively against his.

"Don't I have a choice in the matter?" he said, smiling.

"Nope. I'm about to have my wicked way with you."

"Lady, I surrender."

Again they soared, searching, reaching, creating a tempo as wild as a thousand frenzied drummers. Each burst upon the sphere of ecstasy chanting the name of the other.

Slowly, reluctantly, they drifted back, then Cutter moved away, immediately tucking Hollis close to his side. He covered their cooling bodies with the blankets, then lazily sifted his fingers through her silken hair.

"So sleepy," she said, then yawned.

"Close your beautiful green eyes," he said, smiling at her. "I'm going to hold you right here in my arms. Hollis?"

"Yes?"

"Thank you."

"Thank you?" she said, laughing softly. "That's what a person says when someone passes them the mashed potatoes. What are you thanking me for?"

"For tonight. For being who you are. For trusting me."

Oh, dear God, Hollis thought, not that again. Not now. She didn't want it in that room, in that bed, not tonight. Tomorrow. Yes, tomorrow she'd sort it all through, but tonight was theirs, hers and Cutter's. It was so special, rare, wonderful. Nothing could intrude on this night; not the rain still beating against the window, nor the doubts and fears of reality that would glare in the light of the new day.

"Sleep." He kissed her on the forehead.

"Good night, Cutter," she said, snuggling closer to his warmth. *Good night, my love.*

"Good night, Hollis," he said quietly. *I love you. Man, how I do love you.*

When Hollis awoke the next morning, sunlight was streaming in the window. She knew Cutter would have been up and gone at dawn, yet she indulged in a momentary fantasy of what it would be like to wake up by his side, to be the recipient of his smile, kiss, and touch.

She stretched leisurely, like a lazy kitten, only to frown as her muscles complained of foreign use due to her lovemaking with Cutter.

Wonderful lovemaking, she mused dreamily. Fantastic, unbelievable, beyond-description lovemaking. With the man she loved.

And trusted? her mind asked.

Hollis pushed the distressing question away and went into the bathroom, welcoming the warm water of the shower that eased her aching muscles. Her breasts were tender, and she vividly recalled the ecstasy of Cutter's mouth on the soft flesh.

"Goodness," she said as desire swirled within her. "Change the subject."

A short time later, dressed in jeans and a checked flannel shirt, her hair in two heavy braids, Hollis entered the kitchen. Mattie was peering out of the window over the sink.

"Something interesting going on out there?" Hollis said, pouring herself a cup of coffee.

"Doc Nelson's truck is still here. The longer he stays, the worse it is."

"Doc Nelson? The veterinarian? What's wrong?"

"It's Butterfly," Mattie said, turning to look at Hollis. "She's down sick, really bad off. They think ... Oh, Hollis, they think she's been poisoned!"

Chapter 9

No! Oh, no," Hollis said, shaking her head. She gripped the edge of the counter as a rushing noise roared in her ears. No! her mind repeated. Not beautiful Butterfly. "Poisoned?" she whispered, hardly able to believe the word as she said it.

"That's what Jesse said when he came running in here to get Cutter," Mattie said. "I've never seen such raw fury on Cutter's face. They've been in the barn over two hours now."

"I'm going out there," Hollis said, starting toward the door.

"Don't be underfoot, Hollis. You know Buck never let you come around when anything important was happening in the barn."

"I won't be in the way," Hollis said, then went out the back door.

As Hollis ran toward the barn, her mind whirled from the impact of Mattie's words: Butterfly poisoned. That lovely horse. It couldn't be true. It just couldn't!

Three ranch hands were standing by the entrance to the barn, their expressions grim. Hollis rushed to where they stood.

"Have you heard anything yet?" she said, trying to catch her breath. "Have they told you how Butterfly is doing?"

"No, ma'am," one said. "We're just standing here waiting for someone to come out. We'd best go get to our chores, I guess, but I sure did want to know if Butterfly is going to make it. She's a fine animal, and just as sweet-tempered as they come."

"Where's the foal?" Hollis said.

"Cutter put it on Fancy Dance to nurse. Fancy took it along with her own, no questions asked. The foal's okay, ma'am. It's Butterfly that's bad off. I'd like to get my hands on that sorry son of a...excuse me, ma'am," the cowboy said, clearing his throat. "My mama didn't raise me to be cussin' in front of ladies. All I can say is, the lowlife who poisoned Butterfly is going to pay up. Every cowboy on Gauntlet Run would like to get his hands on that snake in the grass."

"Are you sure it was intentional?" Hollis asked. "Maybe Butterfly got into something accidentally."

"No way," the cowboy said. "She hasn't been farther than the corral since she gave birth. She was poisoned on purpose, no doubt about it."

"Dear God," Hollis whispered.

"Cutter is fuming," the man said. "I've never seen him so hot. I think we best get to work, boys, before Cutter finds us standing around. I wouldn't want to cross him in the mood he's in. Ma'am, we'll stop back by later to see how Butterfly is doing."

Hollis nodded and watched as the three walked away. A knot tightened in her stomach as she overheard their parting conversation.

"Why were you so polite to her, Billy?" one of the ranch hands said. "I'm betting it was her that hired this done to get at Cutter. It was her who had those cattle killed, too."

"Naw, don't think so," Billy said. "She's Buck's daughter, a Champion. She didn't do this to Cutter."

The three disappeared around the side of the barn. "No," Hollis whispered, shaking her head.

She pressed trembling fingers to her lips and drew a deep steadying breath. How many others thought she was guilty? she wondered dismally. How many would point the finger at her, declare her so evil and determined that she would drive Cutter away from Gauntlet Run at any cost? She wouldn't think about that now. The important issue was Butterfly.

Hollis spun around and hurried into the barn, slowing her step as she saw the three men at the end of the aisle. They were gathered at the double stall where Hollis had watched Butterfly give birth. Cutter stood head and shoulders above the others. Hollis's gaze was riveted on Cutter as she moved forward, seeing the tight set to his jaw, his rigid stance. She recognized the veterinarian from years ago and noted absently that his hair was now completely gray. Jesse stood by Cutter and the doctor.

"Cutter?" Hollis said quietly, when she reached them.

"What?" he said, snapping his head around. "Oh, Hollis, I didn't hear you come up."

"How is she?"

"Not good," he said.

"Hello, Hollis," Dr. Nelson said. "It's nice to see you. I just wish it were under better circumstances. We've got a mighty sick animal here."

Hollis watched the horse's labored breathing for a moment. A sheen of sweat glistened on her massive body, which shuddered with every breath.

"Oh, Butterfly," Hollis said softly, "who did this to you?" Tears misted Hollis's eyes, and she blinked them away before she looked at the doctor again. "Is she going to be all right?"

"I don't know," he said, stroking his chin. "I've done all I can. Now it's wait and watch. Cutter, I've got to get over to the Triple Bar. I'll check in with you later. Tell Sheriff Dunbar I'll get him a report on the exact type of poison that was given to Butterfly once I can analyze it in my lab."

"Yeah, okay," Cutter said, nodding.

"Try to get her to take water," the doctor said. "What a waste. That is one fine animal. Well, good luck. I'll talk to you later."

"Thanks, Doc," Cutter said.

"Goodbye, Dr. Nelson," Hollis said.

Cutter sighed wearily and ran his hand over the back of his neck as he stared at the sick horse.

"Hang on, Butterfly," he said, his voice rough. "Fight like hell. Damn it, she can hardly breathe!"

"Not a pretty sight, is it?" Jesse said tersely, looking at Hollis. "Course, it probably doesn't bother you. Butterfly is just a horse. Cutter's horse. Just like the cattle that belonged to him."

"I've had enough of your accusations, Jesse," Hollis said, her voice rising. "You're convinced that I'm some kind of cold-blooded person who would do these horrendous things, and it isn't true. I don't know why you detest me, and I don't care, but I won't listen to your slanderous insinuations any longer."

"Well, la-di-da," Jesse said sarcastically. "You've got no say over me, Hollis Champion. I work for Cutter, not you, and I'm not wearing blinders like he is. I can see you for exactly what you are."

"Get out of here, Jesse," Cutter said, a pulse beating wildly in his temple. "Go make the rounds!"

"Yeah, fine," Jesse said, yanking his Stetson roughly forward on his head. "I could use some fresh air. I'll check back to see how Butterfly is doing." He shot Hollis one last stormy glare, then strode away.

"I'm sorry, Hollis," Cutter said. "Jesse has made up his mind about you, and only time will show him he's wrong. Try not to let it bother you."

"He's not the only one who feels that way. I heard some ranch hands talking. Oh, Cutter, this is a nightmare."

"Come here," he said, opening his arms to her.

Hollis moved into Cutter's embrace and welcomed the strength of his arms as they circled her. Welcomed his heat, his aroma, the power of his muscled body. Welcomed the desire that tingled within her as memories of their exquisite lovemaking flitted through her mind.

"Better?" Cutter said, tightening his hold on her. "Man, you feel good. Smell good, too."

"Butterfly is going to be all right, isn't she? Oh, God, who did this to her? And why? Where's it all going to end?"

Cutter sighed. "I don't know if Butterfly is going to make it, Hollis. She's so sick. I don't have *any* answers for you now, but I'm going to find out who's behind this. The sheriff was here, but he's no closer to figuring it out than we are. You and I are the only ones with motives. Beyond the two of us, it's all a blank wall. I've got to try to get Butterfly to take some water now."

Hollis tilted her head back to look up at Cutter and saw the anger and frustration in his eyes. She'd heard the chilling tone in his voice as he'd vowed to find the party responsible for what was happening on Gauntlet Run. Even though Cutter was looking at her at that very moment, he wasn't really seeing her, Hollis realized. His mind was focused on Gauntlet Run and the evil lurking there. She understood. He was Gauntlet Run.

"Tend to Butterfly," she said softly, stepping out of Cutter's embrace.

Cutter moved into the stall and hunkered down by Butterfly's head. He dipped a rag into a pan of water and patted the horse's mouth while he spoke to her in low, soothing tones.

So gentle and so caring, Hollis mused. Her heart ached not only for Butterfly but for Cutter. She knew what pain he was experiencing as he watched the innocent animal suffering. Dear heaven, this madness had to stop! The culprit had to be caught, the nightmare ended.

"Hollis! Yoo-hoo, Hollis."

Hollis looked up quickly and frowned as she saw an attractive young blond woman hurrying toward her. She recognized Judy, an acquaintance from seven years before. She'd heard that Judy now wrote a "fluff" column for the local paper. It was the last person Hollis wanted to see at the moment.

"Judy?" Hollis said as the woman drew nearer. "What are you doing here?"

"It's good to see you," Judy said, then kissed the air near Hollis's cheek. "It's been a long time. You look marvelous. Listen, smelly barns are not my turf, but I appreciate the scoop on this story about the poisoning of the horse. I'm demanding a byline—that's for sure. Is that the sick horse? It doesn't look so hot. Well, hello," she added, smiling engagingly at Cutter.

"Judy," Hollis said, "slow down and back up. How did you know that Butterfly had been poisoned?"

"I don't recall your having a strange sense of humor, Hollis," Judy said, frowning.

"Just answer the question," Hollis said.

"Well, you called me at home and told me. I came right out. You ranch people sure get up early. This is grim."

Cutter planted his hands on his thighs and pushed himself slowly to his feet. He stepped out of the stall to tower over the two women, a deep frown on his face.

"Judy Barnes," she said, flashing him a hundred-watt smile.

"Cutter McKenzie."

"Ah, yes, you're becoming a household word," Judy said, nodding. "Remind me to give you the address of *my* household, Cutter. Drop by sometime."

"Judy, flirt later," Hollis said. "You're saying I phoned you at home this morning and told you about Butterfly? How do you know it was me?"

"Your voice hasn't changed in seven years, Hollis. Heaven knows I was on the phone to you enough while you were still living here, keeping up with your social outings. Besides, you called me Rude Jude, just like the old days. Why are you asking me these silly questions?"

"Hollis?" Cutter said.

"No," Hollis said, shaking her head vigorously. "No, Cutter, I didn't phone Judy. Mattie told me about Butterfly and I came straight out here to the barn."

"Damn it," Cutter said.

"Whoa, guys," Judy said. "I'm definitely confused."

"That wasn't me on the phone, Judy," Hollis said. "It was someone impersonating me."

"You're kidding," Judy said. "No, you're not kidding. Well, whoever impersonated your voice is damn good at it. Why on earth would someone do that? I can see by that sick horse that it's a legit scoop, right? What's going on here?"

"We've been through this before," Cutter said. "Someone impersonated me, too."

"The plot thickens," Judy said. "Everyone knows you two stand to gain a lot if one of you leaves Gauntlet Run. Obviously someone else stands to gain from this."

"It looks that way," Cutter said, "but we're the only ones with motives."

"Geez, this is incredible," Judy said. "Listen, tell me what you want me to do. We've been friends forever, Hollis. I won't print anything that will cause you further problems. Now...do you want me to pretend I was never here?''

"No," Cutter said, "run the story about Butterfly. If you don't, our charming creep will see to it that someone else does. But don't mention the impersonations. We'll let him or her think we're too intimidated to say anything. We can only hope he makes a mistake. And soon. This creep's getting braver and crueler. We've got to stop him. We *will* stop him!''

"If you get to him first, he'll be mincemeat," Judy said. "Remind me never to cross you, Cutter. Okay, I'll do the story on the poisoned horse. Everyone in the newsroom was buzzing yesterday about a doll that was delivered out here that represented Hollis with a knife stuck in her heart. This is a sicko you're dealing with here, folks.''

"Tell me about it," Cutter muttered.

"We really appreciate what you're doing, Judy," Hollis said.

"Some welcome home you've had, Hollis," Judy said. "When things calm down, we'll get together, okay? I'll pick your brain for my column. It's about time I had Champion doings to print. Kathleen doesn't do much these days beyond a dab of charities. Anyway, it'll be great to see a Champion flitting around Houston like the old days.''

"Oh, well, I don't—" Hollis started.

"Must dash," Judy interrupted her breezily. "Ta-ta, sweetie. And, Cutter?" she said, extending her hand. "I can't begin to tell you what a pleasure it was to meet you.''

Cutter took Judy's hand and smiled. "The pleasure was all mine. Thanks again for your help in this mess.''

"Oh, you just don't know how cooperative I can be," she said ever so sweetly, then hurried away.

Oh, good grief, Hollis thought, Judy Barnes hadn't changed a bit in seven years. She was still an outrageous flirt, but it was hard to dislike Rude Jude.

Cutter chuckled as he watched the exaggerated sway of Judy's hips as she left the barn.

"Interesting woman," he said.

"Judy is Judy," Hollis said. "We went through school together. Cutter, do you think there's more than one person masterminding this thing? That had to be a woman impersonating me on the phone."

"It could have been a very skilled man, Hollis. There's no way to know how many people are planning this. It could be just one person who has well-paid hired help, like the cattle rustlers. Until we can figure out a motive, I don't see us getting any closer to knowing who it is. Unless, of course, we catch him red-handed."

Butterfly whinnied and lifted her head, then dropped it back into the hay as though it were too much effort. Cutter went to her side and pressed the water-soaked rag to the horse's mouth.

"Easy, girl," he said, stroking her nose. "Don't worry about your foal; he's having breakfast with Fancy Dance. Hang in there. You'll be on your feet and out in the sunshine before you know it. You've got to fight this thing. Everyone on Gauntlet Run is pulling for you."

Tears misted Hollis's eyes as she watched Cutter continue to urge Butterfly to take the water. Cutter talked on in a low, rumbly voice, his large hand never stopping the gentle stroking of Butterfly's nose. The horse's breathing was still labored, but she lay still, her eyes half closed as Cutter worked his magic.

Oh, please, Butterfly, Hollis begged mentally, don't die.

Hollis wrapped her arms around her elbows and blinked away her tears. Time lost meaning. The only sounds in the huge barn were Cutter's mesmerizing low voice and Butterfly's raspy breathing.

"Yeah, that's it," Cutter said finally. "You sleep for a while. Sleep, Butterfly." Ah, damn it, he thought, his throat tight with emotion, she was dying. This beautiful creature was dying, and he couldn't do a damn thing about it! He was going to get the bastard who had done this if it was the last thing he did. It had gone too far; his lady had been threatened, and the very essence of Gauntlet Run, in the form of Butterfly and the cattle, had been harmed. It was time the sleazeball paid up. He'd find him and have his revenge before he turned the scum over to Sheriff Dunbar, Cutter vowed.

"I'll get him, Buck," he said. "Just the way you would have done it. I'll get him."

At the chilling tone in his voice, Hollis stared at Cutter and saw the hard set to his features. The fury and tension emanating from him seemed to reach out and touch her with icy fingers, and she shivered. It was as though Cutter were alone, wrapped in a cocoon of his own rage. His eyes were narrowed, cold, his body coiled, ready to pounce like a powerful animal restrained on only a flimsy leash.

Cutter got to his feet, his gaze riveted on Butterfly.

"Cutter?" Hollis whispered.

A muscle jerked in his jaw, and he swallowed heavily before attempting to speak. "She's dead," he said, his voice raspy. "Butterfly is dead."

"No," Hollis said, shaking her head as tears spilled onto her cheeks. "Oh, please, no. Her breathing seemed better, and you'd calmed her down, and . . ."

"She's dead!" Cutter yelled, stepping out of the stall, his eyes dark with pain and anger. "You can't close your eyes and pretend this hasn't happened, Hollis. Butterfly is dead, just like Forever was. Nothing is going to change that!"

"Stop it!" Hollis sobbed.

"For once in your life, face the truth head-on. You drove into Houston last night because *you* wanted to. You pretended there was no danger because it didn't fit your program."

"I—"

"Then you went to bed with me because *you* decided it was time," he raged on.

"Stop!"

"Well, you'll have to face this one up front, right now, like it or not. Butterfly is as dead as Forever was." He grabbed her wrists. "There's nowhere to run from this one, Hollis. Cattle are dead, Butterfly is dead, and that doll you got says that you're next! You can't pick and choose what you want to believe. What will you do? Decide that you trusted me last night, but today maybe you don't, and you'll flip a coin on the subject tomorrow?"

"No!" she shrieked. "Let me go. You're hurting my wrists, Cutter. Let me go!"

Slowly the barn came into focus, then he saw Hollis and his hands, which held her wrists in a viselike grip. Reality slammed into his mind, and with a moan that seemed to rip from his soul, he released his hold on Hollis. He spun around and strode out of the barn.

"Oh, dear God," Hollis whispered, unable to control her trembling. "Oh, Cutter." Tears streamed down her face. "We'll do this together. Don't you see? We'll find out together who did this to Butterfly. Don't go, Cutter, please. Not like this." She ran to the house and flung herself into Mattie's arms, sobbing as she told the housekeeper that Butterfly had died.

"Cutter must be beside himself," Mattie said, fighting against her own tears.

"He's so upset," Hollis said, "and angry. He left the barn, and I don't know where he went. Oh, Mattie, I've never seen him like that, and there was nothing I could do to help him."

"There're times, when you love a man, that you have to know he needs to be alone. You just wait for him to come to you when he's worked it all through."

"I never said I love Cutter McKenzie," Hollis gasped, stepping out of the older woman's arms.

"I've known you since the day you were born, Hollis Champion. You can't hide a thing from me. I can see it in your eyes, in the flush on your cheeks. Oh, you're in love with him, all right. And you've picked a fine man to give your heart to, honey."

"Oh, well, I..." Hollis began, feeling the warmth of embarrassment creep onto her cheeks. "What I mean is, I..."

Mattie smiled. "Buck would be so pleased, the cagey old fox. He accomplished just what he set out to do with the provisions of his will."

"No, Mattie," Hollis said quietly, "not quite. I'll admit to you, only to you, that I love Cutter, but I know he doesn't love me. Buck's wish hasn't come true, not all of it."

Mattie opened her mouth, closed it again, then shook her head slightly. "Not my place to say anything, I guess. Go wash the tears from your face, then I'll fix you something to eat. Maybe Cutter will come in soon."

But Cutter didn't come in during the remainder of the morning, nor through the endless hours of the afternoon. Hollis wandered back to the barn and was told that Cutter had ridden out on the big stallion hours before and had not been seen since. Hollis returned to the house and occupied herself with unpacking the remaining boxes from Mexico. She kept her hands busy, but her mind saw only one image. Cutter.

The seconds, the minutes, the hours ticked slowly by.

Dinner was a lonely affair, and Hollis snapped her head up every time she heard a noise outside the dining room. But it was only Mattie coming yet once more to be certain that Hollis was eating. There was no sign of Cutter.

"Mattie, where can he be?" Hollis said, pushing her plate away.

"Hush, now. Don't fret so. He's on Gauntlet Run, working through his sorrow and anger. He'll come in when he's ready."

"I'm not very hungry. I think I'll go take a long bath, then read in bed. I really need to relax. It's been a very long day."

"Good. You go on, then. Try not to be fussing over Cutter in your mind. He's doing what he has to do, honey."

"I know. I'm beginning to understand that. I just wish I could be with him, help somehow."

"You just go take a long, hot bath, then try to sleep. Things will look better in the morning."

In her room, Hollis turned back the bed and thought of Cutter, of what they had shared there. She shed her clothes, catching a glimpse of her naked body reflected in the mirror, and thought of Cutter. He had touched and kissed every inch of her, bringing her to a height of passion like never before. And she had touched *him*, timidly at first, then with bolder hands as she discovered all that he was.

He was Cutter. Male. Magnificent.

And she loved him with an intensity that defied description.

She ran a tub full of warm water with a generous amount of flowery scented crystals, then submerged herself up to her chin in the fragrant, bubbly expanse. Leaning her head back on the tile wall, she closed her eyes with a weary sigh.

When Cutter came in off the land, what would he say and do? Such pain and fury had raged through him when Butterfly had died. What frustration he must feel to be at the mercy of some sick, devious mind. Gauntlet Run had been violated, harmed by evil, and Cutter wouldn't rest until the wrong had been righted, the culprit caught.

She'd heard him speak in that cold, menacing voice, Hollis mused, of how he would protect his Gauntlet Run. Did his fury extend to the event of the doll because it had been intended for her?

Did he love her as she loved him?

Again Hollis sighed, knowing her questions were not going to be miraculously answered. She thought of Judy Barnes and something she had said that Hollis had dismissed as unimportant. It was something about... Yes, Kathleen. Judy had said that Kathleen was not very involved in the social scene in Houston, to the point where she'd even cut back drastically on her volunteer committees.

Hollis frowned as she pulled the plug in the tub and stepped out onto the thick mat. Kathleen, she recalled, had insinuated that she was as busy as ever, had even said she intended to enlist Hollis's help on some of her committees. But according to Judy, Kathleen had practically dropped out of sight compared to what she used to do. That didn't make sense. If Kathleen had gotten tired of her ongoing volunteer work, why hadn't she just told Hollis so?

Hollis slipped a pale gold caftan over her head, then settled on a white velvet lounge with a book. She left the door partially open to listen for Cutter, and switched the reading light to low, casting a rosy glow over the area where she sat. She opened the book, looked at the first page three times without comprehending a word, then snapped it closed.

"Wonderful," she muttered. Darn it, McKenzie, she fumed, come home. He'd been out there alone for so long. She wanted to see him, touch him, know he was all right. She wanted him to take her in his arms and tell her he hadn't meant the cruel words he'd hurled at her that morning, that they would stand together against the foe that stalked them. "Anything else?" she said dryly, opening the book again.

Well, she mused, as long as she was daydreaming, she might as well go for the gusto. Cutter would walk through that door, swoop her into his arms and declare his endless love. Oh, and ask her to marry him, of course. They would spend the remainder of their days on Gauntlet Run, surrounded by their beautiful children, he would say, and they'd live happily ever after. The end.

"And you, madam," Hollis said to the book, "are cracking up. You're not smack-dab in the middle of a fairy tale."

Hollis clucked her tongue in self-disgust, and reread the first page of the book.

Two hours later, Cutter stepped out of the mud room off the back porch as he donned a clean shirt, leaving it unbuttoned and hanging free of his jeans. His feet were bare and his hair damp from the shower he'd taken to rid himself of the sweat and grime from the hours he'd spent out on Gauntlet Run.

He was too tired to eat, Cutter decided, glancing at the refrigerator. Just plain bone-weary. Besides, the knot in his gut wouldn't welcome the addition of food. During that long day he'd replayed in his mind a thousand times the things he'd said to Hollis after Butterfly had died. He saw over and over the grip of his hands on Hollis's fragile wrists. It seemed almost inconceivable now that he had said such horrible things to the woman he loved.

The pain and fury and frustration that had consumed him at the moment of Butterfly's death were no excuse. He'd lashed out at the first person within his reach, and it had been Hollis; his beautiful, warm, loving Hollis. She hadn't deserved what he'd done to her, and somehow, *somehow*, he had to convince her to forgive him.

And he didn't have one idea in hell how to do that.

He would rather, Cutter decided, go up against four drunken cowboys or take on an angry bull than face Hollis Champion Ramirez. Brute strength, he had. Well-chosen words and a defense against tears glistening in emerald eyes, he did not. Tears that had been caused by him.

"You're scum, McKenzie," he muttered, smacking the light switch as he left the kitchen. "If Buck were here, he'd skin you alive."

He started down the corridor to his room, then saw the light from Hollis's bedroom and stopped, staying out of view, as he realized the door was ajar. Sweat trickled down his back.

Damn it, he raged at himself, he was acting like a kid who'd been summoned to the principal's office. But what could he say to Hollis to repair the damage he'd done?

Cutter inched closer to the door, then drew a deep breath before he peered into the room. He felt as though he'd been punched in the gut as he viewed the beauty of the scene before him. Hollis was asleep, the soft light of the lamp casting a glow over her as though she were floating on a white cloud. Her hair was in disarray, spread out on the velvet lounge and across her breasts on the gold material of the caftan.

Blood pounded in Cutter's veins as he moved into the room to stand above her, his gaze missing no detail of the exquisite picture she presented. His eyes were riveted on her pale wrists, where he'd held her so tightly, too tightly.

After the way he'd manhandled her, he wouldn't have been surprised to see that she had bruises. "Oh, my God, Hollis," he whispered, "I'm so damn sorry!"

Chapter 10

Cutter was calling to her, but she couldn't hear what he was saying. She was in a field of wildflowers and struggled to move, to get up, so she could run to his outstretched arms. The flowers held her, pulled at her clothes, as she tried desperately to tell Cutter where she was. He couldn't see her! He was coming closer and closer, but he didn't know she was there. His lips moved and she strained to hear his words.

"Oh, Hollis, I'm so damn sorry!"

Such pain, in Cutter's voice, such agony. Hollis had to open her eyes. She knew, there in her dream, that she had to open her eyes!

Slowly, slowly, her lashes lifted from her pale cheeks.

"Cutter?"

He hunkered down next to the lounge, a deep frown on his face.

"Cutter? Is that you, or am I still dreaming?"

"It's me. Hollis, I . . ." He stopped speaking as he took her hands in his, staring at her delicate wrists. "I'm so sorry. I don't know what to say to you, how to beg your forgiveness. There's no excuse for the things I said, for grabbing you and hurting you like that." He placed her hands gently back in her lap, then got to his feet. "I'll stay away from you. You don't have to be frightened of me." He turned and started toward the door.

"Cutter, wait." Hollis got to her feet. She shook her head slightly to clear the last fogginess of sleep. There was such pain in his eyes, such a bleakness to his voice. "Please, Cutter, don't leave me."

He stopped with his back to her, the deep breath he took seemed to rip through his entire body. "I've never—" He cleared his throat roughly "—never physically hurt a woman in my life, and I said awful things to you. Saying I'm sorry isn't enough. I won't come near you again."

"Don't do this, Cutter," she said, tears misting her eyes. "I know you didn't mean to say those things, and I know you didn't realize you were holding my wrists so tightly. I've been waiting for you all day, worrying. I'm so glad you're home."

He turned slowly to face her, his jaw set in a hard line as a pulse beat in his neck. "Damn it," he said, his voice gritty. "How can you stand there so damn calm, as if none of it happened?"

"It happened, but it doesn't matter. Don't you see? I know how upset you were about Butterfly, about all the hideous things that have taken place on Gauntlet Run. If Jesse had been standing there instead of me, you would've lashed out at him. If not Jesse, then you would have hit the poor wall again. Oh, Cutter, every man has his limit, and you'd reached yours. That's why you stayed out—to sort it all out. And now you've come home. Oh, please, Cutter, say you've come home to me."

Cutter took a half step toward her, then his gaze fell on her wrists again. He stopped, shaking his head.

"No," he said, his voice strained. "You're doing it again. You're hiding from the truth, believing only what you want. I *hurt* you, Hollis!"

"It doesn't matter!"

"Yes, damn you, it does!"

"All right, fine," she said. In the next instant she pulled the caftan up and away, dropping it onto the floor.

"What in the hell are you doing?" he roared as his eyes raked over her naked body.

"You're determined to lay a guilt trip on yourself, aren't you? Well, never let it be said that Hollis Champion Ramirez didn't help a worthy cause. Here," she said, splaying her fingers on one of her full breasts. "Look right here, Cutter McKenzie. There's a small bruise on my breast. Are you sorry about last night, too?"

"No!"

"Yes, you held me too tightly, and it hurt a little," she said, holding up her hands to display her wrists. "But it just tells me that you're human, that you have feelings— deep, caring feelings. You were angry and hurt, and you reacted. You're not a shell of a man: you have depths, inner strengths and weaknesses. If you walk out of this room, Cutter, it will be because you chose to go, not because I sent you away. I'm asking you—" she lifted her chin "—to stay and make love with me."

Hollis slowly lowered her hands to her sides. She forced herself not to move, not to grab the caftan and cover her nakedness. She was emotionally as well as physically bare as she stood before him, praying her trembling legs would support her and that Cutter wouldn't hear the wild beating of her heart. She watched the play of emotions on his face, in his eyes, and knew he was warring within himself.

The tension in the quiet room was nearly palpable.

Cutter, please, Hollis silently pleaded.

At last, Cutter drew a deep, shuddering breath and stared at the ceiling for a long moment before looking at her again.

"Hollis," he said, his voice oddly husky, "I...I love you."

Hollis blinked once slowly. "I beg your pardon?"

"I love you. I kept waiting for the right time to say it, but I never knew when the right time was, because I've never been in love before," he said, dragging his hand through his hair.

"Cutter, I..."

"Just listen, okay?" he said, raising his hand to silence her. "How am I supposed to make sense when you're standing there stark naked and all I can think about is tossing you onto that bed and... Cover yourself."

"Oh, yes, of course." She snatched the caftan from the floor and held it against her.

"Thank you," he said stiffly. "I didn't intend to fall in love with you, because it would mean that that damn Buck had won, gotten just what he wanted when he wrote his will the way he did. But, hell, let him win the last round—I don't care. All I know is you've knocked me over, lady."

"Cutter, I—"

"Shh, I'm not finished."

"Oh. Sorry," she said, trying not to smile.

"I realize it could appear I'm trying to gain control of all of Gauntlet Run by declaring my love for the woman who holds the other half of this place. I can't change the way things are set up, so all I can do is tell you the truth. Bottom line and up front, I love you."

"I see. May I speak—"

"And I swear to you that I'm going to find whoever is pulling this stuff on Gauntlet Run. I'll keep you safe, Hollis."

"I've never doubted it—"

"I don't know what else to say to you to convince you. Ah, damn it, aren't you even going to comment on the subject?"

Hollis laughed.

"Thanks a lot!" Cutter roared.

"Cutter McKenzie," she said, a warm smile on her face, "I love you with every breath in my body. I've dreamed about hearing those words from you."

"Come here," he said, opening his arms to her.

Hollis dropped the caftan to the floor and ran across the room, flinging herself into Cutter's arms. He lifted her high onto his chest, holding her tightly against him. He slid her slowly, sensuously down his rugged length until her toes just barely touched the floor, then he lowered his head and captured her mouth with his, his tongue parting her lips to seek the sweet darkness within.

Cutter was home, Hollis's mind whispered, and he loved her.

Hollis's last rational thought vanished as Cutter lifted her into his arms, then kicked the door closed. He carried her to the bed and laid her on the cool sheets. After quickly shedding his clothes, he stretched out next to her, his lips melting over hers in a searing kiss.

Desire swirled within Hollis as she returned the kiss in total abandon, her hands roaming over the steely muscles in Cutter's back, along his thighs, up over his tight buttocks. He ended the kiss to seek one of her breasts, gently kissing the tiny bruise before drawing the nipple deep into his mouth, suckling, tasting, heightening her passion and his.

An urgency engulfed Hollis, a need greater than any she'd ever known. The words had been spoken; Cutter loved her as she loved him, and now it was time to seal their commitment with the most intimate act between man and woman. They would be one not just in body: they would mesh their souls, the very essence of themselves, to seal forever their pledge of love.

"Cutter, please."

He shifted to gaze at her flushed face, seeing the smoky hue of her green eyes. He reached for one of her hands and gently kissed her wrist, then repeated the process with the other.

"So damn sorry," he said, his voice rough with passion.

"Don't speak of it again, Cutter," she said softly. "I understand what happened this morning. Just make love to me, now, knowing we love each other. The future is what's important, not the past. Come to me, Cutter."

He filled her. He moved over her and into her, sheathing himself in the honeyed warmth of her womanhood. He filled her body with all that declared him to be a man, and filled her heart and soul with love. They were one.

For them alone, it seemed, the ritual had been created to carry them to the wondrous place, to lift them above all that was reality, to soar beyond reason, time and space. They clung to each other, called to each other, then climbed higher yet in a raging tempo to crash upon the sought-after shore with each other.

Then silence.

And peace.

A gentle floating back into a dreamy state of sated contentment.

"Oh…my," Hollis said with a whimsical sigh. "Oh, my, my."

Cutter chuckled, then moved away, pulling her close to his side. "You're very articulate," he said, his lips resting lightly on her forehead.

"That was wonderful."

"Yes."

"I love you, Cutter."

"I love you, too, Hollis."

"I'm so glad. Cutter, did your stomach just growl?"

"Yeah, I'm starving. I haven't eaten all day."

"Well, I must say, you made fantastic love for a man in such a weakened condition. Would you like an omelet?"

"Who do I have to kill to get it?"

"I'll fix it for you."

"Oh, yeah?" he said, chuckling. "Can you cook?"

"Not very well, but if you're hungry enough, you shouldn't be too fussy."

"Good point. You've got yourself a deal. But first . . ." He claimed her mouth in a long, searing kiss. "Now I'm ready for an omelet."

Cutter got into his jeans as Hollis pulled the caftan over her head. With his arm tightly circling her shoulders, they left the bedroom and went to the kitchen. Cutter made coffee and toast, while Hollis cracked eggs into a bowl and added chunks of ham and cheese. After she poured the mixture into a frying pan, she frowned.

"Cutter?" she said.

"Hmm?" he said as he buttered toast.

"How do you feel about scrambled eggs?"

He peered over her shoulder at the frying pan. "Crazy about 'em. Especially scrambled eggs with stuff floating around in them."

"I've never made an omelet."

He chuckled. "Now she tells me. It might help if you stirred those a bit."

"Oh. Sure. How's this?"

"I'll let you know."

The eggs, Cutter declared, were delicious. And, no, it made no difference whatsoever that some were runny, the rest hard. Hollis threw her arms around his neck and kissed him on the end of the nose.

Hollis sat opposite Cutter at the table and cradled a mug of coffee in her hands. She watched the fascinating play of Cutter's muscles as he reached for a piece of toast and

swept her gaze over his bare chest again and again. Desire
tingled throughout her.

"Hollis?" he said.

"What!" she said, jumping in her chair.

"Did I wake you?" he said, smiling.

"No, I was daydreaming."

"I spent part of today covering the ground where the
cattle were rustled. I realize it has rained since then, but I
was looking for something, anything, that might be a clue
as to who had been out there."

"And?"

"Nothing. I did the same thing in the barn, but came up
empty. No one saw a stranger by the house when the doll
was brought in, and there was no one lurking around the
barn to get to Butterfly. It makes me wonder if one of the
ranch hands is in on this."

"Someone here? On Gauntlet Run?"

"It makes sense. A lot of those guys are drifters, who
just go from ranch to ranch. They don't have any partic-
ular loyalty to Gauntlet Run, Buck or me. I think it's safe
to say that money could talk business."

"Do you have any ideas as to who it might be?"

"No. All I can do is keep my eyes open, watch for anyone acting strange, being in the wrong place. But I really
think the mastermind has help here on the ranch," he said,
then took another forkful of eggs. "Jesse agrees with me."

"Jesse," Hollis repeated, frowning. "Jesse would love
to see me pack up and go back to Mexico City."

"He's just a stubborn old coot. He isn't a suspect here."

"Why isn't he?" Hollis said, plunking her mug on the
table. "He's made it very clear that he despises me. He's
also very vocal about how he feels. I could become so un-
comfortable I'd decide it wasn't worth it to stay. You
would have Gauntlet Run, and Jesse would have accomplished his goal."

"No," Cutter said, pushing his plate away. "It isn't Jesse. He'd never have hurt Butterfly or those cattle. He'll lighten up on you, Hollis. Just give him a little time."

"I just don't see why you're so quick to dismiss him as a suspect."

"Because I trust him," Cutter said quietly. "Pure and simple. Trust, Hollis. You said earlier that you had trouble trusting me because Gauntlet Run was involved in our relationship."

Hollis ran her fingertip around the edge of her mug, then lifted her lashes to meet Cutter's gaze. "I didn't know what to believe," she said softly. "I was angry at myself at first for falling prey to Buck's plan, then I wasn't sure how you really felt. There was a lot at stake here. I'm sorry if it hurts you to hear that, Cutter, but the doubts were really within myself. I've had little experience with men, and I didn't know how to tell fact from fiction."

"And now?"

"I love you so much. You've told me you love me. I saw it in your eyes, heard it in your voice. I believe in you, in what we have together."

Cutter covered her hand with his on the top of the table. "Thank you for that. We have to trust each other," he said, squeezing her hand slightly. "No matter what happens, we have to stand together."

"We will."

Neither spoke as they gazed at each other. Whispers of heat traveled up Hollis's arm, generated from the pressure of Cutter's hand on hers, traveled up her arm and across her breasts, causing the nipples to grow taut beneath the caftan. Cutter dropped his gaze to her mouth, and though he didn't touch her, Hollis could feel his lips on hers. He looked lower at her breasts, which were heavy, aching for his tantalizing touch, the sweet suckling of his mouth on her soft flesh.

"Oh, Cutter," she said, hardly able to breathe.

"I know," he said, his voice gritty. "Oh, yes, lady, I do know." Moments passed, and he slowly drew his hand from hers. "More coffee?" he said, getting to his feet.

"No, thank you." Being in love was glorious! she thought as she watched him move around the kitchen.

"We'll call Judy Barnes in the morning," Cutter said, bringing Hollis from her reverie.

"Judy?" she said as he sat back down at the table. "Why?"

"We'll get an announcement in the paper immediately, saying that we're engaged to be married."

"Engaged?" Hollis said, her eyes widening. "Married?"

"Either there's an echo in this room or you're part parrot," he said, smiling. "Yes, engaged to be married. I want it known that we're a united front. If we're engaged, obviously one of us isn't going to take off for parts unknown and forfeit that half of Gauntlet Run. With luck, our friend the creep will get nervous and make a mistake. Part of his plan, I'm sure, was to make us suspicious of each other, create dissension and tension here. We'll be letting him know it didn't work."

"By saying that we're engaged." Hollis was frowning.

"Yep," he said, then took a sip of coffee.

"But we're not engaged, Cutter."

"We're not?" he said, surprise evident on his face. "Yes, we are."

"I do believe, Mr. McKenzie," she said, narrowing her eyes, "that in order for one to be engaged, one has to have been proposed to, and one has to have accepted that proposal."

"Well, go for it, Hollis. Propose to me," he said, grinning.

"I certainly will not," she said, jumping to her feet.

"Why not?" He crossed his arms over his chest. "You're a woman of the eighties, right? You love me, right? And you know I love you. So? Make me an offer I can't refuse."

"You," she said, poking him on the arm with her finger, "don't have a romantic bone in your body. I have no intention of proposing to you, Cutter McKenzie."

"Well, damn," he said, getting slowly to his feet, "a man has to do everything around here."

"Don't strain yourself," she said, glaring at him.

Cutter chuckled, then his smile faded as he cradled her face in his large hands. "Hollis," he said, his voice low, "will you marry me? Will you be my wife, the mother of my children? I love you, Hollis, with all my heart. You are my life. Will you be my wife, too?"

"Oh," she said, her eyes misting, "that was the most beautiful thing I've ever heard."

"So, answer the damn question!"

"Oh. Yes. Yes, yes, yes, I'll marry you."

"I should hope so," he said, then captured her mouth with his.

The kiss was long and powerful, and Hollis was trembling when Cutter released her. In unspoken agreement, they left the kitchen and returned to the bedroom.

Their lovemaking was slow, sensuous, as if time had stood still and they were the only two people in the universe. With their lips and hands, teeth and tongues, they conducted languorous journeys over each other, kindling the smoldering embers of desire into raging flames. They held back, savoring, anticipating what was to be, until they could bear it no longer. The summit was reached in a maelstrom of tempestuous sensations that swept through them both.

Sated, at last, they lay close, not speaking, hands resting on each other in gentle possessiveness.

"I love you, Hollis," Cutter finally said. "Sleep well."

"Good night, my love," she said.

Within minutes, Hollis knew that Cutter was asleep, as she felt the steady rise and fall of his chest beneath her palm. She inhaled his special aroma, then closed her eyes, allowing pictures of the day to flit into her mental vision.

So much had happened since that morning, when Mattie had told her about Butterfly, Hollis mused.

And Cutter loved her.

Cutter loved her and wanted her to stand at his side for the remainder of their lives.

Hollis sifted that knowledge through the chambers of her mind, nudging away all the unsolved horrors still hovering over Gauntlet Run. She dwelled only on the man next to her, savoring his heat and strength, the very essence of Cutter McKenzie.

With a soft smile on her lips, Hollis snuggled close to Cutter and gave way to the somnolence that beckoned her.

When Hollis awoke the next morning, Cutter had already gone, as she expected. Once they were married, she mused dreamily, she'd adjust to his early hours and get up to have breakfast with him. Married. To Cutter. How wonderful it sounded.

"That was quite a plan you had, Daddy," she said, smiling. "And the best part is . . . it worked!"

Hollis showered and dressed in jeans and a red-and-white checked gingham blouse. She pulled a red V-neck sweater over the blouse, then caught her hair up in a ponytail with a red ribbon. When she entered the kitchen, her eyes widened.

"Cutter," she said. "I didn't expect to see you here."

"I live here," he said, then took a bite of bacon.

"I know, but you're usually out on Gauntlet Run by now." She poured herself a mug of coffee and sat down opposite him at the table and looked at him questioningly.

"I wanted to be here when you told Mattie that we're getting married. She knows something is up, because I don't normally take this long to eat. I thought you'd never wake up. You look cute as a button," he added, smiling at her.

"Cute?" she said with a snort of disgust. "Cute isn't quite the image I would have hoped for. How about sexy, sultry, oozing with femme fatale?"

"That's later, when we're alone," he said, the smile changing to a lazy grin.

"Morning, Hollis," Mattie said, coming out of the pantry. "Cutter McKenzie, are you planning on eating me out of house and home today?"

"No," he said, chuckling, "I've had more than enough. A man surely does appreciate a well-cooked meal, though." Hollis glared at him. "Hollis has something to tell you."

"Me?" Hollis said in a loud whisper. "Why not you? I mean, you can speak English. Just open your mouth and tell her that we're getting married."

"Married!" Mattie shrieked. "Oh, glory be. Saints above, this is wonderful."

"You did a fine job of telling her," Cutter said, trying to hide his smile but failing. "Couldn't have done better myself." Hollis glared at him again.

Mattie hugged them both, dabbed at her eyes with her apron, declared Buck Champion, rest his soul, to be a genius of a man, then started over with the hugs.

"We're glad you're happy," Cutter said. He grabbed Hollis's hand. "We have some calls to make to share our news. Come on, Hollis."

Hollis nearly had to run to keep up with Cutter's long-legged stride as he went down the hall. In the library, he pulled her into his arms and kissed her so passionately her knees began to tremble.

"Good morning," he said finally, close to her lips. "How are you?"

"Fine. More than fine."

"Call Judy."

"What?"

He put her gently away from him. "Call Judy and tell her we're engaged to be married."

"Now?" she said, sliding her hands up his chest.

"Now! Or I'll ravish your body on top of that desk."

"Can we have a vote?"

"I want this announcement to get into the papers as quickly as possible. Tell Judy we haven't set a date for the wedding but that we plan to make our home on Gauntlet Run. Sound excited, thrilled out of your mind, as though you're not giving a second thought to everything else that's been happening here."

Hollis frowned. "This is starting to come across as awfully clinical, Cutter, like a play we're acting in."

"This is important, Hollis. We're pushing the creep, hoping to force his hand. I spoke with Sheriff Dunbar already. There was nothing unusual about the poison given to Butterfly, so he's still at a dead end. He likes the new plan."

"Plan?"

"Of letting it be known we're engaged," Cutter said, as though explaining things to a rather dense child, "that neither of us is blaming the other for what's happened, nor is one of us leaving. The sheriff agrees that the guy might panic, try something rash, then make a mistake."

"I see," Hollis said quietly.

"We still don't know his motive," Cutter said, beginning to pace the floor. "If Gauntlet Run had gone on the open market, our creep wasn't guaranteed to have enough money to win. But whatever his reasons, this announcement should force his hand. Don't tell Judy the rest; just sound like an excited bride-to-be. The fewer people who know about the plan, the better."

"The plan," Hollis said dully. "Just like Buck had a plan with his will."

"His worked, didn't it? Let's hope we're so lucky. What are you frowning about?"

"Oh, I... Nothing." She refused to look at him, she was so angry.

"What is it, Hollis?" Cutter sounded a little impatient now.

"Plans, schemes. Cutter, Buck had one to get me here, to keep me on Gauntlet Run, and even to have me fall in love with the man he chose for me. Now you have a plan to use that love, that commitment to a lifetime together, to catch a criminal. It's wrong to use our love as a weapon!"

"You're being dramatic," he said, frowning as he raked his fingers through his thick hair. "We love each other, and we're getting married. Why *not* use that to our advantage and get this guy out of our lives?"

She thought of Butterfly, of the cattle. "I suppose you're right," she said, throwing up her hands. "But I still feel— Forget it. I'll call Judy and Kathleen."

"Good." He gave her a quick peck on the lips. "I've got to get to work. See you later."

"'Bye," Hollis said as Cutter strode from the room. She walked around the desk and sat down in the soft leather chair. She reached for the phone, then hesitated, her hand splayed flat on the top of the desk.

Somehow, she mused, she suddenly didn't feel like a bubbly bride-to-be. Last night she'd been happier than she could ever remember being. But now she felt like a pawn in some game. Cutter's thoughts seemed to be centered on how the announcement of their pending marriage could be used to catch the culprit. The fact that he and Hollis were going to be husband and wife, were in love with each other, was now taking a back seat.

"You're pouting, Hollis," she scolded herself. Well, darn it, she felt like pouting. She didn't want her love for Cutter mixed up in this cloak-and-dagger scenario. She didn't want the announcement of their engagement to trigger a trap for a weirdo. Love, marriage, lifelong commitment, was sacred. She'd loved Raymond on a different plane, almost like that of a child. Now she was truly a woman in love with a man different from any she had ever known before. And, damn it, she felt like an actress playing a role. She didn't like this one bit!

With a sigh, Hollis reached for the phone and called Judy Barnes.

"Goodness," Hollis said a few minutes later as she replaced the receiver. Judy had been so excited over Hollis's news flash that Hollis had hardly gotten a word in edgewise. Judy had pressed for the promise that she'd be the first reporter to receive details on the wedding plans and hung up with the statement that Cutter McKenzie was the sexiest man she'd ever seen in a pair of jeans. "And with that much," Hollis said now to no one, "I thoroughly agree."

She reached for the telephone again and called Kathleen.

"Kathleen? Hollis. Cutter and I are engaged to be married. We haven't set a date. We love each other. Super, huh? You betcha." She was babbling, she thought.

"You're babbling," Kathleen said, laughing. "A true sign of an excited bride-to-be. Oh, Hollis, I'm thrilled. But wasn't this rather sudden?"

"Sudden? Oh, well, when the love bug bites…it bites," Hollis said lamely. Darn it, she supposed she shouldn't go on to explain that Cutter hoped to jangle the sicko with the announcement. Everything was hush-hush in the cloak-and-dagger world. "Anyway, I wanted to tell you my happy news."

"I guess it goes without saying that you and Cutter will live at Gauntlet Run. Buck certainly knew what he was doing when he set up his will the way he did. His little scheme worked like a charm."

"Kathleen, I was speaking with Judy Barnes. You remember Rude Jude. Anyway, she said that you're hardly involved in any of your volunteer work anymore."

"Judy should mind her own business," Kathleen said sharply. "What I do is none of her concern."

"Well, you know how nosy reporters are," Hollis said, frowning. "From what you said to me, though, I got the impression that you were as busy as you've always been."

"I...I've cut back on my outside activities so I can spend more time with Floyd. He's the most important thing in my life, Hollis."

"Yes. Yes, of course he is," Hollis said, her frown deepening. There was a frantic edge to Kathleen's voice, she realized. Something was definitely wrong. "Floyd is all right, isn't he?"

"Certainly he's all right," Kathleen said. "Why wouldn't he be? I really must run. I'm happy for you, dear. 'Bye."

"'Bye," Hollis said to the dial tone, then replaced the receiver. Kathleen had switched moods too quickly, Hollis thought, and it was very obvious that she'd wanted to end the conversation before Hollis could press her further. Kathleen wanted to spend more time with Floyd? From what Hollis had gathered from Kathleen's previous comments, Floyd was suddenly away a great deal of the time on business. What kind of business? In the past he'd never traveled without Kathleen. None of this made sense. What was Kathleen keeping from her?

"I'm becoming paranoid," Hollis said, getting to her feet. Maybe she was overreacting, she decided. Her nerves were not in the greatest shape after everything that had happened. And to top it off, she was going to marry Cutter McKenzie! She loved him so much, and he loved her, but... Oh, darn it, she did so wish the announcement of their engagement could stand in its own circle of sunshine, instead of under a dark cloud. If only she could feel lighthearted and happy, instead of like a puppet on a string. She had to hold fast to the fact that Cutter loved her, and keep the rest of the nightmare at bay. Somehow.

Hollis wandered over to the other side of the room and stood before the easel. She took a large sketch pad out of a cupboard and propped it against the canvas. Then, with a soft smile on her face, she began to draw.

Hours later, Cutter entered the tack room at the end of the barn and frowned slightly when he saw Jesse.

"Jesse? I thought you took the boys up to the east end to check the fences."

"Billy forgot his gloves. I said I'd come back for them. That kid will come up with an excuse an hour to get out of work. I told him to buckle down or he'd find himself looking for another job."

"Whatever. I just checked on Butterfly's colt. Fine little horse," Cutter said, nodding.

"You know how to breed 'em, Cutter. I just wish... Well, we all feel bad about Butterfly. Sure would like to catch the slime who killed her."

"We will."

"I'll see you later," Jesse said. "Billy won't do a lick of work until I get back out there."

"Yeah," Cutter said absently as he hung a halter on a peg on the wall. "See ya."

As Cutter turned to leave the room, his glance fell on a small white envelope lying on top of an open keg of nails beneath the workbench.

"Jesse," he called, "did you drop a..." Too late. Jesse was gone, he realized, reaching for the envelope.

The flap was open, and inside was a folded piece of paper. Hesitating for a moment, Cutter pulled out the paper and flipped it open, his gaze flickering over the typewritten message:

MCKENZIE:
YOU CAN'T BE EVERYWHERE AT ONCE. I'M WAITING AND WATCHING. DO YOU KNOW WHERE HOLLIS IS? ARE YOU SURE I DON'T HAVE HER AT THIS VERY MOMENT?

"Damn it," Cutter said, spinning around. He jammed the note and envelope into his shirt pocket and took off at a run.

"Hey, do you want me to move Fancy—" a cowboy said as Cutter flew past him.

"Not now," Cutter said, not slowing his pace.

He left the barn and ran toward the house, the pounding rhythm of his feet matching that of his heart.

Hollis! his mind screamed. If anything had happened to her he'd ... No! No, she was fine. She was in the house, and she was fine. She had to be.

Dear God, she just had to be!

Chapter 11

Hollis!" Cutter yelled as he came barreling into the kitchen. "Hollis, answer me. Where are you?"

He ran down the long hall, across the foyer and into the library. Empty. He retraced his steps and went down the corridor to their bedrooms. A few moments later, he burst into Hollis's room.

"Hollis!" he bellowed. "Where... Oh," he said, his voice trailing off as his gaze swept over her.

Hollis had jumped in shock at his entrance, but now, with a scowl on her face, she calmly stepped into a pale blue, silk teddy and drew it slowly upward. Cutter's heated gaze followed the path of the rich material as it covered, then clung to her bare skin. She adjusted the lace, which barely hid her full breasts, then adjusted the thin straps over her shoulders.

"I trust," Hollis said, planting her hands on her hips, "that there is an explanation for your flying through my bedroom door. I don't necessarily expect a reasonable explanation, but give it your best shot."

"What?" he said rather blankly. "Oh!" he said, seeming to snap out of a semitrance. "I was looking for you."

"Do tell," she said dryly. "All of Gauntlet Run must have heard you looking for me. Cutter, what is your problem?"

"That," he said, his gaze sweeping over her again, "is the sexiest thing I've ever seen. What is it?"

"Back up there, Cutter McKenzie, and tell me why you came charging in here. You nearly scared me to death."

"I'm sorry, Hollis. I got this note," he said, reaching in his pocket, "and I panicked. I just had to make sure you were all right."

She walked across the room, took the note and envelope from his hand and read the message.

"Dear heaven," she said.

"You smell good," Cutter said, filling his hands with her thick hair and pressing it to his nose.

"Where was this note, Cutter?"

"The what? Oh, the note," he said, dropping her hair. "On top of a keg of nails in the tack room. It's too late now to be thinking about checking it for fingerprints. I don't suppose our friend left any, though. When I read it, all I could picture was you, and I had to find you. I must say, Hollis, my timing was terrific."

"This isn't funny, Cutter."

"I know," he said, sighing. "I know it isn't. I'll call the sheriff right away. This creep is a fast worker. The announcement of our engagement has probably just gotten to the stands in the afternoon paper. He's responded very quickly, realized we're not at each other's throats and is trying a new tactic. He's fast—I'll give him that."

"You didn't see anyone near the tack room?"

"Jesse was in there, but no strangers were around."
Jesse was in there, he thought. No, he knew Jesse, he amended quickly.

"Jesse?"

"He didn't see the note. I found it after he left." Cutter grabbed the papers from her hand. "There's no telling when it was put there."

"It couldn't have been there long," Hollis said. "The story of our engagement was just printed."

"Oh, by the way, that thing you're wearing is incredible," he said, giving her another thorough scrutiny. "If I wasn't sweaty and dirty I'd haul you into my arms and—"

"Cutter, enough! What about the note?"

"Yeah," he said. "I'll call Sheriff Dunbar. Hollis, don't go outside, and keep the doors locked."

"I can't stand the thought of being a prisoner in my own home, Cutter."

"We don't have any choice. Listen, we'll go into Houston tonight for dinner to celebrate our engagement."

"Really?" she said, smiling brightly.

"Yeah, pick a place where the 'in' people go, where we'll be very visible. Maybe we can push our guy into doing something rash."

"Oh." Hollis frowned. "We're still playing out our roles," she said, disappointed.

"Call Judy and tell her where we'll be so she can get it in her column. The creep may not like it that we celebrated, on the same day we received a threatening note. I'm hoping to force his hand. In the meantime, you stay in the house. Uh, I'd also appreciate it if you'd put some clothes on. I can't take much more of this."

"Then don't look at me."

"Believe me, Hollis, I'd like to do a lot more than just look. I've got to get out of here."

"Aren't you going to kiss me goodbye?"

"No," he said, holding up his hands. "No way. If I touch you, that will be all she wrote. 'Bye," he said, and strode from the room.

"Well!" Hollis said. She flopped onto the bed and stared up at the ceiling. Darn it, she fumed, she hated this. Now they were going out to dinner to celebrate their engagement as part of the ever-famous plan. This dinner should be special, the stuff of which memories were made. But instead, it was just another scene in this show they were putting on. It wasn't fair or right, and she really hated it.

The note wasn't too terrific, either, she mused dismally. The story about her and Cutter's engagement had no sooner hit the stands than the note had appeared—in the same room with Jesse. Didn't Cutter think it was rather strange that Jesse had been there but hadn't seen the note before Cutter did? Cutter wasn't budging on the subject of Jesse's innocence in all of this. Hollis knew Jesse's motive; he despised her! She was sure he'd like nothing better than to see all of Gauntlet Run go to Cutter.

But now it was more complicated than that. The note meant that the guy wanted both Hollis and Cutter off Gauntlet Run. If Cutter became too worried about Hollis, he might pack them up and leave. Then where would Jesse stand? At the mercy of the new owner, who might bring in his own ranch hands. Darn, it was confusing. And it was overshadowing what should be the happiest time of her life. What a rotten situation.

"What would you do, Buck?" Hollis said to the ceiling.

With a sigh, Hollis walked to the dressing table, sat on the padded stool and brushed her hair. She definitely wasn't smiling.

At seven o'clock, Hollis turned back and forth in front of the floor-length mirror and nodded in approval. The rich, burgundy-colored velvet of her slacks and jacket was a lovely shade to complement her fair skin and dark hair, she decided. The cream-colored silk camisole beneath the jacket was feminine and pretty. And under that was the pale blue teddy that had put Cutter in orbit earlier.

It was going to be a wonderful evening, Hollis told herself yet again. She was determined not to allow anything to intrude on her and Cutter and the celebration of their impending marriage. She was going out with the man she loved, and the rest of the world could take a flying leap.

With a decisive nod, she picked up the clutch purse that matched her evening sandals, and patted her hair. She'd woven satin ribbons into her hair braid, then twisted it into a figure eight at the base of her head.

"You're stunning, my dear," she said to her reflection. She left the room in search of Cutter.

And she found him. He was standing in the living room, staring into the roaring flames in the fireplace, and the sight of him took Hollis's breath away. He was wearing a steel-gray, western-cut suit tailored to perfection. The material emphasized the wide set of his shoulders, his narrow hips, the muscles of his long legs. His shirt was the exact shade of his blue eyes, and his tie was gray. He was the most magnificent man she'd ever seen. And she loved him.

"Cutter," she said softly, not even aware that she'd spoken aloud.

He turned to fully face her, his gaze traveling over her from head to toe. Then he extended his hand to her.

Hollis moved forward, her eyes riveted on his face that held no readable expression. She stopped in front of him and placed her hand in his.

"You're so beautiful," he said, his voice low and husky. "And I love you, Hollis, more than I'll ever be able to find the words to tell you."

"Oh, Cutter."

He kissed her palm, then dropped her hand so that he could free his own hand to cradle her face. Then slowly he lowered his head to brush his lips over hers. A soft whimper, a plea for more, escaped from Hollis's throat. Cutter caught the passionate sound in his mouth as his lips found hers again. His tongue sought hers, teasing, touching, tasting. Hollis's knees began to tremble.

Cutter kept his body away from hers. His hands cupped her face, his lips and tongue were mated with hers, but their bodies were separate and apart. He ached with need. A groan rumbled up from his chest.

"Oh, man," he said, lifting his head. "What you do to me should be declared illegal. Forget dinner. Let's stay here."

"'Kay," Hollis said dreamily.

"No," he said, dropping his hands from her face. "We're going into Houston. It's important."

"To the plan," Hollis said, coming back to reality with a thud. "Can't we think about something else for a change?"

"Okay, we'll go to dinner and have a great time celebrating our engagement. Besides," he added, grinning at her, "if we stayed home, you might decide to fix me an omelet, and I'm not sure I can handle that."

It was hard not to stay cheerful around him, she thought. She punched him on the arm. "So, I'm not a great cook. I have other talents."

"I know. Oh, lady, I really do know."

"I paint lovely pictures, Cutter McKenzie."

"Oh, *that* talent. Well, you'll have to show me your etchings some time. I've never seen your work. Hollis, are you wearing that thing you had on before?"

"My teddy? You betcha, cowboy."

"I'm not going to survive this," he said, rolling his eyes heavenward. "I have to sit across from you in a crowded restaurant knowing that beneath that suit you're wearing... I'm dying, I tell you!"

"Tsk, tsk," Hollis said, starting toward the door. "Is that a fact?"

"Damn right it is," he said as he followed her out. And another fact, he thought, smiling to himself was that he loved this woman more with every tick of the clock.

Cutter chose to drive a sleek black sports car that had been Buck's favorite vehicle, and Hollis mumbled something about "boys and their toys." Cutter commanded the powerful car with ease as it covered the miles to Houston. Their conversation was varied and light, sprinkled generously with smiles and laughter.

Oh, yes, Hollis reaffirmed in her mind, it was going to be a wonderful evening.

The restaurant was one of Houston's most exclusive, and Hollis and Cutter were greeted and congratulated by many of the city's prominent citizens. Hollis smiled and waved to people she hadn't seen in years. Beside her, she could feel Cutter tense as they were led to their table. His gaze swept the large room after they'd been seated and handed large, flock menus.

"Don't you like this place?" Hollis asked.

"What? Oh, it's fine, perfect. I just can't help wondering if he's here, watching us, planning his next move."

"Oh, Cutter, please don't spoil this evening. We were having such a lovely time until we walked in here."

"Yeah, okay. I'm sorry," he said, but his eyes darted around the room again.

Hollis sighed.

And the mood was set.

Cutter was there, but he wasn't there, Hollis realized, when their dinners were placed in front of them. He'd retreated within himself again, was no doubt mentally examining every clue they had. This was to have been such a special evening, and it was being ruined. It just wasn't fair.

"Cutter, I thought we were just going to come here and have a great time," she said.

"Hmm?"

"Never mind," she said, pushing her vegetables around on her plate with her fork. "It wasn't important."

"Hey, what's wrong? You look like you just lost your best friend."

"I did. You. You're not really here with me, Cutter. Your thoughts are centered on the person who's trying to drive us off Gauntlet Run. This was supposed to be our night to celebrate our engagement. But . . ." She paused, considering. "No that's wrong. This dinner out was for his benefit from the beginning, wasn't it? You're proving a point to him, showing him we're not intimidated by him. We're not really celebrating at all."

"Yes, we are," he said, frowning. "We're engaged, Hollis, and I'll make it official as soon as I can buy you a ring. We could pick it out together if you'd like to."

"Then what?" she said, a slight edge to her voice. "I call Judy Barnes to describe it, so she can tell all of Houston what it looks like? That ought to fry the crook's bacon. Heaven knows that people who are scared to death don't go blissfully on their way buying engagement rings, right? Oh, and I must sound excited when I phone Judy. You know, the happy bride-to-be."

"Hollis, that's enough," Cutter said in a tight voice.

"That's exactly my point," she said, leaning toward him. "I've had enough. I don't think you understand, Cutter. All my life I've been under someone's control. Even after I married Raymond, I was watched and reported on by Buck's detectives. Okay, I realize now that my father truly did love me and he missed me. But I knew those men were following me, watching every move I made. Buck never let me go, not really. Not even in death. He saw to it through his will that I would come home and stay on Gauntlet Run, where he felt I belonged."

"Hollis, I'm not Buck," Cutter said. "I'm not stepping in and trying to pick up where he left off in controlling your life."

"Aren't you?" she said softly.

A muscle jumped along Cutter's jaw. "What in the hell does that mean?"

"Cutter, this isn't the place to discuss this further. We're obviously not behaving like a dewy-eyed couple in love, and God forbid we should blow our performance! I'd like to go home. I'll meet you in the lobby." She got to her feet.

"Hollis, sit down," he ordered her, his voice just barely under control.

"I'll be in the lobby, Cutter," she said, then walked briskly away.

"Damn," Cutter mumbled, then signaled to the waiter. What was the matter with her? he wondered angrily. She knew what they were facing with that creep, knew the importance of catching him before even more drastic things happened. Maybe Cutter hadn't emphasized the danger of the note enough. Granted, he'd been momentarily side-tracked. He smiled, recalling Hollis in the teddy. But the blatant threat of that note had slammed against his brain during the hours following. He was so tense and wired, he felt like a stick of dynamite about to explode. And now Hollis was off on some tangent about how their acting happily engaged was just part of a performance. Damn it, they *were* engaged, and they *were* happy. So what if they used it as a lever against the scum?

"Your check, sir," the waiter said, placing a silver plate on the table.

Cutter glanced at the paper, paid, then got to his feet. He walked across the crowded room, hoping he had a pleasant expression on his face, as he was very aware that people might be watching his exit. He and Hollis were big news at the moment, and he'd better look like an extremely pleased, newly engaged man.

As part of the performance? he asked himself. Well, sort of—no, not exactly. He *was* happy that Hollis loved him and had agreed to be his wife. There was nothing phony about that.

And, damn it, he was not Buck Champion, attempting to control her. He was trying to protect her, for crying out loud. Ah, hell, why was she chewing him out on this issue tonight? His nerves were strung so tightly, he could almost feel them hum. He had no time for a hassle with Hollis Champion Ramirez!

Cutter moved through the crowded lobby, nodding, smiling, acknowledging congratulations as he searched for Hollis. He found her by the front door, talking to an elderly woman.

"Ready to go?" Cutter said as he approached the pair.

"Yes," Hollis said, not looking at him. "Mrs. Maynard, this is Cutter McKenzie. Cutter, Mrs. Maynard. She knew Buck ever since he was a little boy."

"Mr. McKenzie," Mrs. Maynard said, shaking his hand, "this is indeed a pleasure. I've heard marvelous things about you. I've known the Champions for as long as I can remember. There've been good times and bad on Gauntlet Run."

"Yes, ma'am." Put a cork in it ma'am, he thought irreverently. He needed to be alone with Hollis!

"And now there's to be a wedding," Mrs. Maynard said with a wistful sigh. "Splendid. Soon, I hope, there will be children on Gauntlet Run again. Buck always wanted a large family, but when dear Marilyn died, you were all he had, Hollis. If only Buck hadn't reacted so harshly when Kathleen... Well, that's water under the bridge. It's time to look to the future. You must find the culprit who's been creating trouble on Gauntlet Run, Cutter. I've been reading about it in the papers."

"Yes, ma'am," Cutter said. "We're getting that under control. There's nothing to worry about. Hollis, shall we go?"

"In a minute. Mrs. Maynard, what did you mean when you said Buck reacted harshly when Kathleen... When Kathleen did what?"

"Oh, dear," Mrs. Maynard said, fiddling with her diamond necklace, "have I spoken out of turn? I just assumed you knew about... Well, just forget I mentioned it. It was so many years ago, but I remember it as though it were yesterday. That's a sign of old age, I'm told. I can remember so far back, yet don't know where I set my hankie five minutes ago. Poor Kathleen. She was so young to face that alone. Buck was livid, wouldn't listen to reason. He was more of a father to her than a brother, you know. Kathleen came to me crying as though her heart would break, but there was no changing Buck's mind. Kathleen had no choice but to go."

"Go?" Hollis said. "Go where?"

"To New Mexico," Mrs. Maynard said. "You know, dear, to one of those homes for unwed mothers."

"What?" Hollis whispered, her eyes widening.

"As close as you and Kathleen are, I'm surprised she never told you. Oh, my, she was so young and frightened back then, just barely seventeen years old. I'm truly amazed that she forgave Buck for insisting she give that baby up for adoption. Especially when she and Floyd were never able to have children. Kathleen told Floyd about the baby, of course, when they met and fell in love years later. It didn't matter to Floyd, because he loved Kathleen so much. Can't say as I know who fathered that baby, though. I do believe it was one of the ranch hands at Gauntlet Run. Anyway, now there will be children on Gauntlet Run again. Bless you both. I must join my party. Good night."

"Good night," Hollis said absently as the woman hurried away. "I had no idea that Kathleen had a baby years ago."

"Come on," Cutter said. "Let's get out of here."

Hollis didn't speak again until they were in the sports car and merging into the busy traffic.

"Cutter," she said, "did you know about Kathleen? During those long talks that you and Buck used to have in the evenings, did he tell you about that baby?"

"No."

"I can remember Kathleen going to one specialist after another trying to find out why she and Floyd hadn't had a child. She was very upset by it all, then eventually she just quit talking about it. Oh, how heartbreaking to give up your baby, only to discover you can't have another."

"I don't imagine Kathleen would be too thrilled if she knew someone was spilling the beans after all these years."

"Mrs. Maynard means well. She's really a very sweet woman. This is quite a shock. I wish Kathleen had told me. It might have helped for her to know she could talk to me about it if the memories became too distressing. I realize she was very young, but there was plenty of money to hire someone to assist her. That baby could have been raised on Gauntlet Run."

"You don't know all the circumstances," Cutter said. "Buck must have had his reasons for doing what he did."

"Buck Champion was also very stubborn. Once he made up his mind, that was it."

"That seems to be a Champion trait," Cutter said, chuckling softly.

"Meaning?"

"Meaning you have a stubborn streak, too, Hollis. And before you got sidetracked by Mrs. Maynard, you were working up to having a real whopper of an argument with me," he said, grinning at her before redirecting his attention to the traffic.

"I wasn't trying to start an argument, Cutter. I was merely attempting to explain to you how I feel."

"And I keep trying to get across to you that the sooner we nab this guy, the quicker we can get on with our lives.

Hollis, I'm not Buck. I'm not interested in controlling you."

"I don't like feeling as though I'm playing a role." She turned her head to look out the side window. "I'm being shuffled around like a pawn on a chessboard. It's been this way all of my life, and I can't bear the thought of it following me into my relationship with you, too. I won't do this anymore, Cutter. I won't call Judy or go out to dinner if it serves a purpose beyond what it really means. Tonight wasn't ours. It was just another act in the play."

"Damn it," he said, smacking the steering wheel with his palm. "You're twisting everything around. Hollis, we really are in love. We really are engaged to be married. Why don't you just concentrate on that?"

"Because you won't allow it," she said, her voice rising as she snapped her head around to look at him. "All you can think about is catching that man."

"He's threatened your life," Cutter bellowed. "Damn right I want to catch him. I'll do anything I have to to accomplish that."

"At the cost of my feelings? At the cost of treating our commitment to each other as a weapon against him?"

"Yes, if it has to be that way!"

"No, Cutter. No more. I won't be a part of this. I won't make any more calls to Judy or be seen in the right places with stars in my eyes to prove how happy I am. For once in my life I refuse to be manipulated and controlled, told what to do and when. Catch your crook, but count me out!"

Cutter's hold on the steering wheel tightened until his knuckles turned white. "You're not being even close to reasonable. All I'm asking is that you cooperate for a while."

"I've been *cooperating* all my life. Every time I exhibited a tad of independence, Buck nipped it in the bud. Oh, he momentarily lost control when I left Gauntlet Run with

Raymond, but not for long. I'm sure those detectives were instructed to let me know they were there so I'd be aware that Buck was once more running things. He even reached out his mighty hand from his grave with his will."

"Oh, and I suppose you've decided you're still mad as hell about that," Cutter shot back. "About staying at Gauntlet Run, about falling in love with me."

"No! I was at first, but so were you. Loving you, knowing you love me, has brought me more happiness than I've ever known. Or it did until..." Hollis's voice trailed off.

"Go on—finish!" Cutter said, narrowing his eyes.

"Until you picked up where Buck left off. You're telling me what to do, say, where I'm to go, how I'm to act. You're taking our love, our very private and special love, and turning it into a sideshow. Well, forget it, Cutter McKenzie. The female lead in this play just quit!"

"Meaning?" he ground out.

"I don't want to discuss our love, our engagement, not any of it, until this nightmare is over. I can't bear having to sort through the words and actions, trying to figure out what's real and what's part of the performance. Until that man is caught, everything is on hold—us, our engagement, our commitment. I just can't do this anymore, Cutter. I just can't."

Hollis turned to look out the window again, blinking back tears that threatened to spill onto her cheeks. She had to do it this way, she thought dismally. She felt as though she were drowning in a sea of confusion. And oh, how it hurt. She was keeping the man she loved at arm's length. But she had to. It was all becoming like déjà vu, a rerun of her life under Buck's command. She couldn't live that way with Cutter. Their love had to be free to grow, blossom, and it needed sunshine for that, not the shadows of deception. Did Cutter understand any of what she'd said or how she felt? Or was he so angry that he viewed her outburst as nothing more than a tantrum? Did he love her enough to realize that she desperately needed to be her own person, so that she could love him as a complete woman? The puppet was cutting the strings in order to step forward of her own volition into the arms of the man she loved.

Hollis slowly turned and looked at Cutter. She shivered. She could virtually feel the tension and anger emanating from him. If he gripped the steering wheel any tighter, he'd probably break it in two. All she could do was wait, hope that once he'd cooled off he'd understand what she had said, how important it all was to her. Yes, he'd understand. Wouldn't he?

Cutter turned into Gauntlet Run and drove to the front of the house, stopping opposite the porch steps.

"I can walk from the garage," Hollis said quietly.

"I'll put the car away after I change my clothes," he said tightly. "I need to check on some things in the barn. I'll see you in."

Hollis looked up at him quickly, then swallowed a sigh before it could escape from her lips. Cancel angry, she thought ruefully. Furious beyond belief was closer to the mark. Cutter was going to dump her in the house and go to the barn rather than be under the same roof with her. So far, he definitely did not understand.

In the foyer, Cutter moved around Hollis and started down the hall.

"Cutter, wait," Hollis called. "Don't go. Not like this. I know you're angry, but if we could talk it through, I'm sure we could reach some sort of compromise. Yes, that's it. A compromise."

Cutter turned slowly to face her, yanking his tie loose in the process. He swept his jacket back and planted his hands on his narrow hips. A deep frown knitted his dark brows together.

"Compromise?" he repeated. "A little of this, a little of that? Like trading baseball cards? No, Hollis. No way. We're not talking about a polite situation, such as you cook and I'll clean up. Your life could be at stake here. I don't have time to worry about your frame of mind or your female ego. There's a deranged man or woman out there, who's hell bent on getting us off this ranch. If you don't like the way I'm doing this, it's just too damn bad. I'll do anything I have to to protect you, and, damn it, you'll do as you're told!"

That did it. Hollis could feel the fury building within her, edging aside the ache in her heart and the tears in her eyes.

"The hell I will, McKenzie!" she yelled. "I will never, ever, be dictated to again. Do you hear me? I will go where I please, do as I please, say what I please. You are neither my father nor my keeper."

"No, I'm not. I," he said, thumping himself on the chest, "am your lover!"

"Not anymore you're not," she said, squinting at him. "I won't be kept on a leash, and I won't act out a role in a phony play. As of this moment, I'm free."

"What are you saying?" he said, his voice ominously quiet.

"That I...um..." Hollis said, pressing her hand to her forehead. What had she done? She'd gone too far. She didn't want to be free in the way she'd made it sound. She just wanted to love Cutter as an equal partner in their relationship.

"Well," Cutter said with a snort of disgust, "this has to be one of the shortest engagements on record. Free? Fine. You've got it, lady. All bets are off. You do anything that suits your fancy, and so will I. If I choose to protect you from that lunatic out there, that's my business. If you want to screw things up by telling Judy Barnes we're no longer

engaged, be my guest. You're acting like a spoiled brat!"
He spun on his heel and strode down the hall.

"Oh, is that so?" Hollis yelled after him. "You're about
as sensitive as tree trunk, Cutter McKenzie. You haven't
even tried to understand how I feel. I..." She paused.
"Forget it. No one is even listening to me." She stomped
into the living room and flopped into a leather chair, fold-
ing her arms over her chest.

Spoiled? The nerve of that man, she fumed. She wasn't
pitching a fit; she was expressing her views, trying to explain who she was, how she felt. Which, when dealing with
the great Mr. McKenzie, was like talking to a mule. Stubborn, stubborn, stubborn.

"So, fine," she mumbled, "go catch your crummy
crook. Just don't speak to me while you're doing it."
Don't speak to her? her mind echoed. Or touch or kiss
her? Don't make love to her or say the glorious words "I
love you, Hollis"? Oh, what had she done? Cutter had just
said they were no longer engaged. She'd only meant to put
things on hold, not cancel their future together. "Oh,
damn," Hollis said as a tear slid down her cheek.

Hollis plunked her elbow on the arm of the chair, rested
her chin in her hand and stared into the gray ashes in the
cold fireplace. She and Cutter were at an impasse. Maybe
she should... No! She wasn't going to budge. She refused to take part in that phony-baloney playacting for one
more second. If Cutter would quit screaming at her and
think about it instead, he'd realize that her whole life had
been controlled, and she couldn't marry a man who was
picking up the reins where her father had left off. No, sir.
Cutter McKenzie was definitely acting like a carbon copy
of Buck Champion. It looked as though the creepy crook
wasn't the only one who was proficient at impersonations.

"Impersonations," Hollis said aloud. That meant
something to her somewhere in the back of her mind... A

party. Yes, it had been a party held there in the living room. She could see a Christmas tree and lots of people. The noise had awakened her. She'd heard Donald Duck inside, where the party was, and wanted to see him, so she'd crept out of her bedroom in her nightie and had stood by the living-room doorway. She hadn't been very old—maybe seven or eight—and she'd been tingling with excitement, because she'd known she wasn't supposed to be up.

"Do John Wayne," someone had called, and Porky Pig had been transformed into a drawling cowboy.

"Marilyn Monroe!"

A woman's breathy voice had replaced the cowboy drawl.

Oh, how Hollis had wanted to see this magical person, who could change into whatever he or she wished to be. But she was too small; all she could see were the legs of the big adults.

Hollis had inched to the doorway, she remembered, and peered in but was still unable to glimpse the unbelievable creature her daddy had surely brought from a faraway fairy-tale world.

"Zsa Zsa Gabor!" Hollis had heard a new voice then, and the crowd had cheered.

The group had shifted slightly, Hollis recalled, and she'd craned her neck to see. It was ... It was ...

"Dear God," she whispered, stumbling to her feet. She remembered! She had to tell Cutter, she thought, her mind racing. Maybe it wasn't true—was only a coincidence—but she had to tell Cutter.

Hollis ran down the hall to Cutter's bedroom. Empty. She spun around but halted as she heard the intercom buzz on the phone in her room. She hurried inside and snatched up the receiver.

"Yes?"

"Hollis? Cutter. Come to the barn. I need to talk to you."

"Cutter, I have to tell you something. I just remembered who—"

"The barn, Hollis," he interrupted her, a sharp edge to his voice. "Now!"

"Fine. I'm coming." She slammed down the receiver. "How rude," she muttered, then ran from the room.

Chapter 12

Hollis had gone only a few feet beyond the back door of the house when the heels of her sandals began to sink into the soft ground. The night was too damp and chilly to go barefoot, she decided as she tiptoed her way forward. Now *she* looked like a crook skulking around in the dark.

With a sigh of relief, Hollis left the lawn at last and moved onto the gravel drive leading to the barn. She was past wondering why she was hurrying to meet Cutter simply because he'd barked an order at her. She was eager to tell Cutter what she had remembered about the impersonations, said a part of her mind. But some other section admitted that she was glad Cutter was at least speaking to her, even if he'd sounded like a drill sergeant.

"What's next, Hollis?" she muttered. "You start saluting the man? Ha!"

Hollis entered the barn, welcoming its warmth, then stopped. The only light in the huge building was a single bank of light bulbs just inside the doors. The remainder of the interior was pitch-black.

"Cutter?" she called. "Cutter, where are you?"

His voice came out of the darkness, causing Hollis to jump in surprise. "Back here, Hollis. I'm by the tack room. I'm waiting for you."

"Would you turn on a light?" she said loudly. "I can't see anything."

"Just come down the center aisle. There's nothing in your way. Hurry. I need to talk to you."

"Well, cripes," Hollis said under her breath, "is it too much to ask to turn on a light?"

"Hollis?"

"Yes, all right, I'm coming," she said.

Hollis moved cautiously down the center of the wide aisle. The darkness closed in around her, making it impossible to even see the hand she instinctively held out in front of her. Somewhere to her right, a horse snorted.

"Oh," Hollis gasped. "Cutter, this is ridiculous," she called out. "Would you please turn on a light?"

"Just keep coming," he answered. "I'm right here, waiting for you."

"Brother," she said, then started off again with tentative steps. She'd never known darkness to feel so heavy, so menacing, as if it were pressing against her, making it difficult to breathe. That sound echoing in her ears was her own frantic heartbeat. This was absurd. And she was getting scared. Whatever Cutter wanted to speak with her about, it had better be good.

"Are you doing okay?" Cutter said from the darkness.

"No thanks to you," Hollis shot back. "This is like trying to walk in an inkwell. Cutter, turn on a light."

"No, that will spoil my surprise."

Suddenly Hollis heard what sounded like a scuffle, then a low *"oomph,"* as if someone had bumped into something.

She stopped dead in her tracks. "Cutter?"

"Hollis, run!" he yelled. "Get out! Now!"

"What?" She squinted into the wall of darkness in front of her, totally confused now.

"Keep walking, Hollis," Cutter snarled.

"Cutter?" she said, her eyes widening as her heart thundered beneath her ribs.

In the next instant, the barn was awash with light and Hollis blinked against the sudden glare. As her eyes adjusted, she gasped in horror at the scene before her.

Cutter's arms were held tightly behind him by an enormous man Hollis had never seen before. She stared at Cutter's face and saw the raw fury in his eyes. And saw—dear God, her mind screamed—the blood running down Cutter's chin from the corner of his mouth.

"Oh, my God, Cutter, what—" she started.

"I'm here, sweetheart," Cutter's voice said.

Hollis snapped her head around, absently registering the fact that another man she didn't know was standing next to Cutter and the giant who held him. Then she saw a Gauntlet Run ranch hand she recognized, and Jesse.

"Come closer, lovely Hollis," said the voice of Cutter McKenzie.

"Dear God," Hollis whispered. She saw the gun that was aimed at her, heard the voice of Cutter that came from the last man in the group. "Floyd," she said.

"In the flesh," he said, using his natural voice. "Nice of you to join us, my dear. Of course, you would come when your lover called you, wouldn't you? I was counting on that. Move closer, Hollis. Right now."

Hollis looked frantically at Cutter, who jerked his head to indicate she should do as she was told. But her feet refused to move! She was so frightened. And cold. She was so very cold and—

"Hollis," Cutter said, "do as Floyd says. Come on."

"I said zip it, McKenzie," the man next to him said.

"Let him talk to her for a second, Reb," Floyd said. "Our little Hollis appears to be about to faint, and we don't have time for such garbage."

"I'll get her," Reb said.

"No," Cutter said fiercely. "Don't touch her. Hollis, do as Floyd says. Come closer. Everything is going to be all right. Just do exactly what you're told. There's nothing to worry about."

Penetrating the hazy mist of fear in Hollis's mind, clearing her head, was one question: was Cutter McKenzie nuts? Nothing to worry about? Her uncle Floyd was the evil man who had been doing the horrible things on Gauntlet Run. And now he had a gun, an ugly giant was holding Cutter captive, and his trusted Jesse was one of the bad guys. But there was nothing to worry about! Did Cutter think she was—

"Do you think I'm stupid?" she shrieked. The man holding Cutter flinched. "How dare you tell me there's nothing to worry about, Cutter McKenzie. I'm an intelligent woman. We're in a mess here."

Cutter grinned at her. "Yes, ma'am, you're right. I should've noticed that myself."

"Enough," Floyd said. "Come over here by me, Hollis."

"You're darn right I'll come over there," she said, stomping forward to stand in front of Floyd. "Why? Just answer me that. Why did you do all those horrendous things?"

"Easy, Hollis," Cutter said, a warning tone to his voice. "Don't push it."

"That's good advice," Floyd said, still pointing the gun at Hollis. "You'd do well to listen to your lover, Hollis. Not that it will make any difference in the long run."

"What do you mean?" she said.

"That I'm going to kill you—and Cutter, of course," Floyd said pleasantly. "I hate to see it come to this, but you left me no choice in the matter."

Kill...us? Hollis tried to say, but realized no sound had come out of her suddenly dry mouth. *Kill?* her mind echoed. *No! She loved Cutter, he loved her, they were going to be married, have beautiful babies, be so happy together on Gauntlet Run.* "No," she whispered.

"I'm afraid so," Floyd said with an exaggerated sigh. "If only you two had heeded my warnings and left Gauntlet Run, this wouldn't be necessary. I started with the cattle, thinking Cutter would soon tire of the trouble, take his money, and go. That would have left only you to deal with, Hollis. But you didn't budge either. Then, ah, yes, you two fell in love and became determined to stay on Gauntlet Run together. You shouldn't have done that, you know."

"Why?" Hollis said, amazed her voice was working again. "Why are you doing this, Floyd? If—if we're going to...die, at least we have the right to know why."

"You do?" Floyd said. He frowned, looking slightly confused.

Hollis stared at him. There was a strange gleam in his eyes, an unnatural cadence to his voice. *He's insane!* she thought, her mind racing. She had to keep him talking until Cutter could figure out what to do. *Oh, really? Cutter was being held by a mountain!*

"Yeah," Cutter said. "It's only fair, Floyd. We deserve that much, at least."

"We're wasting time," Reb said. "Let's get this over with. Get some rope, Hank," he said to the ranch hand. "Tie Jesse up first."

"Jesse?" Her eyes darted to the older man.

"I came into the barn," Jesse explained. "I heard Cutter call me, and I came back here just as nice as you please. Course, it was Floyd who'd called me. This ape already had Cutter, then Floyd phoned you on the intercom, Hollis. I've never in my born days heard anyone do impersonations that good.''

"I have," Hollis said. "I heard him years ago at a Christmas party here on Gauntlet Run. I was just a little girl, and I snuck downstairs because I thought Donald Duck was in the living room. I forgot about that party until tonight. I don't think I ever heard you do impersonations after that, Floyd. Until now."

"Buck was furious at me that night of the party," Floyd said. "He took me into his library and said I'd made a fool of myself and of him, by turning his party into a kiddy show. He said Gauntlet Run had class and that I wasn't worthy of being there. He only allowed it for Kathleen's sake. How I hated Buck Champion. I hated him. Do you hear me?"

Hollis nodded quickly, then glanced at Cutter, who mouthed the words "Keep talking."

"You hated Buck because of what he said to you that night?" Hollis said, redirecting her attention to Floyd.

"Not because of that," Floyd said. "I didn't care what Buck thought of me. It's because of my Kathleen that I hated that bastard. All of this—" he waved the gun in the air "—I've done for her. She's all I have, you know. I want her to own Gauntlet Run. She deserves to own it. She suffered so much because of Buck, but I'm going to make it all up to her now. I'm going to give her Gauntlet Run."

Hollis drew a steadying breath. "Gauntlet Run won't replace the baby, Floyd," she said, watching his face.

"Ah, damn," Cutter muttered as Floyd whipped the gun up and pointed it at Hollis.

"Who told you about the baby?" Floyd said, a wild look in his eyes. "Kathleen said she didn't want you to know. She loved that baby. She begged Buck to let her keep it, but he refused. He said the father wasn't good enough for a Champion, was a lowly ranch hand, a no-account drifter. And then what does Buck do? He leaves Gauntlet Run to another ranch hand, to Cutter McKenzie, and to a daughter who didn't speak to her father for seven years. Gauntlet Run is going to belong to my Kathleen!''

"Yes, you're right," Hollis said carefully. "She *should* have it."

"What?" Floyd said.

"We weren't going to stay," Cutter said. "Hollis has property in Mexico. We're going down there to live as soon as we're married. We're forfeiting the ranch. But Floyd, Gauntlet Run will go on the open market. How do you expect to win the bid?"

Floyd laughed. It was a shrill, eerie laugh that made a shiver course through Hollis.

"I've liquidated all of my assets," Floyd said. "I have millions stashed away. I told Kathleen I needed cash for a special deal I was putting together. She let me sell her jewelry, the extra cars—everything we had of value. It's all turned into cash, ready, waiting to be bid on Gauntlet Run. I couldn't let Kathleen do her volunteer work anymore, because they'd go to lunch afterward, go shopping. She couldn't spend the money I had for Gauntlet Run. No, I couldn't let her do that. She'll understand, once Gauntlet Run is hers. It *will* make up for the baby, you see. Buck took her baby, then the doctors said I couldn't have children. So I'm giving her Gauntlet Run, and she'll be happy. She deserves this place."

"Yes, of course she does," Cutter said. "Hollis and I agree with you one hundred percent, Floyd. There's no reason to kill us. We'll go on to Mexico and forget that any of this happened."

"Don't believe him, Floyd," Reb said. "He'll turn us in the minute we let them go. The plan stands like we said. We take them up to the cabin on the far edge of Gauntlet Run and kill them. Everyone knows there've been threats made.

It'll look like whoever it was got tired of playing games. The sheriff can't figure out who it is now, and he won't later, either. We'll have to kill Jesse, too."

"But... But Kathleen will cry if Hollis dies," Floyd said in a whiny voice. "I knew that all along, but if I let them go, Kathleen won't cry. It would be so much better if my beautiful Kathleen didn't cry, Reb. You understand, don't you?"

"Holy hell," said Hank, the other ranch hand, "he's nuttier than a fruitcake. I don't like this, Reb. We're the ones doing all the dirty work. How do we know we're going to get the rest of our money from this loony-tune?"

"I wouldn't count on it, Hank," Cutter said. "Hell, he won't even let his own wife go out to lunch. Every penny Floyd has is going toward the bid on Gauntlet Run. You won't see a dime."

"You could send him a bill, I suppose," Jesse added with a dry chuckle.

"Too many voices," Floyd said, pressing his hand to his head. "I can't think when everyone is talking." He lowered the gun. "You all have to be quiet so I can think. Now, what would Kathleen want me to do?"

While the gun was pointed at the floor, Cutter made his move. He jerked his arms free of the man holding him and rammed his elbow into the fleshy stomach behind him. The man grunted and staggered backward. In the next instant, Jesse delivered a right cross to Hank's chin, sending the young ranch hand sprawling on his backside. Cutter grabbed the front of Reb's shirt, then pulled back his fist to deliver a blow as Hollis lunged for Floyd's gun.

But Floyd was faster.

He circled Hollis's neck with his arm and pulled her back against him, the gun rammed into her ribs.

"Hold it!" Floyd yelled. "I'll kill her right now! I swear I will."

"No!" Cutter released Reb and took a step toward Floyd.

"I mean it, McKenzie." Floyd tightened his hold around Hollis's throat. Hollis gripped the arm, trying frantically to ease the pressure. "Stand still, Hollis," Floyd warned, "or Cutter is a dead man." Hollis stood statue still.

"I'm in charge here," Floyd bellowed. "I'll kill anyone who doesn't follow my orders. We're going to the cabin, just like I planned."

"Damn you," Cutter said, taking another step toward Floyd.

The huge man behind Cutter lunged forward and caught him around the chest, pinning Cutter's arms to his sides. Cutter strained against the viselike hold, then braced himself as Reb stepped in front of him. Reb smashed his fist into Cutter's ribs, causing the air to rush from his lungs.

"Cutter!" Hollis screamed.

Reb swung again and connected with Cutter's jaw, snapping his head back.

Jesse swore.

"Oh, God, Cutter," Hollis said, tears clinging to her lashes.

Reb hammered another, than another, vicious blow to Cutter's midsection. Cutter tried desperately to free himself, but he felt as though he were moving in slow motion as waves of dizziness, nausea and pain assaulted him.

"No," Hollis sobbed. "Oh, please, stop."

Cutter's head snapped back again as Reb's fist found Cutter's jaw. A curtain of darkness fell over Cutter's senses. As his knees gave way, the man released him and he crumpled to the floor.

"Cutter!"

He heard Hollis scream from a far away place, told himself he had to move, go to her, protect her. But then the black veil dropped totally over him, and he was swept into painless oblivion.

"Oh, Cutter," Hollis said, tears streaming down her face. "Floyd, let me go. Let me see if he's all right."

"Fine, fine," Floyd said impatiently, releasing her. "Go fuss over your cowboy lover. Just remember I've got this gun pointed at you. Reb, you and the others get the horses saddled. We'll need large flashlights, too. Hurry. We've wasted enough time."

Hollis ran to where Cutter lay on the floor and dropped to her knees beside him as Jesse did the same, hunkering down on the other side of Cutter. Jesse slid his arm under Cutter's chest and gently rolled him over onto his back. Cutter moaned but didn't open his eyes.

"Oh, God," Hollis whispered, pressing her fingertips to her lips.

Cutter's jaw was already beginning to swell on one side, and blood poured from his mouth and nose.

"His face looks worse than it is," Jesse said quietly. "We got messed up more than that a few years back in a bar in San Antonio. It's his ribs I'm worried about, Hollis. If they're busted and that ape hauls him around too rough, he could puncture a lung."

"Oh, Jesse," Hollis said, her voice trembling, "what can we do to help him?"

"I don't figure Floyd will let us take the time to tape up Cutter's ribs. Damn, they worked him over. They'll pay for this, Hollis. I promise you that."

"You really care about him, don't you?"

"Like he was my own son. Cutter McKenzie is the finest man I've ever known. But then I guess you don't need to be told that. You know Cutter for what he is."

"I love him, Jesse."

"I know. I was wrong about you, Hollis, and I'm sorry for the way I treated you. We'll get out of this mess—you'll see. The game's not over till it's over, as the old saying goes."

"Hurry up with those horses," Floyd yelled.

"Floyd is crazy," Jesse whispered to Hollis. "That makes him even more dangerous. Listen, I know Hank. He's scared by now. He's worked here about six months, and I've seen him around the other hands. He's got the backbone of a jellyfish. He's the weak link, and maybe we can figure out a way to play on that."

Cutter groaned. "Hollis," he said, his voice raspy. He opened his eyes, which were clouded with pain.

"I'm here, Cutter," she said, grasping his hand.

"Damn, that guy has a fist like a sledgehammer. Jesse, we gotta get Hollis out of this mess."

"I know that, boy," Jesse said, grinning. "Grit your teeth for a minute. I want to see how bad you're busted up."

"I'm fine," Cutter said, shifting his gaze to Hollis. "Hang in there, okay?"

"You bet," she said. She smiled and willed herself not to cry.

Cutter sucked in his breath as Jesse gently probed his ribs, a frown pulling the older man's shaggy eyebrows together.

"Damn it, Jesse," Cutter hissed. "That's not bread dough you're kneading there. Get your hands off me."

"Jesse?" Hollis said.

"Busted. Two ribs for sure, maybe more. That sorry son of a— I'd like five minutes alone with that Reb."

"Help me up," Cutter said.

"No, Cutter," Hollis protested, "you shouldn't move."

"I'm not going to have a choice. Better that you two get me on my feet than our friends."

"He's right," Jesse said, sliding his arm under Cutter's shoulders.

"What are you doing?" Floyd roared.

"Just putting him on his feet," Jesse answered. "Don't worry, Floyd. He's in no condition to cause you any trouble."

"Thanks a lot," Cutter mumbled, struggling to sit up. "Ah, damn." He sat back, writhing with pain.

With Hollis and Jesse on either side of him, holding his arms, Cutter staggered to his feet. A hot spasm coursed through his entire body, and he clenched his throbbing jaw as a wave of dizziness assaulted him.

"Wonderful," he muttered. "I thought San Antonio was bad."

"We're ready, Floyd," Reb called.

"Let's go," Floyd ordered the trio, waving the gun.

"Floyd, listen to me," Hollis said. "Cutter is in no condition to ride a horse. Forget about the cabin. Cutter and Jesse and I will leave for Mexico now, and you'll never see us again. Gauntlet Run will be yours to give to Kathleen. Oh, Floyd, think of how happy she'll be. Her eyes will be sparkling, and she'll be smiling that lovely smile of hers."

"Floyd, are we going or not?" Reb yelled.

"Oh, yes, my Kathleen does have a lovely smile," Floyd said, a dreamy quality to his voice. "She's so beautiful. She'll be wonderful as mistress of Gauntlet Run. This is where she belongs. Once she's here, Buck will have to bring the baby back, won't he? Isn't that right, Hollis?" He slowly lowered the gun as he cocked his head to one side like a little boy. "I'm going to play with the baby and have fun. Okay? Is that okay, Hollis?"

"Yes. Yes, you'll have a wonderful time," Hollis said, her voice trembling. "It will be you, Kathleen and the baby, here on Gauntlet Run."

"I'll teach the baby to play peekaboo," Floyd said in a singsong voice. "And hide-and-seek." The gun hung loosely from his fingers at his side. "And we'll have ponies—me and Kathleen and the baby."

"Now, Jesse!" Cutter yelled, lunging forward.

In one motion, it seemed to Hollis, Jesse yanked her out of the way by the arm as Cutter slammed full force into

Floyd, causing the two of them to crash to the floor. The gun slid away, and Jesse picked it up, pointing it at an advancing Reb.

"You move, you're dead," Jesse said. "Do me a favor and move. Hank, bring your buddy the ape over here. It's all over but the shouting."

"Kathleen," Floyd yelled. "I want my Kathleen." He burst into tears as Cutter rolled off of him with a groan, clutching his ribs. "Why isn't my Kathleen here?" Floyd sobbed, covering his face with his hands.

"Cutter?" Hollis said, hurrying to his side. She dropped to her knees beside him, tears streaming down her face.

"Free," he said. "Free." Then he closed his eyes and went limp.

"Cutter?" she said.

"Hollis," Jesse said, "call the bunkhouse on the intercom and wake up those worthless no-goods. Get 'em over here to watch these jerks. Then call the sheriff and the paramedics. We gotta get Cutter to a hospital."

"Yes, of course," Hollis said, scrambling to her feet.

"Jesse," Hank said, "please, please, don't call the other hands. They'll take me apart. Jesse!"

"Should've thought of that sooner, boy," Jesse said.

Floyd rocked back and forth on the floor, crying quietly.

Hollis made the calls, then hurried back to Cutter's side, cradling his hand in both of hers. She was vaguely aware of the sound of men thundering into the barn, the harsh exchange of words. She saw only Cutter, heard only his shallow, raspy breathing as he lay, unmoving, on the cold floor.

Free, her mind echoed over and over. That was what Cutter had said before he passed out. That was the word she'd hurled at him in the house. Why had he said it now? Had he thought it through, decided that was what *he* wanted after all? To be free? Oh, dear heaven, no!

Jesse came to Cutter's side and dropped to one knee. "The hands took our friends outside to wait for the sheriff. Guess Floyd isn't going to hurt anyone. He's a sad case. How's our boy here?"

"He hasn't moved, Jesse," Hollis said, a sob catching in her throat.

"He'll be fine. It'll take more than a couple busted ribs and a Technicolor face to hold him down for long. It's all over, Hollis."

"What?" she said, looking up at him quickly.

"The trouble here on Gauntlet Run. It's over. Now you and Cutter can get on with your lives together."

"I hope so," she said softly, "but—"

"I hear sirens." Jesse got to his feet.

"I want to go to the hospital with Cutter, Jesse," Hollis said.

"I'd hate to be the guy who tried to stop you," he said, chuckling. "You pulled this out of the fire, you know, talking to Floyd the way you did so Cutter and I could make our move. I'd hate to think what might've happened if they'd gotten us to that cabin. Well, no sense worrying about it now."

"Kathleen?" Floyd was saying. "I want Kathleen."

"Poor guy," Jesse said.

"Kathleen is going to be devastated by all of this. They've been devoted to each other for so many years," Hollis said.

"Yeah, well— Hey!" Jesse yelled. "Back here."

Two young men carrying metal boxes ran down the aisle.

"Paramedics," one said.

"Well," Jesse said, "take your pick. We've got a beatup cowboy and a sad, sad mental case. But gentlemen? That cowboy is Cutter McKenzie. He's Gauntlet Run. I got thirty hands outside that want to see him as good as new."

"Excuse me, ma'am," one of the paramedics said, smiling at Hollis, "but I need to get closer here, consid-

ering the fact that my life is at stake. Taking on twenty-
nine cowboys is my limit, so I'd best see to it that I fix this
one up.''

"Yes, of course." Hollis moved out of the way.

"They worked him over, huh?" the paramedic said,
flipping open the box. The other paramedic was speaking
gently to Floyd, who continued to whimper for Kathleen.

"Jesse thinks Cutter's ribs are broken," Hollis said
anxiously.

"All right," the man said, nodding. He opened Cutter's shirt and slipped the shirttails out of his jeans.
"Whew!"

"Oh, God," Hollis whispered.

The paramedic put on a stethoscope and pressed it to
Cutter's chest, moving it every few moments. Hollis waited
nervously.

The paramedic removed the stethoscope and looked at
his partner. "I'm going to need an ambulance here."

"Yeah, me, too," the other man said. "I'll call in."

Cutter groaned and opened his eyes.

"Take it easy, Mr. McKenzie," the paramedic said.
"Don't move if you can help it. I'm going to take your
pulse and blood pressure. We'll have you off that cold
floor in no time at all."

"Hollis," Cutter said, closing his eyes again.

"Yes, I'm here, Cutter."

"Don't . . . want . . ." he said, his voice weak. "Need . . .
Free."

"He's out again," the paramedic said. "It's just as well.
He's got to be in a lot of pain. Whatever he needs to be free
of, I hope it isn't a hospital. They'll be keeping him awhile
once we get him there."

No, Hollis thought miserably, fresh tears filling her eyes.
Cutter hadn't been referring to a hospital. It was her; she
knew that now. He wanted, needed to be free of her.

Chapter 13

*F*ree.

The word beat against Hollis's brain the moment she opened her eyes the next morning. Her thoughts immediately centered on Cutter and the almost unbelievable events of the previous night.

The trip to the hospital in the ambulance had been a frightening experience, with the driver racing along the roads with the siren screaming and lights flashing. Cutter had drifted in and out of consciousness, mumbling Hollis's name, but not speaking beyond that, not saying again the word that sat with a heavy chill on Hollis's heart: free.

In the emergency area at the hospital, Cutter had been whisked away on a stretcher, leaving Hollis to thank the paramedics and give the admitting nurse information about Cutter. Mattie, who'd been awakened by the arrival of the sheriff and paramedics at Gauntlet Run, had insisted on coming to the hospital with Jesse in one of the pickup trucks. A weeping Floyd had been taken to another room in the hospital, and Hollis had faced the task of calling Kathleen.

"Poor Kathleen," Hollis said now, pulling the blankets up to her chin. But Kathleen had been so brave, she mused, so determined to stay by Floyd's side and get him the best help available.

"I'm so sorry, Hollis," Kathleen had said, hugging her. "Floyd has been acting strange, and I've been terribly concerned, but I had no idea he was ill. I hope you and Cutter can find it in your hearts to forgive him."

"Of course we will," Hollis had reassured her.

"I must go speak with the doctors now," Kathleen had said. "I'm just so sorry all this happened. It's hard to believe that Cutter has been hurt and it's Floyd's fault."

"Cutter is going to be fine," Hollis had said. "Both Jesse and the paramedic said so. You go to Floyd. He needs you, Kathleen. He loves you very much."

"Yes. Yes, I know," Kathleen had said, her eyes brimming with tears. "He's going to get well, and I'll be there every step of the way. He's my life, Hollis."

Hollis had watched Kathleen disappear down the corridor, had seen the square set of her aunt's shoulders, the proud lift of her chin. The Champion stubbornness would stand Kathleen in good stead this time, Hollis had decided. And someday, maybe, Kathleen and Floyd could reclaim their happiness.

Hollis had joined Jesse and Mattie in the waiting room, where Jesse had been leaning against a wall, and Mattie had been twisting and untwisting her handkerchief.

"Cutter won't want to stay here," Mattie had said. "He's threatened in the past that they'd have to hog-tie him to keep him cooped up in a hospital."

"He's in no shape to argue," Jesse had said, chuckling. "He'll be glad to have a soft bed and a good night's sleep. Course, tomorrow they may hear him hollerin' to the next county to be turned loose. Cutter's not one to be held down.''

"What's taking so long?" Hollis had asked anxiously. "Couldn't they tell us something?"

"They gotta X-ray his ribs, I imagine," Jesse had replied. "He's going to be fine, Hollis. He'll be sore as hell, and ornery as a wounded bear, but there isn't a cowboy worth his salt that hasn't been in a brawl. Cutter will just be fighting mad that he didn't get to take a few licks at Reb. An honest fistfight is one thing, but this was something else again."

Time had seemed to mock Hollis as she'd alternated between looking at the clock and the doorway to the room. Although it had seemed like an eternity, it had been less than an hour when the doctor appeared. He was big and burly and had a shock of white hair.

"Evening, folks," he'd drawled. "Y'all waitin' to hear 'bout Cutter?"

"Yes," Hollis had said, hurrying toward him. Mattie and Jesse were right behind her. "How is he, Doctor?"

"Dr. Fred Jerome," the man said, extending his beefy hand.

She'd introduced herself.

"Champion? I knew your daddy. Fine man was Buck Champion. Hated to hear of his passin'."

"Thank you," she'd said. "Please tell me how Cutter is."

The doctor had chuckled, a deep, rumbly sound that seemed to have come all the way from the soles of his feet. "That cowboy is mad as hell, that's how he is. Doesn't want any part of our fancy establishment."

"I knew it," Jesse had said, smiling and shaking his head.

"We're keeping him overnight, though, whether he likes it or not. He's got four fractured ribs. He's suffered a trauma to his entire body, and I'd like to observe him for a few hours. I don't expect any complications, though. He's in fine shape, healthy as a horse."

Hollis had asked to see him then.

"You can look at him," the doctor had said, smiling. "I gave him a pain shot, and he's out cold for the night. Saves my nurses havin' to listen to his naggin' 'bout goin' home, too. You folks can pick him up 'bout eleven tomorrow mornin', providin' my gals don't murder him first. He's an ornery cuss.

"He'll have to take it slow when he gets home," the doctor had continued. "Broken ribs take their own sweet time healin'. All I can do is tape him up and turn him loose, then figure on the pain and a tad of common sense to keep him held back."

"Don't count on it," Jesse had said.

"Yeah, I know these cowboys." The doctor had chuckled. "I'd like a quarter for every one I've patched together. They're a breed unto themselves. Well, good night, y'all."

"You go look in on Cutter if you like, Hollis," Jesse had suggested. "We'll wait here for you, then I'll drive us all home in the truck."

"Oh, but you must want to see him," Hollis had said.

Jesse had stroked his chin. "Can't say that seeing Cutter McKenzie sleeping like a baby would be the thrill of my life. Go."

"Yes, Hollis," Mattie had said, "you go on. I'm going to try to find Kathleen and see if I can convince her to go home for some rest. Bless her heart, she's had such a shock. I'll meet you back here."

"All right," Hollis had said, hugging Mattie. Then, on impulse, she'd hugged Jesse, who'd appeared extremely embarrassed. "I won't be long."

Hollis sighed and pushed back the blankets on the bed. She swung her feet to the floor and stared into space, envisioning Cutter in her mind the way he had looked when she'd entered his dimly lit room.

Tears had misted her eyes as she'd stood by the bed gazing at him. The sheet was pulled to his waist, the white tape encasing his chest standing out in sharp contrast to his burnished skin. The bruises on his face didn't seem so ominous as they'd been in the barn. The swelling had lessened and the blood been cleaned away. His hair tumbled boyishly onto his forehead, and Hollis brushed it back with trembling fingers.

"I love you, Cutter McKenzie," she'd whispered.

And, now, in the quiet solitude of her bedroom, she said the words again in her mind, her heart. Oh, how deeply she loved him.

Hollis felt the now familiar ache in her throat that said tears were threatening once again. She shook her head and went into the bathroom, welcoming the soothing warmth of the water in the shower as it caressed her body.

She was still tired, she realized. Physically and emotionally drained. She'd slept restlessly when she'd returned to Gauntlet Run, haunting nightmares of the events in the barn twisting through her mind. And soon she would drive into Houston and pick up Cutter at the hospital.

What would he say to her? Hollis wondered as she began to dress. What should she say to him? The shadow of evil hanging over Gauntlet Run was gone, the mystery solved. There was nothing standing between her and Cutter and their life together. Nothing but the word "free."

With yet another sigh, Hollis finished dressing in a soft yellow wool skirt and a yellow and white sweater. She brushed her hair until it shone and left it to tumble down her back the way Cutter liked it.

In the kitchen, Hollis poured herself a mug of coffee and had just sat down at the table when Mattie came out of the pantry.

"Oh, hello, Hollis," Mattie said. "I'm glad you slept late. You still look tired, though."

"I'm fine. I'll be driving in to get Cutter soon."

"Oh, well, that won't be necessary," Mattie said. She smoothed her apron, keeping her eyes averted from Hollis's.

"What?" Hollis said, jumping to her feet. "Why? Has something happened to Cutter?"

"No, no," Mattie said, waving Hollis back onto her chair. She sat down opposite her. "Jesse was in here to get Cutter some fresh clothes. Cutter had phoned him, said he was ready to come home, and asked Jesse to drive in to pick him up. Jesse left over a half hour ago."

"I see," Hollis said quietly, staring into her mug.

"Hollis, don't look so glum. Cutter's hurt, might need help getting into his clothes. A man's pride is a fragile thing. Stands to reason he'd want Jesse there rather than you. Everything will be fine once Cutter gets home to Gauntlet Run."

"No, I...I don't think it will be," Hollis said, her voice trembling. She got slowly to her feet. "I'm going to go paint for a while."

"Honey, what's wrong? What happened between you and Cutter?"

"I can't talk about it right now," Hollis said, trying desperately not to cry. She hurried from the room, leaving a frowning Mattie staring after her.

In the library, Hollis brushed an errant tear from her cheek, drew a steadying breath and walked to the easel. She flipped open the sketch pad and studied the drawing, then propped it against the window. A short time later, she had donned a smock, mixed oils on a palette and, with a determined lift to her chin, began to paint.

Cutter stared out the side window of the Mercedes, not really seeing the lush, rolling land within his view.

"This is some fancy car," Jesse said. "I figured you'd appreciate a smooth ride. Me? I'll take a good ole pickup truck anytime."

"Mmm," Cutter said.

"Want to talk about it?"

"About what?" Cutter turned his head to look at him.

"About why I came in for you, instead of Hollis. About the fact that you haven't said two words since we started home. I realize you're not feeling up to par, but I figure it's more than that. You know, Cutter, I was mighty wrong about Hollis Champion. She's a fine woman."

"Yes, she is," Cutter said, looking out the side window again.

"So? Do you want to talk about it?"

"No."

"She's waiting for you, at home, at Gauntlet Run."

"She's there, Jesse, but, no, I don't think she's waiting for me."

"That's crazy, boy."

"Give it a rest, Jesse," Cutter said wearily. "I don't want to talk about it."

"Well, hell's fire," Jesse muttered.

Free, Cutter thought. Damn, that word was haunting him, taunting him. Hollis wanted to be free. It was over, finished—their engagement, their commitment, everything. He'd be a fool if he assumed he could pick up where they'd left off, just because the threat of Floyd's sick mind had been removed from their lives. No, Hollis had made it clear that she would not answer to him in any way, that she no longer wanted to be a part of their relationship. He had no desire to control her life as Buck had done, but Hollis didn't believe that. She wanted to be free.

So, now what? Cutter asked himself. Damn it, he loved her, wanted to marry her as soon as possible. Fat chance. She was probably packing right now, getting ready to return to Mexico.

"Hell," Cutter said. Jesse rolled his eyes heavenward.

No, now wait a minute, Cutter mentally went on. If Hollis left Gauntlet Run, she'd forfeit the house due to Buck's will. She was too stubborn to leave. And as long as she stayed, he had a chance to win her back.

Because, Cutter thought suddenly, he had an edge.

"Jesse," he said, a smug smile tugging onto his lips, "speed it up a little, will you? I've got important business waiting for me at Gauntlet Run."

"I've got the hands tending to everything, Cutter. You're supposed to be taking it easy."

"My business is personal," Cutter said, his smile growing bigger. "It's of the feminine variety—big green eyes and beautiful black hair."

"Oh, well, in that case," Jesse said, pressing on the gas pedal, "I'll just hustle us right on home."

From the library window Hollis saw the Mercedes coming up the long driveway that led to the house. She quickly draped a cover over the canvas, cleaned her brush and palette and removed her smock. Her knees were trembling when she entered the foyer just as Cutter was coming in the front door.

"Hello, Cutter." She stopped several feet away from him.

"Hollis," he said, nodding. He closed the door behind him.

"Are you all right?"

"Yeah, I'm fine. I've had worse than this. How about you? Did you survive the ordeal in the barn without any aftereffects?" This conversation was dumb, Cutter thought. Hollis looked pale, drawn, as if she hadn't slept well. He wanted to hold her in his arms, tell her that she was safe now, that the evil had been removed from their lives. Yeah, he wanted to make love to her, but first he'd just hold her, drink in her aroma, savor the feel of her soft curves pressed against him. But, no, he had to play it cool, loose, see if there was any indication that she wished she hadn't said she wanted to be free. He had to size up the situation in order to know how rough a road he had to travel to make Hollis his again.

"*I'm* certainly all right," she said. "You're the one we were so concerned about. And Floyd, of course."

"Kathleen came by my room at the hospital this morning. I assured her we wouldn't be pressing any charges against Floyd. I assume that's agreeable with you?"

"Yes, of course. Thank you. He's ill, not a criminal."

"Yeah."

Their eyes met and held, blue eyes and green, searching, seeking answers to questions that screamed in their minds. Neither spoke. Tension and heat seemed to weave between them, tempting, pulling, one beckoning to the other.

Cutter cleared his throat, breaking the eerie spell. "I'm glad you're all right, Hollis. I would've done anything to spare you that scene in the barn."

"Please don't worry about me. Just take care of yourself. The doctor said you had to take things slow and easy."

Okay, Cutter thought. He was getting the *verbal* message. He wasn't to worry about her, just focus on himself. Separate entities. Hollis over there. Him over here. Not together. Not one. Separate. And free. Well, he had news for Hollis Champion Ramirez.

"I think I'll rest before lunch," he said. "See you later."

"Yes." She watched as he disappeared down the corridor. She pressed her fingertips to her lips to silence the sob that threatened to escape. And to silence the plea that would beg Cutter to take her in his arms, hold her, kiss, touch her. He was acting as though they were near strangers, instead of two people who'd made love and declared their love. He had meant it. Cutter was free. "Oh,

God, Cutter," she whispered. "I love you so much. I need you, Cutter McKenzie."

She couldn't stay here, Hollis thought frantically. She couldn't watch Cutter from afar, aching for him, wanting him. What was the purpose of meeting the six-month time frame of Buck's will? To gain ownership of the house on Gauntlet Run was to sentence herself to a lifetime of loneliness within those walls. A lifetime of having Cutter so near, yet just beyond her reach.

What would happen, she wondered, if she flung herself into Cutter's arms, told him she loved him, would always love him? No, darn it, she wouldn't do it. She had her pride. He'd made his feelings clear when he'd walked in that door. She was a Champion and would conduct herself with dignity. And stubbornness? No, she wasn't being stubborn: she was facing facts, being realistic. The man she loved had had a change of heart, and she would act accordingly. She would leave Gauntlet Run.

"And I've never," Hollis said with a sniffle, "been so miserable in my entire life."

Cutter lay on his bed, his hands laced under his head as he stared up at the ceiling. He was annoyingly tired, his jaw throbbed like a dull toothache, and his ribs felt as though they were on fire.

And he was smiling.

In the shimmering depths of Hollis's eyes, he had seen what he needed to know.

She still loved him.

Standing between them now was Hollis's pride and stubbornness. Those were the two ingredients that had kept her and Buck apart for seven wasted years. Cutter knew that, and that gave him the edge, the winning hand.

With a satisfied nod, he drifted off to sleep.

When Cutter didn't appear at lunchtime, Hollis ate

alone, then returned to the library, where she painted for the remainder of the afternoon. She was thoroughly depressed, she realized, and a breath away from bursting into tears at any moment.

At dinner, Mattie announced that Cutter had emerged from his room for a late lunch and wouldn't be eating with Hollis. Cutter looked marvelous, considering the beating he'd taken, Mattie had chattered on. Didn't Hollis agree?

"Yes," Hollis said, then stabbed a potato with her fork with more force than was necessary.

"Something wrong?" Mattie said, all innocence.

"No," Hollis said sullenly.

"That's good," Mattie sang out, then left the dining room.

"Nothing is wrong," Hollis said to the potato. "Other than the fact that my heart has been smashed to smithereens."

The next day was a repeat performance. The only evidence that Hollis had that Cutter was even in the house was when she heard him open or close his bedroom door. Once he'd come down the hall singing off-key. Singing, for crying out loud, she'd fumed. Well, she was glad *somebody* around there was chipper. Being all-fired "free" certainly did wonders for Mr. McKenzie's frame of mind.

"The jerk," Hollis had mumbled into her pillow.

In the late afternoon of the following day after Cutter's return to Gauntlet Run from the hospital, Hollis stepped back from the easel and cocked her head to one side, then the other.

"It's finished," she said. And it was the best work she'd ever done. She'd painted it not only with her hand but with her heart. It was her parting gift to Cutter, and now that it was complete, she would leave. She would leave Cutter McKenzie and Gauntlet Run.

Hollis cleaned up her supplies, then wandered across the foyer and into the living room, her heart aching. Her breath caught in her throat as she saw Cutter by the mantel, lighting a fire.

"Oh, I—I didn't mean to intrude," she said from just inside the room.

Cutter got to his feet and turned to face her. "Come in. I thought a fire would be nice. It's chilly out today."

Hollis walked slowly forward, her gaze taking in every inch of Cutter. The bruises on his face were hardly noticeable, the swelling completely gone. He was wearing black western-cut slacks and a black western shirt with pearl snaps. His hair was a thick ebony glow on his head, and the darkness of his clothes made his tan appear deeper, like bronze reflecting the rich colors of the leaping flames in the fireplace. He was magnificent. He was Cutter. And she loved him.

"Cutter," she said, stopping about six feet away from him, "I . . . I'm leaving Gauntlet Run."

"Oh?" he said, resting one arm on the mantel. "I take it you plan to be away for longer than twenty-four hours. I mean, why else would you be telling me?"

"I'm leaving…permanently, returning to Mexico," she said, lifting her chin.

This was it, Cutter thought, feeling a trickle of sweat run down his back. The showdown, ten paces at high noon, guns drawn. He was even dressed for it, all in black. And there stood Hollis with her stubborn Champion chin tilted in the air. The rest of their lives depended on what he said and did now. He could only hope, pray, that his edge, his ace in the hole, would be enough. How he loved this woman!

"Well, Hollis," he said, shoving his hands into his back pockets. "I'm afraid I can't let you do that."

"I beg your pardon?"

"You're not leaving Gauntlet Run."

"Now, wait a minute here," she said, closing the distance between them and glaring up at him. "Who do you think you are?"

"I am," he said, his voice low as he looked directly into her eyes, "the man who loves you, the man you love. I am someone who saw Champion pride and stubbornness keep a father and daughter apart for seven years—seven long, heartbreaking years. Because of what I witnessed, I have an edge, a trump card."

"I don't understand," she said, hardly breathing.

"I have pride and I've been known to be stubborn, but Hollis? Not this time. I'm not going to be part of a repeat performance of what happened between you and Buck. I'm not going to lose you the way he did. I'm pushing aside my pride and stubbornness and baring my soul to you. I'm telling you that I love you more than life itself. I'm saying I want you physically and emotionally. I need you, Hollis, as my wife, the mother of my children, my partner, my best friend. I'm asking—*I'm begging*—you to stay here with me."

"Oh, Cutter, I love you so much," Hollis said, tears filling her eyes. "I would have done it. I would have left you, just as I did Buck, on the basis of my pride and stubbornness. How can you forgive me for that?"

"There's nothing to forgive. Listen to me," he said, cradling her face in his hands. "You are a Champion, Buck's daughter, and you should be proud of that. I'm not trying to change you into someone else, nor am I trying to control or manipulate you. All I'm saying is that this time, *this time*, channel that determination toward me, us, the life we can share together. Will you do that?"

Tears spilled onto Hollis's cheeks. "Yes," she said, nearly choking on a sob. "Oh, yes. I didn't want to leave you, Cutter, but I didn't know how to stop myself. The Champion pride was consuming me, just as it did Buck, pulling at me, forcing me to go."

"I know," he said, trailing his thumbs back and forth across her tear-stained cheeks. "I saw it happen to Buck, too. I heard the pain in his voice when he spoke of you. I knew how much he missed you. I learned an important lesson from what you two suffered. Yes, a man's pride is important, but it takes a bigger man to know when to set it aside."

"And you did, for me."

"Yes."

"Oh, Cutter, I love you. Thank you for saving me from myself."

"You're entirely welcome," he said, lowering his head toward hers, "but don't thank me. Just love me."

The kiss was long and powerful, and passions soared. The kiss spoke of the lonely hours of the past days and the need to push away the hurt and confusion. The kiss was hungry, heated, urgent and frenzied. It was tongues meeting and senses being filled with tastes, aromas, the feel of hard muscle against soft flesh.

"I want you so damn much," Cutter said, lifting his head. "These past few days have been hell. I was giving you time and space to work things through on the outside chance you'd see that your pride was standing between us."

"But I failed to do that," she said, her voice unsteady.

"I'm not that surprised. You're Buck Champion's daughter."

"And so, it was up to you. Oh, Cutter, you had to do it all. I didn't even meet you halfway."

"I'm not keeping score. We have the rest of our lives for give and take, compromise. No, wait a minute. There's something you can do for me right now. It would mean a lot to me, Hollis."

"What is it?"

"Sit tight," he said, walking to the end table and picking up the receiver to the telephone. He punched in some numbers. "Jesse? Now. This is it." He replaced the receiver.

"This is what?" Hollis asked.

"Come on." He took her hand and led her from the room, down the hall and into the kitchen.

"Dinner in ten minutes," Mattie said.

"Okay," Cutter said. "We have to go out back for a moment."

"Oh, my," Mattie said, "is it that time already?"

"It is," Cutter said with a decisive nod.

"For what?" Hollis said.

"Bless you both," Mattie said, sniffling into her handkerchief. "I'm so happy."

"Cutter, what is going on?" Hollis said as he hauled her outside the back door.

And then she stopped.

Jesse stood there smiling, a lightweight rope in his hands that led to a spindly legged little horse.

"It's Butterfly's foal," Hollis said.

"Hollis," Cutter said, his voice slightly husky, "I want you to have him. I'm asking you to accept this colt as your own to tell me, show me, that you've put the hurts of the past away and you're willing to start fresh, look to the future, with me. Will you do that, Hollis? For us?"

"Yes! Oh, yes," she said, stroking the colt's nose. "Hello, baby," she said to the foal. "Hello...Forever."

Cutter released a rush of air and only then realized he'd been holding his breath. Rest in peace, Buck Champion, he thought, glancing heavenward.

"Let's go, Forever," Jesse said. "It's dinnertime. Can I tell the hands there's to be a wedding on Gauntlet Run?"

"Yes!" Hollis and Cutter said in unison.

"'Bout time," Jesse muttered leading the colt away. "Thought those two would never come to their senses."

Dinner was, Hollis decided, a ridiculous event. Neither

she nor Cutter could remember to eat, and they lost track of the thread of conversation when their eyes met. Mattie threw up her hands and left them alone.

"I want to make love to you, Hollis," Cutter said, trailing his thumb over her cheek.

"Yes" was all she managed to say.

They left the room with Cutter's arm tightly around her shoulders.

"Cutter," she said, looking up at him, "what about your ribs?"

"You'll just have to be gentle when you ravish me," he said, waggling his eyebrows at her.

As they started down the corridor, Hollis hesitated. "No, we belong in the master suite. You and I, together, are Gauntlet Run, Cutter. Those rooms are ours now."

In the master suite, Cutter made a fire, then turned to Hollis, extending his hand palm up. She placed her hand in his, feeling the calluses, the strength, gentleness and heat as he curled his fingers around hers. They shared a smile, one of love, of greater understanding, of commitment. A smile of victory after a battle well fought, a gauntlet run and conquered. And it was a smile of peace, contentment, of having journeyed far to be at last at home.

Then the smiles faded, and blue eyes and green grew smoky with desire, with need and want. Clothes were shed, and Hollis frowned as she saw the heavy tape wrapping Cutter's chest.

"Don't worry about it," he said, then claimed her mouth.

They sank onto the plush carpeting in front of the hearth and rediscovered the mysteries of each other. In a sweet foray of lips, tongues, and hands, they caressed, kissed, touched and tantalized until they could bear no more.

"Cutter, please."

"Yes."

He came to her with all that he was: strength tempered with gentleness, an earthy honesty that spoke of raw need, a desire to give before receiving what she would so willingly offer. He came to her as man, as Cutter, and Hollis sheathed him in the velvety warmth of her femininity. She was woman to his man. She was Hollis. She was his.

Their senses swirled as their bodies meshed, carrying them away as the tempo raged on—building, higher, harder, stealing the very breath from their lips.

"Cutter!"

"Yes, Hollis, now!"

They spilled into oblivion as though hurled into a wondrous place created only for them for when they were one. They were suspended there in pleasure, lingered, then drifted slowly back. Cutter shifted his weight from Hollis, then drew her close to his side, where she rested her fingertips lightly on the moist tape.

"I love you so much, Cutter," she said, her head nestled on his shoulder.

"And I love you," he said, running his fingers through her silken hair. "I think we should drink a toast of thanks to Buck at our wedding."

"I'm sure that when he wrote his will he didn't doubt for one minute that things would work out the way he planned. It just wouldn't occur to him once he made up his mind."

Cutter chuckled. "Yep, he was something, all right. Buck Champion was a helluva man. I'm proud to have been his friend."

"And at long last, I'm proud to have been his daughter. Cutter, your stomach is growling again."

"We didn't eat much dinner."

"Mattie made peach cobbler. We could go get some and bring it back here in front of the fire."

"Sold."

Cutter pulled on his pants, and Hollis slipped into his shirt, which fit her, she declared, like a tent. As they walked down the corridor, she grasped Cutter's hand.

"Would you come into the library for a moment?" she said. "I have something for you. It was ... Well, it was to be my gift to you as I said goodbye. Now it's the perfect way to thank you for giving me Forever to raise as my own."

"Lead on, ma'am."

In the library, Hollis flicked on the lights, then walked to the easel, realizing she was suddenly nervous.

"I'm not a professional painter, remember," she said, turning the easel to face him. "It's just a hobby that I enjoy, but I thought you might like to have ... What I mean is—"

"Lift the cloth," Cutter said, smiling.

Hollis did as she was instructed, then stepped back, chewing on her lip as she watched Cutter's face. His eyes widened, he opened his mouth, but when nothing came out, he snapped it closed again. He walked slowly forward, his gaze riveted on the canvas.

"My God," he said, his voice oddly husky, "it's Butterfly. Oh, Hollis, she looks so alive, so vital, so real. You captured her right there on that canvas for eternity. I had no idea you were so talented. Thank you for this. Butterfly was very special to me. I'll cherish this always."

Hollis moved to his side, snuggling close to his warmth as he held her tightly.

"I'm glad you like it," she said. "We'll hang it here in our home on Gauntlet Run, and we'll raise her foal together. Forever will be ours to share."

"And our love will be ours to share—forever," he said, then lowered his lips to hers.

* * * * *

ATTRACTIVE, SPACE SAVING BOOK RACK

Display your most prized novels on this handsome and sturdy book rack. The hand-rubbed walnut finish will blend into your library decor with quiet elegance, providing a practical organizer for your favorite hard-or soft-covered books.

Only $9.95

**Approximately
16" x 8"
when assembled**

Assembles in seconds!

To order, rush your name, address and zip code, along with a check or money order for $10.70* ($9.95 plus 75¢ postage and handling) payable to *Silhouette Books*.

Silhouette Books
Book Rack Offer
901 Fuhrmann Blvd.
P.O. Box 1396
Buffalo, NY 14269-1396

Offer not available in Canada.

BKR-2A

*New York and Iowa residents add appropriate sales tax.

Silhouette Intimate Moments

Starting in October...

SHADOWS ON THE NILE

by

Heather Graham Pozzessere

A romantic short story in six installments from best-selling author Heather Graham Pozzessere.

The first chapter of this intriguing romance will appear in all Silhouette titles published in October. The remaining five chapters will appear, one per month, in Silhouette Intimate Moments' titles for November through March '88.

Don't miss "*Shadows on the Nile*"—a special treat, coming to you in October. Only from Silhouette Books.

Be There!

IMSS-1